PROMISE ME

BELINDA BENNA

vinci
BOOKS

Vinci Books

vinci-books.com

Published by Vinci Books Ltd in 2026

1

A CIP catalogue record for this book is available from the British Library.
Paperback ISBN: 9781036733810
The EU GPSR authorised representative is Logos Europe, 9 rue Nicolas Poussion, 17000 La Rochelle, France contact@logoseurope.eu

By Belinda Benna

Marie & Lukas

Promise Me

Show Me the Stars

Halifax Harbor Hospital

A Glimmer of Hope

A Twist of Fate

Miracle Glow

Love and Other Dreams

The Dreams We Share

The Sky We Seek

The Colors We Desire

The Dance We Remember

The Stars We Chase

Prologue

FIVE YEARS EARLIER

My eyes follow the cotton-white shapes of the clouds above us, I watch them drift on and wonder where they're going. "I wonder what it feels like to sit up there and look down at the world?" Without taking my eyes off the sky above us, I move closer to Lukas.

"Definitely not as good as being here with you." He lifts his arm and lets me rest my head on his shoulder.

The picnic blanket is too big for just the two of us, lying this close together. Still, I snuggle even closer to him. Because being with him gives me more warmth than the autumn sun tickling my cheeks. And his skin smells more enticing than the tall wildflower meadow where we're hiding from the world together.

I feel for his hand, gently stroke his skin and finally lace my fingers with his. "Do you think that as long as we're together, nothing else matters?"

Lukas covers the crown of my head with so many little kisses that I lose count. "Mhm," he murmurs and takes a deep breath. "I just need to have you with me. Hear your laughter, look into your eyes and watch how your honey-blond hair shines in the sun. Then nothing else is important anymore."

I'm not actually sentimental, but now I have to swallow. Because I can hear his heart beating and know exactly what it wants to tell me with its rhythm. "We could go anywhere. Watch the giraffes in Africa roaming the savanna together. Climb Machu Picchu together…"

"…bathe with dolphins off the coast of Portugal…" He rests his cheek on my head and strokes my upper arm so tenderly that I have to sigh.

"…and watch the northern lights in the eternal night above Iceland's horizon." I sit up, look into his chestnut-brown eyes and can't do anything but smile at him. "We can go to the end of the world together. And much farther still." Lovingly, I run my hand over his short, brown hair.

"Is that what you dream of?" he asks, looking at me as if there's nothing he'd rather do than make my wishes come true.

Instead of answering, I press my lips to his. Very slowly and gently, as if what we have is as fragile as this moment. And yet I know one thing for sure. "I dream of you. Of us staying this happy forever and nothing ever tearing us apart," I breathe against his mouth and kiss him again right away.

"You can have me," he murmurs with a crooked grin on his face. "Forever."

Now he takes my hands in his. The mild autumn wind makes the sleeves of his blue T-shirt flutter, and far away I hear it rustling through the leaves of the birch-lined avenue.

We do nothing but look at each other, and nothing more is necessary. Because we don't have to say what we feel. Because we both know that happiness will never leave us.

This moment is far too beautiful, I mustn't let it slip away, I don't want to forget it. "Wait a second. Don't move. Stay exactly as you are."

Quickly I rummage my camera out of my bag and capture the moment in a photo.

"Look," I say with a smile and drop down beside him again. Together we look at Lukas's face in the golden light of the autumn sun. Behind him stretches a lush green, sprinkled with white and violet dots.

"Take another one. This time of both of us."

He rests his forehead against my cheek and I hold the camera up. Even before I press the shutter, he starts to speak. "I want to be with you, wherever you are," he whispers, while my finger finds the shutter button as if on its own.

Goosebumps spread over my whole body; I'm trembling, even though this autumn day is warm.

The photo no longer matters. I turn my head to the side, nuzzle my nose against his and gaze deep into his eyes. There I can see everything of him. Every spark of feeling and all his wishes.

"Forever." The word leaves my lips almost soundlessly. Then we kiss, so intensely as if we wanted to seal our promise with it.

Chapter One

We stay silent. Because there are no words in this world with which we could offer each other comfort. Surrounded by an oppressive quiet, Grandma and I do the only thing we're still capable of. We sort out sweaters, fold trousers and lay them in black plastic bags. We're careful, treating the clothes like a treasure we have to look after.

Because that's what they are.

Not everything, but a great many of the things that belonged to Grandpa go into bags and boxes. Countless cartons now stand in Grandma's living room. Soon they'll be gone; only our memories will stay with us. The beautiful and the ugly ones, the amusing and the sad.

Out of the corner of my eye, I try to make out in Grandma's face what she's feeling. She looks tired, her nose is swollen. The wrinkles on her forehead seem to have deepened over the past few days, and the rosy cheeks that used to be so full have sunk in and turned pale.

Now, with her index finger, she lovingly traces the pattern of a dark brown knitted sweater. Exactly at the spot where, just a few days ago, the wool still touched Grandpa's chest, she pauses. I see her upper body bend forward, and I'm at her side in an instant.

I hold her as tightly as I can. Still, it's not enough, I can feel that so clearly. Nothing I do could help her.

"Why?" Grandma whispers in a choked voice. "We still wanted to…"

What am I supposed to say to her? I can hardly grasp it myself. Grandpa's stroke came as a surprise to all of us.

"I'm so sorry," I force out helplessly and guide her to the sofa.

There we sink down among the countless cushions she sewed and embroidered herself. Just as I used to do as a child at her place, she now lays her head on my shoulder. Her blond hair, streaked with gray, nestles softly against my neck.

"It was less than two months until his retirement. Our new life would have begun with the summer. We counted the days, we were so full of anticipation. And then…" Suddenly her voice turns completely matter of fact. That's probably the only way she can even talk about it at all. "We wanted to have breakfast together on the porch, climb every mountain in Austria, and redesign the garden with our combined forces. We wanted to get some geese and rebuild the chicken coop." She shakes her head, a tear rolls silently down her pale cheek. Then she looks straight at me with her bright-blue eyes. "Do you remember what he always said?"

Of course I remember. I grew up here with Grandma and Grandpa while my parents were doing their pilot training and then went off to conquer the world. I saw Grandpa come home late in the evening on his workdays. He was often tired, worn out, and empty. Whenever

Grandma and I tried to talk him into taking a break, we heard only one single word from him.

"Later," I murmur wistfully.

Grandma exhales loudly. "He had an answer ready for every question. But whenever I wanted to know from him when this 'later' was supposed to come, he just held me silently in his arms."

I wish I could do something for her, but what could possibly comfort her? No one can bring Grandpa back for her; their time together has run out forever.

"Later never comes," she says in a choked voice, and I can't hold back my own tears anymore either.

So the two of us sit on the sofa in my grandmother's living room, surrounded by lemon-yellow curtains in front of dollhouse-like windows and cheerful photo collages on the walls. The cheerful mood of this room no longer reaches us. We're like the plastic bags and the contents of the half-full boxes scattered in front of us on the wooden floorboards. Black. And separated into pieces that will never be put back together again.

We're both trapped in this dark bubble, and yet only one thing matters to me. That Grandma will feel better again.

So I stay with her, even though I should have left for work long ago. I support her, encourage her, and help her pack away Grandpa's life, even if it feels absurd to me to do it. After a good hour in which we've worked side by side in silence, I can't put off our goodbye any longer. "Is it okay if I head to work? Will you be all right?" I ask carefully.

She forces the corners of her mouth up. At least she tries to, even though she doesn't have to. Not for me. "Of course, go on, love."

Immediately I feel bad about leaving her behind. But my boss wouldn't give me today off; after all, I'd already taken the last three days of vacation to be there for Grandma. And if I don't leave right now, I'll never manage to get everything done that has to be taken care of today. "I'll get in touch again later," I say in farewell and give her an encouraging nod.

"Later." Her gaze drifts off into the silent emptiness of the living room.

"I'm always here for you, you know that. We'll get through this together." Just like before. Grandma and I had managed everything together. We were a team, welded together so tightly that nothing could tear us apart.

A strained smile flits across her face. Only for a brief moment, but that's already more than I'd hoped for. "Say hi to Lukas for me. Tell him thank you again for his help. He's an angel."

"Of course." Once more I pull her tightly into my arms.

With a heavy heart I leave her alone and head to work. At top speed I cross half of Vienna and reach the company entrance a good forty minutes later. Even if it feels unimaginable right now—once I cross this threshold, I have to function. Because there's no room here for personal matters, no space for grief, and no time for pain.

I take one last deep breath, then open the door of the fully glassed main entrance and walk straight toward the locker rooms.

There I run into my favorite colleague and friend, Alex.

Elegant as a dancer, she tilts her head to the side and looks me over. "You're late."

"I was with Grandma." I don't want to say more, because immediately I see her in my mind's eye, sitting alone on the sofa. Her shoulders slumped, surrounded by crumpled tissues. Her sadness threatens to overwhelm me, and along with it my own feeling of helplessness.

Alex's voice pushes into my thoughts. "How is she?" she asks in that compassionate tone that only makes it harder for me. Then she drops down onto the narrow wooden bench next to my locker and looks at me closely.

Instead of answering, I just shake my head.

She motions for me to sit next to her and immediately wraps her arms around my shoulders. Her short-cropped hair tickles my ear, and her sweeping earrings lie cold against my skin. "Let me know if there's anything I can do."

"Distract me," I force out with difficulty, because that's the only thing that will get me through this day. Luckily there actually is something I can cling to. So I push Alex a little away from me and fish my phone out of my bag. "I still have to show you something."

Alex instantly raises her eyebrows and turns her gaze to my phone's screen. Not without pride, I show her one picture after another. I wish I could feel the way I did again in that moment two weeks ago, when I discovered the house you can see in the photos. But looking at it today brings hardly any joy to this gloomy day. Still, I try to bring the moment back to life in my memory. Because I need something beautiful to hold on to.

For years, hidden behind a wooden fence, only the roof of the house had been visible. But two weeks ago a "For Sale" sign suddenly hung on the gate. Curious, I peered through one of the broken slats, and all of a sudden, there it was.

The house of my dreams. Nestled in a wildly overgrown garden.

So far, I've only told Lukas about my discovery; this morning I took pictures of it for him. The gray-blue painted wooden façade forms a beautiful contrast to the white shutters. It not only has the perfect size, but also floor-to-ceiling windows, and on the solid wooden front door hang two wrought-iron lanterns with heart-shaped loops. A veranda runs along the entire front side.

"Lukas and I could sit there on rocking chairs and look up at the sky together." A sigh escapes my mouth. The image is like a warm coat wrapping itself around my sadness. "And there in the back there'd still be room for a garden pond, see?" I point to the barren-looking area to the right of the house. In my mind I'm there, far away from the plain cloakroom at our workplace where we're sitting right now. At least a little removed from my worry about Grandma and from the grief over Grandpa's death, which I still haven't processed either.

"An American country house." Alex's voice sounds reverent. "Just perfect."

"Our search would finally be over." I look at the pictures one last time, then send them to Lukas. "He's going to be thrilled." I wish I could smile, the way I would on any other day.

"Who? Lukas?" Alex's face takes on that special expression she always shows me when I talk about him. A mix of longing and incomprehension.

"The love of my life," I confirm with a nod. We've been together for five years now, and he still makes me so happy that I can hardly put it into words. It's enough just to look at him or hear his voice. It's enough to smell the scent of his skin or lean against his shoulder. Lukas and I, we're a dream couple, and I don't care in the slightest how cheesy that sounds.

What if he goes before me too? What if, like Grandma, I one day stand at his grave and can't understand why our time together ended so quickly?

Awful. I don't want to think about that at all.

"Yeah, yeah, straight out of Hollywood," Alex comments loudly. With her lower lip stuck out, she gives a barely perceptible shake of her head. Then her gaze drifts to the delicate watch on her wrist. "Unfortunately, I have to inform you that in the real world it's already half past ten."

I feel a bit as if Alex has just dumped a bucket of ice water over my head. I flinch. "The boss is probably already here."

She looks at me, wrinkling her nose. Even though she stays silent, I know exactly what she's thinking. So I squeeze my feet into the uncomfortable high heels I wear for work. It's not like I have any other choice.

"Dark cherry red," I say, starting our daily guessing game, just to have at least a bit of normality I can cling to.

"Varicose vein violet." She says the word with complete seriousness, yet her lips twitch suspiciously.

I'm sure Alex has the same image of my boss in front of her eyes at this very moment. His hairless head, overheated, maybe even smoking, but in any case covered in dark cherry red and varicose-vein purple.

Just thinking about it, I can practically feel a weight pulling the corners of my mouth down, and if I didn't know better, I could believe it actually got a little darker in here over the last few seconds.

"I'd most like to hide from him. Especially today." My voice is thin.

"We'd all like to do that," Alex says sympathetically, closing her locker. "Believe me, we totally admire how you keep going. Every. Single. Day."

I shrug, my shoulders suddenly feeling heavy. As if something were sitting there that's at least as massive as the boss himself. I can't let that happen. I want to stay positive; anything else is pointless anyway. "Last week he was really nice, even though he found a mistake in my presentation."

"His wife probably let him get some for a change before work." I actually love my best friend's bone-dry sense of humor, but today I can't even laugh about that.

My head sinks onto Alex's shoulder, as if I can't carry it on my own any longer. The honey-blond hair of my chin-length bob falls into my face and veils my view. Still, I know exactly where I am. In the place that's heaven and hell at the same time. Where I rise and crash as if I were on a never-ending roller coaster. "I just don't understand him. Maybe I'm simply too inexperienced for this job at twenty-five."

"You do your job brilliantly, and besides, I'm sure he's having a good day today." If Alex meant to sound convincing, she failed spectacularly.

Still, I force the corners of my mouth up. "Absolutely."

"Then let's get started." With these words, Alex springs up from the bench and reaches out her hand to me. Thanks to her help, a few seconds later I'm standing just as straight as a soldier, even though I have no idea what battle I'll be marching into today. I quickly run my fingers through my hair so everything sits neatly. As the marketing director's assistant, I can't afford a messy hairstyle.

Just as I'm about to close my locker, my phone beeps. It's definitely a message from Lukas. I instantly feel better.

"This is it! We absolutely have to go see it," I read out loud. "PS: Anything special on your desk today?"

"Oh, come on." Alex can sound as incredulous as she likes, I don't care. "This has to stop at some point," she protests loudly.

I raise my hand defensively. "Don't worry, we argue sometimes too." I slip the phone into the pocket of my elegant wool dress and close the locker. Then I march off. I'm far too curious about what's waiting for me on my desk. With Alex in tow, I walk down the corridor with its glossy tiles, past the elegant seating area with the oversized palm for people waiting, toward the office that Alex and I share with three other secretaries.

We've barely entered the room when it becomes more than clear what Lukas meant. In the midst of black folders, anthracite swivel chairs, and silver-gray desks, a colorful bouquet of flowers is on proud display, and I can smell its fragrance from here.

"Wow." I clap my hands over my mouth; Alex lets out a snort.

"I guess today is the anniversary of the first forehead kiss," she remarks in amusement, maybe with a hint of jealousy.

Absentmindedly, I shake my head. "He wants to cheer me up, that's all."

"That men like that still exist…"

Unimpressed by her words, I hurry to my desk and bury my nose in the bouquet. It smells like an entire meadow of flowers, of daisies and violets, of grass and even a little like the forest. My eyelids drift shut; I can't do anything about it. And I don't want to, because right now countless memories flood my mind. All of them as delicate as the petals brushing against the bridge of my nose. I need this kind of escape from reality more than anything else.

"Ms. Berger!" Sharp as the blade of a Japanese knife, the boss's voice cuts straight through my daydreams that had just been distracting me so wonderfully.

A murmur goes through the office; my colleagues immediately duck behind their screens and pound wildly on their keyboards. No one wants to end up in his sights. No wonder, because so far it has ended badly for everyone.

I look up from the bouquet of flowers. The boss stands in the doorway, solid and imposing like a rock. His face is still pale. But there is a dangerous gleam in his eyes, and the vein at his right temple is already standing out.

This is bad. Really bad.

"What is this supposed to be?" he asks, his gaze fixed on my flowers. His voice is not angry. On the contrary, it sounds calm and matter of fact. And yet there is a menacing undertone in it that I know all too well. "Your private life has no place in the office; this is where we work."

I nod, every muscle in my body tensing. My hands curl into fists and my discreetly manicured fingernails immediately dig hard into my palms.

"Why are you just standing around like an idiot?" he hisses at me as well. "Clear that away. Go on!"

"Of course. I'm sorry." With trembling fingers, I reach for the vase to put it on the filing cabinet next to my desk. It almost slips from my hands; I just manage to keep it from tipping over. The glass slams down onto the surface with a loud clang. Individual leaves come loose from the bouquet and float downward in slow motion. We're probably all staring at them right now, and every one of us knows what will happen when they land on the filing cabinet.

No. Please don't. Not today.

The boss needs only three steps, then he is standing right in front of me. "Give me that," he barks at me and yanks the bouquet out of my hands.

Normally he'd snap at me for making everything dirty in here, throw out a few contemptuous words, and then leave the office with a bright red face.

But of all days, today something different happens.

Five pairs of eyes watch him in disbelief as he rams the bouquet into the trash can with all his might. The flower heads bend to the side with an audible crack, and in the same moment it feels as if my heart is breaking along with them.

He's trampling on the one thing in this world that matters most to me. Lukas.

Why would he do something like that?

Desperately, I blink the rising tears out of the corners of my eyes. My lips are trembling, so I press them together so no one will see.

"Good, that's taken care of." He straightens his jacket and wipes his hands, damp from the flower water, on my colleague Sandra's desk chair. "Bring me my coffee. Now."

What else can I do but nod? That's exactly what I do, or at least I think I do, while he turns on his heel to leave the room. He disappears from my field of vision, and not a second later it feels as if the whole office can breathe again.

Alex immediately storms over to me. "Forget that idiot," she says, running her hand over my upper arm.

I tear my attention away from the dead bouquet in the trash can. "How?" The words leave my mouth as fragile as parchment. My gaze wanders through the office. In my colleagues' faces I see pity and understanding.

"He won't last much longer anyway." Sandra sounds convinced, but she's been saying exactly that for months and nothing has happened so far. There isn't a single sign, not a spark of hope.

"Why are you so sure about that?" I ask, even though I know perfectly well that no answer could possibly comfort me.

Sandra gives me a conspiratorial look. "I heard something," she whispers to me. "His end is near, believe me."

With every fiber of my body I want to do that, because there's one thing I know for sure: I can't endure this daily roller coaster of emotions much longer, and there's nothing I could still try myself to put an end to it. Even my complaint to the managing director two months ago didn't bring any improvement. On the contrary, it only led to my boss making my life even harder since then. Of all times, now of all times, the memory of my conversation with Grandma catches up with me. Waiting for something hadn't worked out for her.

"So when is his end going to come? Later?" I ask bitterly and head for the tea kitchen. If the boss doesn't get his coffee soon, I have no idea what he'll come up with next.

Not three minutes later I knock cautiously on his office door. Through the glass panel I see him turn toward me along with his elegant desk chair. He waves me in, and when I enter with the tray in my hand, he suddenly seems friendly and in a good mood.

Unbelievable.

I have to make an effort not to stare at him in bewilderment, because he absolutely can't stand that.

"You're a treasure, Ms. Berger." His gaze moves happily back and forth between the coffee pot and me.

Is he really behaving as if nothing out of the ordinary had happened today? As if not he but his evil twin had just killed my bouquet of flowers?

However it is, I'm not going to let anything show. In silence, I set the sugar dispenser and the little milk jug down on his expansive desk, of course in exactly the arrangement he prefers.

He leans forward and props himself up on his arms. A peaceful expression lies over his face. "Shall I tell you a secret?"

Instead of answering, I just nod and interrupt my work. After all, he expects my undivided attention whenever he speaks.

"I've never had such a great assistant as you." Is that actually joy I see in his expression?

"Thank you, that's nice to hear." Searching for the reason for his good mood, I let my gaze wander around the office. On the computer screen I spot the itinerary for his next business trip, which I had to put together for him so urgently last night. Even though I was on vacation. I couldn't even drive Grandma home myself in order to make the impossible possible.

"What are you staring at?" His forehead creases into frowns.

Now everything has to happen fast, or his mood will flip in a split second. With a frantic movement I pull the coffee cup off the tray and open the pot. Fortunately, out of the corner of my eye I see that he's turning to the documents on his desk. I exhale as silently as possible. Then I let the coffee run carefully into the cup so I don't spill a drop.

Suddenly he whirls around so violently that his arm bumps into mine. He jerks me and the coffee pot with him. Helplessly, I have to watch as the brown liquid spreads across the desk. It soaks through most of the documents and leaves unsightly stains on his keyboard.

My boss shoots up from his swivel chair at once. The furrow between his eyebrows grows deeper with each labored breath. "Can't you be more careful?"

I stare at him in disbelief. I didn't make a mistake. He was the one who…

"What a bloody nerve!" He demonstratively holds his tie right under my nose, its light blue background speckled so it looks as if he'd taken a bath in a puddle.

"I..."

I don't get any further, because he immediately cuts me off. "Unbelievable, this incompetence." Now he's really yelling. Starting at his neck, an intense color rises into his face.

Dark cherry red.

Excuse me? I'm incompetent? Because he shoved me while I was pouring the very coffee he could easily pour for himself every day? "I'm sorry, but that wasn't my fault." Did I really just say that out loud? Probably, otherwise why would that dark cherry red be spreading all the way up to his forehead?

"Why are you standing in the way, then?" He fixes me with an accusatory stare, and I notice a twitch at the corners of his eyes. It looks as if his rage is sending electric impulses right there.

All at once, frustration surges up inside me, hot as magma. It presses so forcefully against my throat that I don't know if I can keep it from bubbling out of me today.

"Will you finally do something!" he cries, feverishly stacking documents on top of each other to save them from the coffee that is relentlessly making its way across the surface of the table.

I can't.

Even if I wanted to, there's a resistance in me that forbids me to help him. My nerves are too frayed today to endure this humiliation on top of everything else. All I can do is stare at him with pressed lips and quivering nostrils.

Suddenly he stops what he is doing. With a wildly jumbled stack of papers in his hands, he scrutinizes me. His eyes are as gray as a November morning, they make me shiver and still can't do anything against this heat inside me. "Are you aware that you're risking your job here?"

I should flinch. Try to make it up to him. Soothe him and apologize. But none of that happens. Instead, my lips just part, and out comes the magma that has been seething inside me for far too long. "That. Was. Your. Fault," I say, enunciating every word. Then I straighten my back and take a step toward him.

Neither his furrowed brows nor the throbbing vein at his temple impress me. Not the corners of his mouth, pulled downward in a tight grimace, and least of all the color of his face, which suddenly, although it should be impossible, grows even darker.

As if he had to get rid of excess energy, he kicks his pompous leather swivel chair aside with his foot and squares up in front of me. "Say that again." His voice is conspicuously calm, his tone dangerously biting.

In an instant I feel nothing but a sense of futility. This is ridiculous and as unimportant as very few things in this world. He shouldn't be this angry, and above all he should finally stop treating me like a doormat. I clench my fists, my breathing turns heavy. I definitely won't back down, and I don't even need strength to do it. Stubbornly, I do what he so politely asked me to do. I repeat my earlier words. "That was your fault."

For a moment there is silence between us. We look at each other, each of us searching the other's features for clues. The fine hairs on my forearms stand on end, as if the air in here were electrically charged. A cold shiver creeps through my whole body in slow motion. But even that can't stop me. Not today.

"So you really do want me to fire you, is that it?" The mighty Goliath stands in front of me as if turned to stone. He always gets what he wants because no one ever stands up to him.

That ends right now. Because suddenly something becomes clear to me with a force that overwhelms even me.

Later never comes. Waiting for it makes no sense.

The wall of reason that I have so carefully built inside myself over the past few years starts to crack. One stone after another crumbles away from the massive structure, and what emerges between the clouds of dust takes my breath away.

Right there, behind that wall, lies a new future. I can lead a happy life not only in my free time. I can do something better than locking myself up in this prison day after day.

So he wants to throw me out? No, that's definitely not how this is going to go. "That won't be necessary," I answer, without taking my eyes off him. My voice is serious, just like my expression.

I do it. As if in a trance, I take a step toward him. We almost touch, and although I'm quite a bit shorter than he is, I suddenly feel very tall.

"I quit," I hear myself say.

Chapter Two

"Please send it out today." I try to speak clearly so that the person on the other end of the line will definitely understand. Then I let myself drop back into my desk chair. This call has already been going on too long, my ear is burning, and my arm is almost numb.

"Yes. By express delivery," I confirm once more, patiently, even though my nerves are more than frayed by now.

At least the customer support at the small-parts supplier finally seems to accept my request and tells me that the urgently needed car body screws will be here tomorrow. I thank them politely and, exhausted, set the receiver back on the phone.

That's taken care of. Thank God. Relieved, I let my gaze wander around the office. My colleague Bernd is mumbling absentmindedly to himself at the desk opposite me, just like always, and in the next office the other members of my department are discussing who should handle the difficult complaints in the future. The hectic rustling of paper, the dull thud of high heels on the carpet, and that mix of coffee smell and electrosmog trigger a feeling of home in me after so many years. It reminds me a bit of rush hour at the train station, with the difference that the rush here lasts all day.

"Done?" Bernd must have noticed that I've ended my call after all, and he looks up from his screen expectantly.

I nod, see his broad grin, and have to smile myself.

Then I turn back to my work, because the next purchase requests are already lying on my desk. I've sorted them by urgency, and if I don't want to get home so late again today, I should get on with them right away. As motivation, I treat myself to a piece of chocolate and let it melt on my tongue with relish.

Soft and sweet.

Like Marie.

I can't help thinking about her, and not for the first time I imagine myself standing at the altar, waiting for her. She's wearing a simple white dress, has daisies in her hair and that incomparable, sunny smile on her face. Her eyes fixed on me, she floats toward me, and the only thing I can still think is that she's the one.

Should I finally dare to do it?

Even though I don't have time for it, I pick up my phone. I've been putting this decision off for far too long. And that even though I know exactly who can help me find the right answer. Anna, my best friend since childhood, always has advice for me.

I push myself up from the chair. "I'm taking a quick break," I say to Bernd, who acknowledges the information with an approving grunt. I take my jacket from the coat rack and march toward the cafeteria.

As soon as I open the glass door to the courtyard,

refreshing spring air streams toward me. No one is here, only a few birds wander across the concrete tiles between the standing tables, searching for leftovers. I dial Anna's number. With the ringing tone in my ear, I lean against the facade of the company building. It's cold, and even the rays of the March sun don't have enough strength to warm me.

There's a click on the line. "Hey. Everything okay, darling?" Anna sounds less like a person than a rubber ball bouncing up and down in a frenzy. In the background I hear pots clattering, interrupted by a regular beeping. She's working, and she's not going to stop just because I've called. Even if she wanted to, as a chef she has no other choice. "How are you? Has Marie calmed down?"

"No one can really grasp that it's actually supposed to be true. It happened so fast," I answer thoughtfully. "Marie's grandma is like a mother to her. She's the one who taught her how to ride a bike and drove her to school. Together with her grandpa, she was always there for Marie. Of course Marie is doing everything she can right now to be there for her grandma."

"Sometimes fate strikes without warning, throws everything into turmoil, and leaves nothing but chaos behind." She talks as if she were a wise old woman, even though, like me, she's only twenty-seven. "Marie will get through this, I'm sure of it."

Of course she will. My Marie can handle anything.

"You're brooding, right?" comes the cheeky remark from the other end of the line. "Come on, out with it." The way she pushes me has something loving about it, almost motherly. That's Anna. No matter how long I rummaged through my memories, I wouldn't find a single moment when she wasn't the best friend I could possibly imagine.

"I'm wondering if maybe it's finally time…"

I immediately hear Anna whistle enthusiastically. "Absolutely!" She sounds so convinced that I don't even know what to say. "What do you think, how long have I been waiting for it to finally happen?"

I run my hand through my short-cropped hair. Just thinking about actually doing it makes me nervous. "But it never occurred to you to give me a hint?"

"No, you had to figure that out on your own." She ends her sentence with a sound that makes it seem like she's blowing out a candle. I can practically see her in front of me. Strands of hair have fallen from her messily pinned-up dark hair into her line of vision. She's trying to blow them away because her hands are busy with something else. She's probably assembling an immersion blender, pinning the phone between her shoulder and her ear while she uses her hip to shove a kitchen drawer closed.

"Some friend you are," I say, pretending to be offended. Whatever reason she had for keeping quiet about this, now she has to pay for it.

"No, not some friend—your best friend," she corrects me in a schoolmarmish tone.

"All the worse." An amused grin spreads across my face.

On the other end of the line it suddenly goes quiet. She pretends to think. Or she dropped the phone. Maybe into the soup she was just about to purée. "Get to the point. You definitely need my help."

Of course she's right. "I really don't know anything about rings." It's quite possible that that's exactly what kept me from asking for Marie's hand for so long. Along with this baseless nervousness and the fact that I have absolutely no idea how to ask her. It has to be unique, original, and romantic. After all, this is Marie we're talking about.

"Me neither. We'll just hit the jewelry stores together,

then we're bound to find the one ring to… love her." Anna's amused giggle pulls me back to reality and calms me down at least a little. "Just tell me when and where, I'll be there."

I can rely on my best friend. Always. We make plans for tomorrow afternoon. "Thanks, Anna. For everything," I say in farewell, and end the call with a relieved smile on my face.

With my gaze turned to the sky, I put the phone back in my pocket and pull the zipper of my jacket up higher.

My fingers have grown cold by now; I rub them together and, with every second they grow warmer, I realize a little more what's going to happen soon.

Marie is going to be my wife.

Of course she'll want to marry me, there's no doubt about that. Still, my breathing grows heavy when I think about the moment I'll ask the all-decisive question.

Because it has to be perfect.

She deserves nothing less. But where is the perfect place, when is the perfect moment, and what are the perfect words?

Even though I'm sure of myself, a pressure spreads across my shoulders. It travels over my chest and settles right in my stomach. Heavy and hard like a stone, it lies down there. My thoughts whirl around wildly.

Individual scenes and different situations appear before my mind's eye. The flower meadow from back then, behind the Gloriette at Schönbrunn Palace. Does it even still exist? And if so, when will it be in bloom? Or would the ice-cream parlor in the city center be a better place for the proposal? The one where, full of youthful high spirits, we immortalized our love on the underside of a table? To help myself concentrate, I push my fingers under my glasses and pinch the bridge of my nose.

Marie's pictures from this morning come to mind. The dream house!

What if I persuaded the realtor to arrange a one-of-a-kind viewing? I could put candles everywhere and then, as if by chance, stroll past the house with Marie. The garden gate would be open, and I would suggest taking a look inside.

She wouldn't have the slightest idea what was coming.

Once we're inside the house, I'll ask her—on my knees, maybe, and with the most beautiful ring in my hands you could possibly imagine.

Excitement rises in me at once. The stone in my stomach crumbles to dust, and in the very next moment I can't feel it anymore.

That moment will be wonderful. Wonderful and perfect. Just like Marie.

There's still a lot to do before then. I immediately run through the to-dos in my head. Taking care of the house is the first item on the list, so I dig out my phone again and take a closer look at Marie's photos. They're mostly useless close-ups. An artfully carved front door, the wooden steps up to the porch, and the low-hanging branches of the tall weeping willow, under which a swing is hidden.

Typical Marie. She has an eye for those little things other people would overlook.

Smiling to myself, I keep searching. Then I find a shot that shows the whole house. On the white-painted pillar of the porch hangs a sign. I zoom in closer and, sure enough, I can read the inscription.

Gartengasse 23.

I don't need to know anything else. My mission can begin.

Chapter Three

I could feel Alex's questioning gaze drilling into my back. And she wasn't the only one staring at me. All my female colleagues watched as I cleared out my desk.

They stayed silent, and so did I. Because I could hardly believe myself what had just happened.

One by one, I let the framed photos of my loved ones, the colorful pens I had brought from home, the box of tissues, and a few cosmetics wander into the cardboard box in front of me. As if I were frozen in shock inside, I didn't know what to think. I had no idea what I felt, and even less what would happen next. But I was sure of one thing. Telling the boss what I thought of him had been right.

"Do you have everything?" The security guy had been accompanying me ever since I signed the termination papers and left the boss's office. I wasn't allowed to take a single step on my own anymore.

They thought I would steal company secrets. As if there were anything here I actually wanted.

Shaking my head, I crouched down and pulled open the

bottom drawer of the desk that would no longer be mine in just a few minutes. Apart from a stack of notepads, it was empty.

I'm done here. For good. "We can go."

When I look up at my companion dressed in gray, I spot Alex in the background. Tears are crawling down her cheeks, and I don't know whether she's crying because of me or for me. I give her an encouraging nod; after all, there's no reason to be sad. Then I take a deep breath, because what comes next isn't easy for me, despite everything.

I'm being led away. Like a dangerous criminal.

"Bye." A little awkwardly, I give everyone a wave, then I turn to Alex. "We'll talk on the phone, okay?"

She nods with her lips pressed together. I can see she's struggling to understand what's happening right now.

"Everything's fine." I quickly pull her into my arms. Because I feel like she needs it. And also so I can whisper something in her ear. "This is the end of *Later*."

She probably has no idea what I mean. But I myself know it all too well. Even as the words leave my mouth, I feel tears rising inside me. They push to the surface, and I immediately understand what they mean.

They're a sign of relief, a symbol of my soul finally being able to breathe. Relentlessly they send a feeling of freedom and release through my body that travels all the way to the tips of my little toes. Never again will anyone insult me because I ordered the wrong food, booked the wrong flight, or chose the wrong font. In one stroke my boss has lost his power over me for good. Even his ridiculous warning that I wouldn't find a better job than this one can't touch me. Because it's simply not true.

I step out of Alex's arms. With my head held high and a

liberated smile on my face, I leave the office that, in recent months, had felt like nothing but a prison to me.

I walk away without looking back.

Not a second after the soles of my shoes touch the shiny tiled floor of the corridor, murmuring starts up in the open-plan office behind me. My female colleagues sound like an aggressive swarm of bees attacking a cherry tree in spring.

"This way, please." The security guard nods toward the exit.

"With pleasure," I say and march off with the small cardboard box in my hand. He won't have to force me to leave this damned place. I'm doing that entirely of my own free will.

All at once everything happens fast. I hand in my keys and step outside through the glass main entrance. My boss doesn't show his face again. He's probably too cowardly, but I don't care. Even if he were watching me as I walk toward the tram stop right now, it wouldn't matter to me.

It's twelve o'clock, the sky above me shines in its most beautiful blue. In the midst of birdsong and surrounded by the intense scent of the broom shrubs growing along the sidewalk, it feels as if nothing but adrenaline is coursing through my veins. The afternoon is mine, and I immediately know what I want to do. I'm going to spend it with Grandma. She needs to get out of her house, where everything reminds her of Grandpa, and think about something else. At least for a few hours. The prospect of being able to help her makes me smile despite all the sadness over Grandpa's death. So I take my phone in hand and dial her number.

Twenty minutes later I'm sitting in the tram toward the old town with an elderly married couple and a mother with a stroller. I only managed to persuade Grandma to meet me there with a trick, but I did it. My attempt to reach Lukas, however, fails spectacularly. He's surely in the middle of a heated discussion with one of his suppliers, negotiating prices or complaining about quality issues. I can practically see him in front of me, sitting at his desk and gesticulating wildly. Where the dark frame of his glasses touches his cheeks, his skin glows with energy. If I were with him now, I'd kiss that spot and then wander further down until I reach his soft lips. At least I can imagine it while, at the other end of the line, all I hear is the monotonous beeping of the ring tone and Vienna's streets race past me in fast motion. A wistful sigh leaves my mouth, a longing feeling floods my chest. I want to tell him in person later what happened this morning, but how much I love him, he should know that right away. And that I miss him every second he's not with me. So I write exactly that to him in a message.

When I arrive at Stephansplatz, I get off, help the mother with her stroller, and give the old lady, who steps onto the cobblestones overcautiously, a smile. Both look at me suspiciously, as if they can't understand that there are still polite people.

"The way you treat the world is the way it will treat you." That's what Grandpa always said, and it dawns on me how grateful I should be that he passed his values on to me. In so many ways he was a role model for me; only his "later" is something I won't be adopting. And today I took the first step toward that.

A wistful smile spreads across my face just as the next tram arrives. Grandma gets off, I run toward her and pull her into my arms.

"Here I am," she says in a matter-of-fact voice. "Where's the surprise?" Her eyes are still glassy from all the tears she has cried in the past few days. There isn't a trace of vitality in her face, the corners of her mouth droop limply.

I know it's my job to be strong for her. So I smile at her and hope that a little of it will rub off on her. "I quit."

"Good, darling, that job wasn't right for you anyway." There's no warmth in her words; she sounds more like an emotionless newsreader. I guess it's her way of dealing with what happened.

I don't want to take her grief away from her; I couldn't anyway. But my idea of distracting her with a stroll through town suddenly seems ridiculous. In her little house on the outskirts, though, she'd probably sink even deeper into her sadness.

I don't want to let that happen, and even if this isn't perfect, at least it's an attempt. Exercise and fresh air will do her good.

"Come on, let's walk along the Graben for a bit." I link my arm through Grandma's and we start to stroll.

As long as we're wandering through the city center, browsing in bookshops and studying the displays in the shoe stores, she doesn't say much. When I stock up on nail polish in the latest colors at the drugstore, she just stands next to me, apathetic. "Dark cherry red or varicose-vein violet?" I ask her in an exaggeratedly cheerful tone, holding up two little bottles.

Her gaze wanders back and forth, undecided. Then she shrugs.

"I vote for dark cherry red. Like my boss's head when I quit today." I give her a mischievous grin.

Something actually stirs in her face. It's only a tiny twitch at the corners of her mouth, but I know what it means. Nothing could make me happier in this moment than this reaction.

Alex should see her progress too, so I snap a photo of Grandma, me, and the nail polish. When I look at it, I realize that Grandma is even smiling a little in it.

And me? I look strangely content, my chestnut-brown eyes shining. Because I was able to be there for Grandma, just a little. And because a whole new life is lying ahead of me. Even if I have no idea where it'll take me, one thing is clear: hardly anything has ever felt so right.

I send the photo to Alex, we stroll on through the store, sniff every single kind of shower gel and let our fingertips glide over the prettily decorated packaging of the exclusive creams.

When we leave the drugstore with bags stuffed full, Grandma's expression is at least a shade brighter. "Thank you, darling," she says, and at last her voice has that motherly sound again that I like so much. "Come on, let's grab a little something to eat together." I nod toward the bakery across the street. I know she's hardly eaten anything in the past few days.

Grandma gives a tired smile. "The chickens are waiting."

My gaze jerks to my wristwatch. Sure enough, it's already 4:30 PM. "I'll come with you and help you."

At the same moment, Grandma takes my hands and looks at me intently. "You've already done enough for today."

I definitely haven't. Letting her go alone can't possibly be right. Or does she need time to herself?

"Yes." Grandma answers the question I never actually asked. That's how it is with the two of us; we only have to look at each other to know what the other is thinking. I study her face closely. I see how she nods at me with the corners of her mouth lifted and know I won't be able to talk her out of her plan.

Even if she'd rather be alone, I hug her tightly once more. "We'll talk on the phone then…" At the last second I bite my lip so that the *later* that's on the tip of my tongue can't slip out of my mouth.

Later doesn't exist anymore. Not for her, and not for me.

We say goodbye to each other and I watch her run along the cobbled street until she disappears around the next corner.

It had been a good afternoon. I'd managed to distract her a little, and things would definitely get easier for her again. Days, weeks, and months would pass. Time would be on her side, and I would stay by her side anyway.

An intense feeling of confidence spread in my chest. In spite of all the sadness, it made me so happy that I decided to visit the little bakery across the street even without Grandma. To celebrate the day, I treated myself to tramezzini and a whole bottle of sparkling wine just for me.

Is it strange to raise a glass to myself?

No, I decided, and toasted myself in my thoughts.

To Grandpa. And to the end of *Later*.

Chapter Four

Full of anticipation for the evening off with Marie, I stepped into our apartment. As usual, I was overcome by the feeling that we were living on a rainbow. Most of all here in the hallway. When I moved in with Marie just under four years ago, everything was still colorful. Luckily, I'd managed to talk her into painting the walls white, but she had insisted vehemently on keeping the brightly colored doorframes of the adjoining rooms. She'd had that incomparable radiance on her face, the one that always convinced me in the end.

"Lukas?" Accompanied by the hum of the extractor fan and the clatter of pots, Marie's bell-like voice floated from the kitchen to me in the hallway. It smelled of that rice I loved so much, and my stomach reacted at once. I set my bag down and slipped my shoes off my feet.

Before I could even head toward Marie, she poked her head out of the azure-blue kitchen door and beamed at me blissfully. "Hello there, my prince."

"Someone's in a good mood." If there's one thing I'll be

powerless against for the rest of my life, it's her smile. Even after five years together, it still feels as if the sun rises when she beams like that. "Did you have a nice day?" I ask skeptically anyway, because I know the chances of that aren't high after her grandpa's death.

"Mhm." There's something mysterious in her voice. She's as jittery as a toddler at Christmas.

I wrap my arms around her hips and pull her close to me. "Are you going to tell me about it too?"

"Mhm." She nods and rises up on her tiptoes. Our lips touch, and instantly I forget all my worries. There's no room left for anger, bills, or annoying coworkers. I can practically feel the world around us slowing down. Her cheek smells like an entire peach tree, and there's an unusual taste on her tongue.

"Have you been drinking?" I ask, amused, after I pull away from her.

She answers my question first with a mischievous grin. "A whole bottle."

I can hear all too clearly how heavy her tongue is. But before I can tease her about it, at least a little, she covers my face with little kisses. I like the feeling her lips leave on my skin. So soft, as if she were brushing my cheeks with a feather. Still, I find it hard to relax.

There's something strange about this. Marie is my sunshine, and it's great to see her smile. But she's only ever in this good a mood on weekends or on vacation. And her grandpa's death had stubbornly overshadowed her radiance lately. For days I tried in vain to cheer her up. Something must have happened today. Something special. Or is it just the alcohol masking her sadness?

"Did you take the day off on a whim?" I phrase my

question gently so I don't remind her unnecessarily of last week's tragic events.

"Something like that," she mumbles. Her kisses wander on toward my neck.

Involuntarily, I close my eyes and take a deep breath.

It smells burnt.

I don't want to do it, but I have no choice. Gently, I push Marie away from me and nod toward the kitchen. "I'm afraid..."

She gives me a mischievous grin. "Oops," is all she says, then she gives me one last quick kiss and staggers off down the narrow hallway.

Shaking my head, I watch her disappear into the azure-blue kitchen doorway with an awkward little jump, looking as if she's diving into the sea. "I'm just going to hop in the shower, okay?" I call after her and undo the top buttons of my shirt.

"I wish I could join you," comes her voice from the kitchen, and I immediately have to smile. Her desire to be close to me isn't the only reason I'm with Marie. I could list at least a thousand traits that just make her lovable. Her willingness to help others, the cheerful way she goes through life. The way she listens to me and laughs with me, the way she kisses me and is there for me. In my mind I go through these and other reasons as I stroll past the cherry-red bedroom door toward the orange-painted entrance to the bathroom.

Chapter Five

I scrape the rice that isn't burnt yet out of the pot and smell it. Thanks to Lukas, at least that's okay. Sometimes, I'm sure a lot of things would go wrong if it weren't for him with his good sense and clear thinking. Whenever I get lost in my thoughts, he keeps an eye on the important things.

We're a dream couple.

Absolutely.

"It must be pretty bright up there on your cloud." Alex's comment suddenly pops into my head as I push the rice to the side.

Oh damn, Alex!

I glance frantically at the big bright yellow clock above the kitchen door. It's seven in the evening by now; I should have called her ages ago. Maybe I shouldn't have treated myself to quite so much sparkling wine; then my head would be less foggy. I quickly grab the crusted pot and fill it with water. Then I grab my phone and dial her number. I don't even hear a single ring before Alex picks up.

"Finally!" She sounds like she's been staring at her

phone for hours, willing it to ring. “Tell me everything,” she demands, her voice tinged with a craving for juicy details.

A hissing sound pulls my attention away. The vegetables are boiling over. “Damn. Hang on a second.”

Thank God our kitchen is tiny. With just one step I’m at the stove and pull the pot off the burner. Right after that I realize I forgot to flip the chicken breast in the pan. I haven’t even opened the kitchen drawer when an impatient sigh comes down the line.

“We have to be quick, Leon will be here any minute.” Just a moment ago her voice had been urgent, but now it has taken on that very special tone. That’s how she sounds these days when she talks about Leon.

“Is someone in for a hot night?” I try to control my tongue, but it doesn’t really work.

“And someone else has had a boozy afternoon,” Alex remarks, amused. “But that’s not the point.” There it is again, that demanding yet affectionate tone. She wants answers, that much is clear.

I awkwardly rummage a fork out of the drawer and use it to turn the meat. The underside already looks pretty dark. “I’ll never be a cook,” I say ruefully.

“And what on earth does that have to do with your resignation?” In my mind she throws her arm theatrically into the air. “You’re not planning to retrain and start working in a restaurant, are you?”

“Definitely not.” How absurd that idea is, is obvious from the state of my kitchen. Between the yellow patterned curtains and the brightly tiled walls there isn’t a single spot that’s clear and clean. Cutting boards, dishes, and empty packages are strewn all over the pale wood of the countertop. Individual grains of rice have found refuge in the grout between the floor tiles.

It's still quiet on the other end of the line.

I know Alex well enough to recognize that she's having one of her spontaneous brainwaves. A thought that suddenly appears and won't let her go. "You know what?"

"What?" I turn down the heat on the stove and lean back against the kitchen cabinets so the room doesn't spin quite so badly around me.

"From now on, anything is possible for you. There are no limits, you can do whatever you want with your life." I know that rapturous tone. It's exactly the one I always used when I dreamed about quitting my job.

"That's exactly right," I confirm, a broad grin on my face.

"So, if I were you, I'd take some time off. When else are you going to get the chance? You could learn to knit. Or take up ballet."

I can't help grinning. "And learn to ride a unicycle."

"I'm serious, Marie." She lowers her voice conspiratorially. "This is your chance, and it won't come around again anytime soon. There is something you've always wanted to do, isn't there?"

I didn't have to think about her question for a single second. "Travel." Even I could hear the dreamy sound in my voice, because in my mind I was already on my way. "South Africa. Greenland. Canada," I listed, seeing the wide steppe of Kruger National Park, huge ice floes, and the untamed wilderness of the Yukon before me. Then I paused for a moment, because an image appeared in my mind that made all the others fade.

Red earth. Colorful cloths. Golden bangles.

"India," I breathed longingly.

"Exactly." She sounded like she was slapping her thigh in excitement. Suddenly her doorbell rang. "Leon's here.

Tomorrow we'll have lunch together and talk everything through properly," she said, out of breath.

Her excitement was simply adorable. "Sounds like a plan." It was better that way anyway, because in my current state I probably shouldn't be making any decisions.

I wished the newly in-love lovebirds a lovely evening and said goodbye. Then I let my gaze wander around the kitchen and tried hard to concentrate.

What was left to do? Turn the meat, season the vegetables, open the wine, and set the table. I started with the meat, but as soon as I took the salt from the cupboard above the stove, my thoughts drifted off again.

Back to Alex and Leon. Even if it had taken years, in the end it seemed she, too, had found the love of her life. Just like that, while shopping, they had suddenly stood facing each other one day. In front of the refrigerated section, by the dairy products. The thought made me smile, and the very next moment the memory of my first encounter with Lukas surged up inside me.

Back then, five years ago.

I was twenty, had just moved into my apartment, and could go out for as long as I wanted without anyone watching me. All at once I felt terribly grown-up. Today I have to chuckle at myself, but back then there was nothing more amazing for me than hitting the town with Alex. On that one special evening, we stormed a new trendy bar in downtown Vienna. As it quickly turned out, thanks to the heated party atmosphere in the vaulted cellar, we had only one option. We had to dance.

Right now the memory overwhelms me. I feel as if I'm back there, reliving the best thing that has ever happened to me.

The steady bass thumps in my ears and from there

forces its way through every cell of my body. With my eyes closed, I move in the middle of the ecstatically dancing crowd to the rhythm of the music. With no sense of time. There's only me, the beat, and what it does to me.

It could have been minutes, or it could have been hours that have already passed. I don't know. All I can still feel are my feet. They burn as if with every step they were touching the floor of hell. I give Alex a sign, limp over to one of the tables at the edge of the dance floor, and drop onto the free spot at the end of the bench. Even though I know it's a mistake, I slip out of my high heels. The pain in the soles of my feet disappears and leaves behind such a liberating feeling that I close my eyes in pleasure with a relieved sigh.

The very next moment someone presses against my upper arm. "Excuse me," a male voice says.

"Look, she's asleep," another one can be heard saying. I can only hope he isn't eyeing me right now like an exhibit in a museum.

"Hey, Sleeping Beauty, you okay?" the first one asks, sounding slightly concerned.

Hopefully he doesn't get the idea to wake Sleeping Beauty from her deep sleep with a disgustingly wet kiss. Just to be safe, I open my eyes and look straight into the friendly face of a man who's probably about my age. His short brown hair sticks out in every direction. It's quite possible that there are chestnut-brown eyes hiding behind his glasses, but it's too dark to be sure.

"Everything's fine, my prince, I'm just resting my legs here. You men have no idea what that can do to a person." I point at the high heels next to my feet with both index fingers and pull a pained expression.

The hint of a smile appears on his face. His eyes sparkle, which, combined with the angular lines of his jaw, makes him suddenly look stunningly attractive. "I can see you have to endure a hell of a lot. May I buy you a drink to make you feel better?" His smile turns into a broad grin.

I can't help but beam at him. "I'd love to."

"Coming right up, Sleeping Beauty!" With a mock bow, he spins on his heel. I watch him as he makes his way through the crowd with his arms raised. Bright flashes of light keep flaring up, letting me catch glimpses of his face. His head bobs to the beat of the music, a mysterious smile playing around his lips.

Not even five minutes later, he's standing in front of me with a glass of Campari orange in his hand.

Bull's-eye. However he knew that.

With a grateful smile, I take the glass from him. "So, my prince, what's your name, anyway?"

He takes a big swig of his beer before he answers. "Lukas."

Lukas? How awful. The name doesn't suit this anything-but-average guy at all, the one who's now making himself comfortable next to me on the bench.

"No, I don't like that." I give him a furtive grin. "I'd rather call you Max."

Lukas bursts out laughing. "Your wish is my command. Should I keep calling you Sleeping Beauty, or are you going to tell me your name too?"

"But Sleeping Beauty is my real name." I wink at him cheekily. This conversation could be fun.

"I see. Then you're already ancient, right? You've probably been dreaming away for several centuries. Good thing I finally woke you up. Poor you, you probably have no idea what time you've ended up in."

He wasn't just cute, he was quick-witted too. I liked that, and suddenly I wasn't so sure anymore whether it really was only the deep bass of the all-dominating music that was making my chest vibrate. "You're mistaken about that. I've been awake for a while now and even managed to find my way around in this world, even if I had my problems with it at first." Awkwardly, I reach for the straw in my drink because I can't manage to take my eyes off him for even a second.

Maybe he felt the same way. With a smirk on his lips, he looked at me without a break. "All right. Tell me how you make a living in this world. Is there such a thing as a Sleeping Beauty job?"

The fact that he went along with my game spurred me on to top form. "Unfortunately, I couldn't get hired anywhere as Sleeping Beauty. Some even thought I'd be better off in a mental hospital than in their company. So I bowed to reality and work as a maid. Incognito, so to speak."

He knew that wasn't the truth; I could see it in his eyes. Still, he kept pretending this was a getting-to-know-you like any other. He had a sense of humor, but what else was behind his exterior, which seemed to be getting more and more attractive? It was a bit as if the lighting were changing, softening his skin and making his eyes shine. "And what do you do when you're not waking up fairy-tale characters in the middle of the night?" I asked him cheekily. By now there was a permanent grin on my face.

"I'm a general assistant," he answered with utter seriousness. I was probably looking at him pretty stupidly right then; at least that's what his amused smirk told me. "It doesn't make me rich, but I love the adrenaline and all the female fans around the world who adore me."

There was something in his gaze. An incredibly sweet, mischievous sparkle that went straight to my heart. It lost its rhythm, turned restless and wild. Strange—I had only known this Lukas for a few minutes, yet already my body was doing whatever it wanted.

That didn't change over the next few hours either. We chatted about our fictional lives without either of us making any attempt to set the record straight. And the longer the evening went on, the less I wanted to anyway.

Entangled in our construct of freely invented stories about the past, present, and future plans, the moments multiplied when tingling shivers ran down my back. Always whenever he looked at me longer than necessary or we touched each other as if by accident.

"Hey, general assistant, can you dance too, or doesn't that give you enough adrenaline?" I asked him challengingly hours later.

Without answering, he took my hand and pulled me onto the dance floor. The mood of the partying crowd was at its peak, the speakers were turned up to the max. But I no longer noticed any of that. It felt as if all of it were staying outside. As if the two of us were no longer here, where we were moving to the beat of the music. The pounding bass bounced off an invisible wall in front of us, the fog and neon lights didn't reach us. It was as if the two of us were all alone.

As if pure magic were at work.

I dance only for him. He wraps his arms around my hips and gently pulls me toward him. We move closer and closer. In the rhythm of the music we melt into one another, and suddenly he is everywhere. I feel his body, smell the tart scent of his skin.

Our eyes meet, and what I see captivates me. His eyes, fixed on me and radiating so much warmth. The happy smile on his lips. And his face, suddenly so close. Only a few millimeters are left between us.

All at once everything stands still. I stop breathing. I can't think anymore. I only know one thing: it just has to happen. Right now.

I rise up on my tiptoes. I already feel his lips, softer than anything else in this world. Tenderly and with infinite feeling he returns my kiss.

An endless fireworks display spreads inside me. Nothing on this planet matters anymore. Only he and I still exist, tightly entwined on the dance floor, far away from this world.

Even today, five years later, that memory is still so close to me, as if I had just experienced it. And I feel with absolute clarity what both of us already knew back then without saying it out loud.

Lukas and I belong together. Forever.

Blissfully, here and now, I put the saltshaker back in its place and take two plates out of the cupboard. But in the very next moment my mood darkens, because I have to think of Grandma and Grandpa. The two of them were together all their lives, their love was deep, and they wanted nothing more than to enjoy that. But in one blow, the time for everything they had still planned was taken from them.

What Lukas and I have can't last forever either. One of us has to go first, the other will be left behind alone.

Like a shadow, this dark thought cuts through my otherwise boozy, happy mood.

No, I don't want to imagine anything that terrible.

Luckily, things will be completely different for the two of us. Because today I took the first step toward declaring war on Grandpa's "later." For Lukas and me, "later" doesn't exist; instead, from now on we'll live our lives as if every day were our last.

I arrange the vegetables on the plates and hum again the tune we were kissing to back then, a trance-like song about the sky and the sand, underpinned by a thumping bass. All of a sudden I can't help but dance. Just like back then. With a blissful smile on my lips and a warm feeling in my chest.

Chapter Six

With her eyes closed, Marie stands at the stove, waving a fork through the air. Her hips sway seductively from side to side. She sings, and her head bobs to a beat that I can feel instantly as well.

I walk up to her, press myself against her back, and match my movements to hers. “Hey, Sleeping Beauty,” I whisper in her ear.

Without stopping her dance, Marie leans her head back onto my shoulder so I can kiss her cheek. At the same moment she opens her lids and beams at me in that incomparable way. I feel warm, not just in my chest but all through my body.

“I love you,” she says in a feather-soft voice, turns to face me, and traces my cheekbones with her fingers, all the way down to my lips.

What I’d like most is to shout that one question straight out into the world, so loud that everyone can hear it. But it’s still not the right moment, and I have to get the ring first. So

I kiss her, to keep the words from accidentally spilling out of me.

When we pull apart, she gives me a conspiratorial grin. I know at once that she's already waiting to tell me something. Is it about us too? "Let's eat," she suddenly says, grabs the prepared plates, and disappears with them into the living room.

With the cutlery in my hand, I follow her into the small, cozy room. I immediately notice that she has tidied up. The cream-colored wool blanket lies perfectly folded on the gray sofa. She's even fluffed up the purple cushions and arranged them in the corners. She must have been home earlier than usual today. Along with her conspiratorial manner, it's another sign that something isn't the way it usually is. What on earth has happened to her in the last few hours?

"All right. Tell me what's going on." Aside from my own curiosity, I can clearly see how jittery she is. Still, she seems to be waiting for me to sit down at the round dining table.

She herself remains standing. Her gaze wanders to me; she practically pins me in place to have my full attention. Then she raises her arms as if she were a TV host presenting the next show act.

"I quit." She not only looks but also sounds as if she's announcing a sensation to me and, damn it, that's exactly what it is.

I stare at her in disbelief. My head can't process what it just heard. "You did what?"

Accompanied by an emphatic nod, she drops onto her chair and reaches across the table for my hand. "It's done. Over. Finished." Everything about her radiates as if she were seeing fireworks for the first time. Excitedly, her fingers wander over the back of my hand. "I was even put on paid leave, isn't that fantastic?"

Is it? I have no idea. She seems damn happy. And terribly drunk. "Um…" I'm still too confused to say anything at all.

All at once she furrows her brows. "You're not happy at all," she says, disappointed.

"Of course I am. I know how hard things were for you at your job." She did so much to improve her miserable situation at work; all of it was in vain.

When her attempt to transfer to a different department also failed four weeks ago, she was completely discouraged. Still, she should never have quit so thoughtlessly. What on earth got into her?

I quickly close my fingers around hers, stop their nervous movements, and hold them in a firm grip. "I'm still surprised."

As if she were thinking for a moment about whether she can trust me, she tilts her head to the side and studies me. "At first I was too, after all, everything happened so fast. But now…"

"What about now?" I lean across the table toward her. There's only one right answer to this question. Namely, that she's going to start looking for a new job right away. How else are we supposed to make our plan of having our own house come true?

At once a dreamy expression appears on her face, her cheeks turn pink. "I don't have the slightest idea," she says, staring into the nowhere above us. "Absolutely anything is possible."

"My Sleeping Beauty is dreaming." I can't hide the sarcastic tone in my voice.

She immediately pushes out her lower lip. "Am I not allowed to?"

"You are," I answer quickly, but in the same moment my

nervousness overwhelms me. Because the truth is that not everything can have a place in real life. Marie knows that. I certainly don't want to spoil her joy. Not after the sad days she's just been through. Still, there's one thing I have to make clear right away. "Luckily we're dreaming the same dream," I add. Then I pick up my fork and load it with rice.

"You mean the dream house?" Out of the corner of my eye I see Marie also tucking into her food.

I nod. "Exactly." If we want to buy it, we'll both have to work hard for it. Quitting doesn't exactly fit into that picture. While I'm still searching for the right words to tell her that as lightly as possible, she beats me to it.

"That's not going to work with just one salary." She sounds deflated, as if she had suddenly, in one blow, become a little more grown-up.

It hurts to watch her suddenly let her head hang on the other side of the table. Listlessly she pokes at her vegetables, pushes individual peas together into a pea family and perforates the carrots. I don't want to see her like this. Still, I can't think of anything to cheer her up. "I did the math today. Even if we just go by the average price per square meter for houses in this area, we'll have to cough up a small fortune." For us to get a loan, we definitely need two salaries. That's a fact; numbers never lie.

She takes a deep breath and attempts a crooked smile. "Well, then I know what I have to do now. And what I have to do later." Strange, the way she says the word "later." It sounds as if it caused a painful tug on her palate.

Seeing her sad expression instantly dampens my mood as well. I quickly push myself up from the chair and walk around the table. When I reach her, I wrap my arms tightly around her upper body. "I wish it were possible to just have everything. I'd go to the end of the world for that and then a little farther." I thought, life is made up of compromises, but I didn't say it out loud. Marie understands what I mean, I'm sure of it.

She strokes my forearm. "I know that, don't worry," she whispers in a trembling voice.

I hug her once more and cover the crown of her head with small kisses. I just want her to shine again; that's all I wish for. I pull back a little and look deep into her eyes. "Are you okay?"

There it is again, that sparkle. Not like usual, as if an entire starry sky were trapped in her gaze. More like the brief flash of a single star. "But of course." She nods, but I still don't get a smile.

Chapter Seven

No sooner has Lukas taken his last bite than he looks at me expectantly. "We should clear the decks in the kitchen."

Like always, I wrinkle my nose. "Or we could open another bottle of wine," I suggest, not without ulterior motives. Earlier I let myself get talked down by Lukas's common sense far too quickly. "I'll clean up the kitchen tomorrow, I've got time, as we all know." I give him a conspiratorial wink.

He can't help but give in, I can see it in the softness of his gaze. "All right, let's make a toast."

Hurriedly, I stack the used dishes and carry them into the kitchen. There are dirty pots on the stove, but I ignore them. Tidying up right away would shorten our evening together, and that's definitely not what either of us wants. I can't help smiling because one thing about my future already comes to mind that I'm sure of. Lukas will always be a part of my life. Even if he never stops writing those endless to-do lists to hang on the fridge and ticking off the open items one by one. Today I ignore them, open the fridge door, and take out a bottle of the Pinot Blanc that Lukas's parents make at their winery in Burgenland.

I fill two glasses and pause for a moment. The artificial light from the lamp breaks on the wine, sparkling golden. So beautiful that I wish I could capture this sight. Of course that's nonsense, so I shake the strange thought from my head and walk back into the living room, where Lukas has now made himself comfortable on the sofa. In his hands I spot our weekly planner.

"If you're going to be at home from now on, would you drive the car to get the tires changed? Would that be okay? The appointment is the day after tomorrow at eight in the morning," he says.

I set the glasses down on the low white lacquered coffee table and snuggle up to him. I don't care about the stupid weekly planner. I'd much rather talk to him again in peace about the possibilities of our future, but I know how important it is to him to be well organized in everyday life. "No problem. What else needs to be done?"

"Great, thanks." He moves the task from his column to mine and lets the pen wander further over the paper. "Next Thursday at 8:00 AM the plumber is coming because of the faucet in the bathroom, and there are also two house viewings on the schedule. Tuesday and Thursday evening, each at 6:30 PM. On Friday you have a hair appointment at 3:00 PM with Iris, and after that we wanted to go to the movies with Bernd and his girlfriend Lisa. The film starts at 8:30 PM, but we're meeting at 6:00 PM already for pizza. You won't forget the Spanish class on Saturday at 1:00 PM anyway, will you?" Lukas's cheeks are practically glowing as he goes through the appointments one by one. "I'll note down for you that you have to make a photo appointment. For new application photos," he murmurs, and immediately enters the task for next Monday in the column of my to-dos.

I can't help swallowing at the sight of the planner. It's overflowing. There are hardly any days when we don't have something to do.

Is that supposed to be my *later*?

I don't think so. The weekly planner should take a break for a change. My mission for this evening is a different one, so I reach for our wineglasses and hand one of them to Lukas.

"We wanted to celebrate." I clink my glass against his. "What are we drinking to?"

Even though he can hardly tear himself away from his favorite pastime, he does it. For my sake he puts the tablet aside and gives me a warm smile. "You decide."

"To freedom." No sooner have the words left my mouth than that feeling from this afternoon is back again. That certainty that from now on something new will begin for me. A better life. No matter what Lukas said so thoughtlessly earlier, I'm going to find out together with him what's actually possible.

For a moment he furrows his brow, but I skillfully ignore it. Instead, I give him an encouraging nod, take a sip of white wine, and nestle my back against his chest. "Let's dream. Like we used to," I ask him longingly.

He immediately wraps his arms around me. "But what for?" He sounds cautious. And there it is, that reasonableness that has crept so clearly into his voice over the past few years.

"Because we haven't done it for far too long," I say with conviction and sink even deeper into his embrace. There's no place in this world where I feel more at home than this close to him. With a contented sigh I close my eyes, and suddenly it's as if countless ideas are shooting through my head like fireworks rockets. Some fizzle out in the darkness, others light up this one sky that only I can see. The dream-house rocket explodes in my head. Beautiful golden glittering stars rain down on me.

"It would be great to move into our dream house soon. I can already see us sitting together on the porch, looking at wildly growing rosebushes in the garden." A warm shiver runs through my whole body. Not just because Lukas twines his fingers with mine and lets his thumb wander gently across my palm. The idea of living happily with him in this house forever is wonderful.

Even so, doubts overwhelm me, making the sparks from the dream-house rocket burn out far too quickly in the darkness.

"But is it even worth the sacrifices we'd have to make for it? Wouldn't toiling away for years for the money also mean that we'd have to keep putting off the beautiful sides of life?" I abruptly open my eyes and look up at Lukas. "And in the end, doesn't it actually not matter where we sit and what we see, as long as we're together?"

No sooner have I spoken the words than Lukas tilts his head to the side. "Of course it's worth it," he says without hesitating for even a second, and although his thumb is still stroking my skin, it suddenly feels different to me. "Just because we both work hard doesn't mean our life isn't beautiful."

"There's something to that. We could be happy in that house. Very happy." I can't help but smile, yet another thought pushes its way up inside me. "But how are we supposed to enjoy it if we're at work all the time?" For years we've been trying to reconcile our obligations and our longings. We fail. Again and again. It's time to finally change that. "There are completely different paths open to us, too. What about America, Japan, and Tasmania?" New rockets shoot through my head in split-second intervals. Blue, orange, and bright green. They show me all the colors of this world, so radiantly beautiful that I can hardly get enough of them. "You still remember what we used to dream about, don't you?"

All at once there is melancholy in his gaze. Accompanied by a slight shake of his head, he pulls me a little closer to him. It is as if he wants to hold on to me so I won't despair at the words he is about to say. As if he wants to give me support because he is just about to take something else away from me. "We were young and naive. Back then we didn't know what life meant. We weren't aware that we had to take responsibility. We hardly had any bills to pay and even fewer obligations."

In an instant, the shimmering, colorful fireworks rockets in my mind burn out. Lukas is right, we can't just go on a trip.

"You have to work," I say, sobered, and yet I don't want to give up that quickly. "What if you took some time off? We could be on the road for half a year, and after that we'll just jump back into the rat race."

That's it! The perfect idea. Immediately I see the two of us driving along the Algarve in a camper van. Lukas is behind the wheel, his head bobbing to the beat of the reggae music blaring at full volume from the speakers. And me? I stick my arm out the window, feel the warm slipstream brush over my skin, and feel like I haven't in far too long. Free.

As much as the excitement about this idea spreads inside me, it seems to touch Lukas just as little. "You know that's impossible. Even if I got approval, time off like that has to be prepared for months. First we have to find someone to cover for me, and then they have to be trained..."

Must, must, must. I don't hear anything more than that, and although I don't want to give this word any power over me, it overwhelms me effortlessly even without my consent.

Grinding my teeth, I push myself away from him. "So you don't even want to try?" I ask accusingly.

"We can't just run away. And if you want to build something, you have to work for it. That's just how life is, we all have to accept that. You too." He sounds far too reasonable.

There it was again. That terrible must. While I feel the urge to drain my glass of wine in one go, my sky turns dark. Because I no longer know what to think. What am I allowed to dream of, and what can I wish for?

Do I really have to keep working as a secretary? Making coffee, filing documents, preparing presentations. Booking flights, placating the boss, fending off annoying appointments. The very thought of it makes me shudder instantly. Resistance rises in me at once.

Shaking my head, I tug at the hem of my sweater. "For six long years I've done nothing but run after my superiors as if I were their maid. I kept quiet and smiled, lowered my gaze and made myself invisible. All that was missing was a little frilly apron, nothing else." It can't go on like this. Isn't there another way? Couldn't I at least earn my money doing something I enjoy?

"You're exaggerating. Your job has its good sides too, don't forget that."

Lukas's insistent tone makes sure my sky stays dark now. No exciting new idea rises up in me, nowhere does even the tiniest light shine. Still, at least one thing becomes clear to me. "I want to take a bit of time. Just a few days, maybe a week. To at least find a job where the advantages outweigh the downsides. Financially that's not a problem, after all I'll still get my usual salary for the six-week notice period," I say firmly. "If I don't come up with anything, I can still just take any old job."

Later is never, I immediately hear my grandma's sad voice whisper. As if she wanted to remind me that this attitude is wrong.

But what in heaven's name is right?

Obviously relieved, Lukas breathes a kiss onto the crown of my head. "Do that, Sleeping Beauty. And let me know if I can help you."

I nod. Maybe I don't know right now what I want to do with my life, but soon that will become clear to me. I just need time. To think. Without distractions, without stress and without obligations. Just me alone with my ideas of *Later*, neatly sorted, ranked by priority and checked for how feasible they are.

Suddenly the sky inside me grows brighter, as if the sun were climbing over a horizon I can't even see. Warm orange light threads through my thoughts. It's a sign of hope that's just now growing inside me like a delicate plant. So I dare once more to ask myself the all-important questions. What do I want my life to look like from now on? What do I want to do, where do I want to be?

Which *Later* could begin now?

Chapter Eight

I step into the jewelry store and immediately feel as if I've landed in a cave whose walls are covered in gemstones. Everything around me sparkles gold and silver. Overwhelmed, I turn in a circle, but that doesn't help either. "Phewww" is all I can say, then I throw Anna a pleading look for help.

A mischievous smile lies on her narrow lips, and she points her index finger at the print on her gray sweater. "I put this on just for you today."

My eyes wander downward. Yes, we can is written there in dark blue capital letters. That and the funny grimace forming on Anna's face actually help me relax. "Where do we start?"

Thoughtfully, she rubs her chin. I almost have to laugh; with her boyish gestures she always reminds me of a construction worker. Her outfit does the rest; in the baggy jeans and casual sweater she looks anything but feminine. She probably came straight from working out; she isn't wearing any makeup, and her dark brown hair is pulled back into a practical ponytail.

"With Marie, of course." Her voice sounds so wonderfully sure that I would never doubt her words. Motivated, she claps her hands. "What's her favorite color?"

I don't have to think long about that. "Sunshine yellow." Just like her smile.

Instead of looking at the numerous display cases in front of us herself, Anna marches straight over to the salesman, who, in his dark suit, is standing behind the counter like an inconspicuous statue. "We'd like to see all the rings with sunshine-yellow stones, please," she says, and energetically pushes up the sleeves of her sweater.

"With pleasure." The gentleman with the graying hair immediately springs into action, pulls various drawers out of the cabinets, and sets them one after another on the glass display cases in front of us. "Here on the right we have everything in yellow gold. Then silver, platinum, and finally white gold." His hand moves in an elegant sweep over the rings that lie before us like sparkling treasures.

My God, there must be more than a hundred different pieces. How am I ever supposed to find the right one among them?

Too fast to actually see anything, my gaze jerks from one ring to the next. My hands start to sweat; I feel as if today were already the day I'll drop to my knees in front of Marie.

Anna immediately notices what's going on with me and lays a calming hand on my upper arm. "We need a few minutes," she tells the salesperson, who nods understandingly and withdraws. Then she focuses on the rings and pulls one from its dark velvet cushion to take a closer look. "What do you think of this one?"

I look at the slim silver band with a pale yellow, round

stone set on it. "Too ordinary," is the first thing that comes to mind, "and it doesn't shine nearly enough." For Marie I need something special, not just any old rock.

"All right." With an understanding nod, Anna puts the ring back in its place. "Do you already know when and where you want to propose to her?" she asks, letting her gaze wander over the selection.

"I have a vague idea." Lost in thought, I pick up a ring. I like the square-cut stone, but everything else about this piece is too bulky. That doesn't suit Marie. "When I ask her, it has to be one of a kind, you know?"

"Lukas, the meticulously planned perfectionist." She shakes her head, her ponytail loosening. "No matter what you do, for Marie it will always be perfect," she reminds me gently and lets her fingers continue to wander searchingly over the rings. "She loves you. Like crazy."

"And I love her." In my mind I see her sunny smile before me. A gust of wind blows her honey-blond hair into her face. It catches on her lips and tickles her cheeks. "Like crazy."

Smirking, Anna nudges me in the side with her elbow to pull me out of my daydreams. "Focus, darling. We've got a mission to accomplish here; dreaming is for when you're asleep."

"Exactly." Dreams have no place in real life, and no one knows that better than I do. My thoughts jump straight to Marie and what she said last night in her drunken haze about our old pipe dreams. A familiar feeling of bitterness threatens to overwhelm me. I push it away, because it doesn't belong here.

"All right then, tell me: what's the plan?" Anna asks, continuing her search for the perfect ring. The one that will put a watery shimmer in Marie's chestnut-brown eyes and a reverent tremor in her voice.

I clear my throat. "There's this house that would just be perfect for us. Marie sent me pictures." I fish my phone out of my pocket and show her the photos.

Anna looks at her with her lower lip jutting out and a vigorous nod. "Oh là là. That's where you want to do it?"

"That was the idea. But we can only get in together with the realtor. So I wouldn't be able to prepare anything. It would just be a measly proposal in an empty house in the company of someone neither of us knows." I let my phone slide into my jacket pocket and turn to the pieces of jewelry. Hesitating, I grab the next ring, but put it back right away. Too dull. "I guess I need a new plan, but what kind?"

She immediately pulls her shoulders up so far that her neck disappears. "You'll have to ask someone else about that. I don't know much about romance."

That was true. Apart from a few ultra-short relationships and the odd one-night stand, she didn't have much to show for herself in the love department. So I had to keep puzzling it out on my own. "Maybe the realtor can be persuaded. If I manage to organize a few candles beforehand and could do the viewing with Marie alone, it might be an option. Or I carry the ring with me all the time and surprise her with the proposal at a moment when she least expects it."

"Does it really make sense to ask her in the house when you don't even know yet if you're going to buy it?" she asks, rubbing her chin thoughtfully.

"You've got a point." Uncertainty spreads through me at once.

"Just go look at the house and let your gut feeling decide about the proposal," she says, then gives me a conspiratorial look. "Wait, the gut-feeling thing just gave me an idea." Her light-blue eyes light up. Without taking her gaze off me, she lets her hand glide over the rings in front of us, as if she were a medium trying to sense their energy.

Suddenly she stops. "That's the one."

Curious, I watch her sinewy fingers touch the sparkling thing and lift it up. A second later she presents me with the surprise ring, beaming. The first thing I see is an elongated, sunny yellow stone. It's surrounded by small diamonds and set in a band whose delicacy would look fantastic on Marie's finger.

That's the one. It's perfect.

"I'll take it," I hear myself say, and with those words it becomes real. Marie and I, we're going to take the next step. Wedding, our own home and, who knows, maybe even kids soon. Miniature versions of us, two or three little beings made from the two of us. That's a goal. That's what we dream of.

"You sure?" Anna's brow is furrowed, her gaze drops. "How do your feet feel?" she wants to know.

I smile away her doubts, and that's not hard for me at all. "So warm, like I'm holding them out toward a crackling fire," I answer. Because it's the truth.

Chapter Nine

Hardly has the waitress taken our order when Alex can't wait any longer. "I've got to say, that was pretty wild yesterday." She looks as if she's about to tell me about a scandal in the Swedish royal family. Her hands drum impatiently on the wooden tabletop between us.

With a dismissive wave of my hand, I shake my head. "A resignation isn't that unusual, is it?" I speak quietly, because I don't want anyone to overhear this. After all, we're not even a hundred meters from my old workplace, and the place is packed with former colleagues. They're not supposed to know how surprising it was even for me and that I still can hardly grasp it. It doesn't feel real; the night hasn't changed that.

"Maybe. But the way you did it, that had a real Hollywood vibe. Totally in the heat of the moment! Or had you been seriously thinking about it for a while and just didn't tell me, your very best friend?" She leans over the table, eyes fixed on me. Her usually elfin face turns into a demanding grimace in the yellow light of the hanging lamp.

I can't help rolling my eyes. "Have the colleagues really been tearing into it? How many theories are going around?"

Her grin tells me everything; she props her chin in her hands and glances around. "Well, I've heard one or two things. The fact that the boss sat in his office for the rest of the day after your resignation with a face as red as a beet really fired up everyone's imagination. Most of them think you hurled every swear word at him that we collected for him over the past few months, and then he fired you on the spot." Alex is so excited she can hardly sit still. Her whole chair shakes with the twitching of her legs. The fact that our drinks are served at that exact moment doesn't make things any easier for her.

"Well then, that's probably how it went." I wink at her conspiratorially, lean back and take a long, satisfied sip of my Coke.

"Yeah, right, as if I'd believe that. How did it really happen? Did he fire you? Or did you do it yourself? Please, Marie, come on, tell me already!" She clenches her fists, probably to stop herself from grabbing me by the arms and shaking the information out of me.

My thoughts wander back to the moment when I decided to give my life a new and irrevocable direction. Once again that oppressive feeling spreads inside me, I feel this unbridled rage and at the same time I hear Grandma's voice. *Later* never comes, she reminds me with sober sadness. And I decide that she's wrong. That I'm not going to make the same mistake Grandpa did, that I want to live my life and not just watch it pass me by.

Alex can know about it. But it's none of the other people here in the restaurant's business.

"Is that really so important? It's over, that's all that matters." I let my gaze quite obviously drift over to the colleagues from the accounting department, who are just having their dessert served at the neighboring table.

Alex nods knowingly. "I've already told them you're living the life of your dreams now. And I told the boss too. You should've seen the color drain from his face. White as snow!" Her grin is contagious, and I can easily imagine how much she exaggerated in her account. "So, out with it. What's your plan?"

I wish she would ask me a question I can actually answer. Because in truth there's still only one thing I know for sure. "A lot of things are possible," I say absentmindedly. I still have to figure out what my *later* is supposed to be. Somehow.

Alex immediately shakes her head so vigorously that her long pink feather earrings almost dangle against the tip of her nose. "No, that answer is no longer accepted. Don't dodge the question, or I'll have to keep you here until you have no choice but to tell me." Her expression is determined, and I know her well enough to know what that means. Only the waitress, who sets our soups down in front of us at that moment, buys me a little time. Too little. I have to come out with the truth.

"Honestly?" I draw the word out and let my spoon sink into the soup. Even though I keep my eyes fixed on the orange-tinted contents of the bowl, I can feel Alex's impatience. "I've thought about turning one of my hobbies into a job. But as nice as gardening with Grandma is, I can't imagine it as work. And my Spanish course is a total flop anyway. So languages are out too. I guess I'll just have to keep looking; I'm sure something will come to me. For now I'm going on vacation, and everything else will fall into place."

"How nice! Where are you going? Tajikistan? Transylvania?" I can see her excitement growing with every word.

Her euphoria settles heavily on my shoulders, and I have no idea why. "Nowhere." Even I notice that my voice has lost its energy.

Of course Alex raises her eyebrows skeptically. "That sounded very different on the phone last night." Her spoon is still lying untouched next to the soup bowl, all her attention on me. "What happened to your ideas? Where did the 'anything is possible' attitude go?"

I shrug because I feel a little helpless. And overwhelmed. The night was restless, and my thoughts still are. "Lukas can't just take time off like that. And Grandma shouldn't be on her own right now either."

For a split second Alex studies me as if she were trying to look through my eyes into my soul. She wants to know what's going on in there. But how could I let her see it when it's only a blurry picture even for me? "Mhm," she murmurs, then finally turns to her soup.

I do the same, put a heaping spoonful in my mouth, and savor the sweet carrot flavor that spreads across my palate at once.

"I'm going to miss this restaurant." There's melancholy in my voice; I can hear it clearly. Not everything about my job was bad. Not my coworkers, and certainly not this place. We sat at this table and ate together day after day. My fingers wander over the wooden surface and catch on a notch. The spot where Alex rammed her fork in months ago, when she was gesticulating so wildly while telling me about the end of her relationship with that pigheaded Harald that she forgot everything around her. Inch by inch I feel my way forward, and it's as if someone suddenly turned my senses up to full volume. I hear the clatter of plates with almost painful clarity, smell the mix of curry and frying oil, feel the dry warmth of the radiator beside me, and see the pale yellow stripes the artfully curved lamps cast across the tabletop. Out of nowhere, an uninvited thought sneaks into my head.

It's over. None of this will ever come back.

"Are you okay?" I hear Alex ask, as if from far away.

I swallow. Why do I suddenly feel as if something is stuck in my throat? Even though it can't be bigger than a pea. It's there. And along with it comes the worry that the thing might grow. I quickly shake these confused thoughts from my head and smile at my best friend. "Of course."

An uneasy silence spreads between us. To distract myself, I take a spoonful of soup. But what just a moment ago still held an intensely sweet carrot note and a hint of ginger is suddenly a bland mix of vegetables and bouillon cube. What's happening here?

I'm probably just imagining things. It's time for a bit of normality. And a change of subject.

"Tell me about last night. Did Leon finally stay over?" I try a crooked grin.

Alex's expression brightens, and I know at once that I've picked the perfect topic. From her smirk I can tell how much she has to tell me, and I give her an encouraging nod.

In the rest of Alex's lunch break, I hear everything. With flushed cheeks and a glorious glow on her face, she describes every second to me in the tiniest detail. Seeing her so happy makes my strange mood disappear again. We gush about love together, my heart feels light and my throat loosens.

"I'm so happy for you," I say as I hug Alex goodbye. "You absolutely deserve this happiness."

She sighs wistfully. "I do. And so do you. Not just with

Lukas. With everything that's coming for you." Alex pushes me away from her and looks at me intently. "A new future, Marie. A life you get to choose for yourself."

I nod so exaggeratedly hard that my hair falls into my face. "Anything is possible," I confirm, but just a moment later I feel it. The pea in my throat is back, and it seems to have grown. The little green thing has turned into a grape-sized lump. With a rough surface.

Alex doesn't notice. She gives me one last squeeze. "I really have to go. We'll talk, okay?"

"Sure." This moment feels like a farewell, even though it isn't one. Alex and I will stay friends, we'll keep seeing each other. A part of me doesn't seem to understand that and sends me tears that, luckily, only gather in the corners of my eyes.

Why on earth is this happening? There's absolutely no reason to get sentimental.

While I struggle not to let the salty liquid spill over, Alex heads off. I'm left behind on my own. In the middle of the sidewalk. In front of our regular restaurant, which from now on won't be that anymore. And all at once I no longer know where I'm supposed to go next. There are no more appointments scheduled for me in our weekly planner today.

There's nothing I have to take care of, just lots of things I could do.

At last I have what I'd wished for for so long. Still, this new kind of freedom doesn't feel the way I expected.

I'd always wanted to do things. Go on outings, ride my bike, learn to dance salsa, or read books. But it only rarely happened, because I spent too much time at work or tied up with other obligations. This is my chance to make up for some of that. But which of those things would actually be fun for me over the next few hours?

Grandma. I could spend this afternoon with her again and once more make sure she at least smiles a little.

I quickly rummage my phone out of my handbag and dial her number. It rings for a long time, then she finally picks up and greets me in a dull voice.

I don't dare ask how she's doing; after all, I can hear how she feels. "Do you want to do something together today?" I sound overly cheerful. "We could go to the Naschmarkt and try everything we've never eaten before."

"That's sweet of you, but . . ."

"No excuses, we're going to have a great afternoon." A bit impetuously I cut her off, sounding as if I were practically begging her.

On the other end of the line I hear a long sigh. "I have a doctor's appointment."

Is she telling me the truth? Or is she afraid of being a burden to me?

"I'll go with you. And after that we'll head out together," I suggest, because I'm not going to give up that easily. Yesterday she smiled for a moment, and today I want to see that smile again.

For a moment Grandma is silent. It's as if she's looking for an excuse so she won't have to accept my offer. "That's really not necessary," she says at last, and I notice how hard she's trying to sound casual. She doesn't manage it. "Enjoy your afternoon to yourself. We can see each other tomorrow."

She sounds sad, I can hear it clearly. Her mood washes over me. The fact that she doesn't want to let me help her puts a heavy weight on my chest. I make another attempt, but she can't be persuaded. In the end I have no choice but to say goodbye to her.

Indecisive, I shift from one foot to the other with the phone in my hand. I can't stay here in the middle of the sidewalk in front of my regular restaurant, which from now on no longer is one. So I march to the tram stop. Like yesterday, I take the line that brings me to the old town. Shopping was fun; why shouldn't I stroll along the shopping street again for a bit? Who knows, maybe I'll find something there that catches my attention—a clue that shows me where my *Later* is hiding from me?

As the tram stops at one station after another, I try not to think about anything at all.

I fail miserably.

My head is full of questions, and nowhere do I find any answers.

When I reach Stephansplatz, I walk over the cobblestones between horse-drawn carriages and groups of tourists toward Mariahilfer Strasse. A feeling of pointlessness spreads inside me; more and more I lose the desire to keep going. Up ahead is my favorite boutique. The coat in the display window is pretty, but too expensive. And I've already bought the colorful scarf. So why should I look around in there?

To make matters worse, clouds move in front of the mild spring sun and make my surroundings a little darker. The colors lose their brilliance; the house fronts, usually so pleasantly bright, suddenly seem to be covered with a gray veil.

What am I even doing here? I don't know, but it's definitely not right. This isn't *Later*, it's nothing at all.

A bitter feeling of disappointment sends a heaviness through my whole body. I feel as if concrete blocks are pulling my arms down and my legs are trudging through quicksand. Every step is laborious. And more exhausting than the one before. So I drag myself back to the tram stop. It would hardly surprise me if it started to rain. Because that would be more than fitting for what's going on inside me right now. As if a thunderstorm were breaking over me, terrible thoughts flash through my head.

What if I made the wrong decision? What if I don't find what I'm looking for and end up with nothing at all?

What if everyone only talks about happiness, but in truth it doesn't exist at all?

The wind of change that had seemed so lovely yesterday is now blowing against me with full force, surrounding me and tugging at my dreams. So hard that suddenly I'm no longer sure where they're taking place and what they're about.

Chapter Ten

It's quiet. Too quiet.

That's the first thing I notice when I close the apartment door behind me. I walk down the short hallway toward the living room and once again reach for the small package in my pants pocket. It's still there. Of course it is, and yet it's hard for me to believe. I did it, the first step toward a marriage proposal is taken, and I'd love nothing more than to ask Marie on the spot if she wants to be my wife. Then I could immediately see her surprised radiant smile and hear her cheerful laughter.

Maybe today is already the perfect day after all?

Marie is obviously not at home; I could decorate the apartment and run one of her beloved bubble baths for her. Or prepare a picnic right in the middle of the living room, which I now enter. Here, over the cream-colored high-pile carpet, I could spread the checkered picnic blanket, and there on the white-lacquered shelf I could set up candles. I'd have to push the sofa a little to the side. I haven't even finished the thought when I'm already placing my hands on the anthracite-colored fabric of the couch. Just to see whether my plan is even feasible.

At that moment I see Marie.

She's asleep on the sofa. Her mouth is slightly open, her hair is tousled. There are chocolate-brown smudges on her cheek and black streaks under her eyes. In her baggy sweatpants and faded T-shirt she looks a bit neglected. But also insanely cute.

I want to kiss her on the spot, so I walk around the sofa. Only then do I notice the chaos. All around her lies crumpled packaging from different kinds of candy. On the coffee table there are half-full cardboard containers with Chinese characters on them.

I sit down next to her on the sofa and lean over her pretty face. "Wake up, Sleeping Beauty." Gently, I stroke her upper arm.

"Hmmm." For a moment her eyelids flutter. She nods, but seems to drift off again right away.

Should I let her sleep? Unsure, I look at the mountain of trash surrounding us. The edge of the ring box in my pocket presses so hard against my groin, it's like it wants to remind me that it's still there. I let my fingers wander tenderly over Marie's forehead, but I don't get the usual purring in return. She stays still.

I should give her a few minutes; she seems to really need a break. She must have been at her grandma's again and used up all her strength helping her.

First I stash the ring safely in my nightstand, put the leftovers in the fridge, and gather up the trash. Just as I'm wiping the soy sauce stains off the coffee table, something stirs beside me.

"Lukas?" Marie sounds confused. She rubs her eyes and looks as if she can't believe I'm here.

She looks so ravishing that I immediately drop the cleaning cloth and lean over her. "Good morning," I say softly.

A pale imitation of her usually sunny smile is all I get from her. Then, with a weary groan, she pushes herself upright.

I sit down next to her and put my arm around her shoulders. "Are you not feeling well?"

With a sigh, she lets her head drop against my chest. "Don't know," she answers with a shrug, "I feel sick. And I'm tired."

The nausea is easy enough to explain, considering all the candy. But I don't understand the tiredness. "How long did you sleep?" My fingers wander tenderly under the sleeve of her T-shirt and stroke her upper arm. Her soft skin feels warm, maybe too warm. "You're not getting sick, are you?"

Instead of an answer, all I get is a listless shrug.

"Is there anything I can do for you? Do you want some tea? Or should I carry you to bed?" Since I can't think of anything better, I kiss the crown of her head, right at the spot she likes.

For a moment it's as if she first has to think about the questions, then she finally says something. "No, I'm okay. I mean, health-wise."

What does she mean by that? Even though I don't get it, an unpleasant feeling moves through my stomach. Like fog, it has hardly any substance, and yet it's there. "What is it then?" I murmur into her hair. I try to sound loving despite my confusion.

She takes a deep breath. "I need a break."

"A week, that's what we agreed on yesterday. Seven days at most, that's how we discussed it and that's how I entered it in our planner."

Now she pushes me a little away from her and lifts her head. She looks straight at me, her gaze demanding my full attention. "Or more."

It's only two words, but they're like gasoline for the ever-burning fire of fear inside me. It flares up, no matter how hard I try to tell myself I'm overreacting. "What are we talking about? Days, weeks, months?" Do I sound panicked? Maybe.

With a tired smile, she lays her hand soothingly on my chest. "Two weeks, maybe three." She looks as if she has to summon all her energy just to keep her eyelids from closing.

All I can do is brush her hair out of her face and kiss her with all my love. "The agreed-on week isn't even half over yet," I remind her when we finally pull apart again. "How can you already know you'll need more time?"

"There are just too many possibilities." Her intense gaze meets mine. "And I want to find something that's a perfect fit for me."

Of course it would be better if she started looking for a new job right away. After all, we want to buy the house, and for that we need money. From the phone call with the realtor I already know that with our savings of 50,000 euros we have just enough reserves to put down the deposit. We still have to earn the rest. But the way she's looking at me right now, I'm not capable of reminding her of that. "I understand," I say instead.

Behind the tired veil in her eyes I see gratitude, and maybe even a spark. "Thank you, my prince." At last she smiles at me.

Once more I pull her close and hold her as tightly as I can. Because deep down I feel that this is what she needs right now. And I do too.

Chapter Eleven

The fine, steady rain drums on my umbrella, making a sound as if a thousand people were all wildly beating tiny drums at once. Even though I would have preferred to stay at home like I did the last seven days, I came here to the city park. The toes of my sneakers are damp, a cool wind cuts through the fabric of my jacket, and although nature should be green at the end of March, it looks gray to me. Still, I try to force a smile. For Alex, who is already waiting for me on the other side of the pond and is waving so emphatically it's as if she were trying to guide a plane into its parking position.

Maybe I should walk toward her faster, but my legs are tired. When I finally reach her, I earn a shake of the head for my lack of energy.

"Too late," she says in that schoolmarm tone she always uses when she has to wait for me.

"How long have we known each other? Fifteen years?" Alex nods. "And I've never been on time. Why don't you just give up?" I sound just as worn out as I feel.

Immediately, an impressive collection of wrinkles forms on my best friend's forehead. "What's wrong with you?"

I really don't like the way she tilts her head to the side and studies me with a mixture of incomprehension and curiosity.

With a dismissive wave of my hand, I let my gaze wander to the pond beside us. To where the ducks have settled in a sheltered cove. They hate the rain too, even though it beads off their feathers.

"I'm fine, it's just this weather that's getting to me."

Out of nowhere, Alex pulls me toward her. "You look terrible," she whispers in my ear and gently strokes my back.

She's really exaggerating. "I'm just not wearing any makeup." Even though I want to sound casual, I don't manage it.

"How long have we known each other? Fifteen years?" Of course she throws my own words back at me. She lets go of the hug. Her arms may release me, but her gaze doesn't. "Stop lying to me. That baggy outfit, the uncombed hair, and your damn gray complexion are clearly not in your favor."

I look down at myself. I really am anything but well dressed. "We just wanted to go for a walk, not conquer the catwalks of the world." It's another feeble attempt at being funny. But that one fails miserably too.

On top of that, Alex isn't fooled for a single second. "Tell me what's going on with you." She links her arm through mine and pulls me along. "It's easier when we're moving, I promise."

Is it? Uncertain, I take the first step, but it feels just as heavy as the steps before. I breathe in the damp spring air and listen to the crunching sound our shoes make on the gravel path. Alex strolls silently beside me, only her warmth resting on my upper arm, right where we're touching. As if from far away, I register the other people in the park, notice dogs barking and smell the muddy scent rising from the meadows.

A deep sigh leaves my mouth, then I tell Alex what's going on inside me. "Anything is possible. That's what I thought. I wanted to start over, begin a life that makes me happy, and stop waiting for *later*. I thought quitting my job had opened doors."

"It did." Alex sounds as sure as a person can be. "I politely pointed that out to the boss too, when he was bragging to the colleagues that you'd definitely regret quitting."

There's a reason this woman is my best friend. I can all too easily imagine how my old boss, and probably quite a few people on the team, want to see me fail. Alex stands up for me. Gratefully, I let my head drop onto her shoulder as we move on just as slowly as the bands of cloud in the sky above us.

"Unfortunately, not a single door has opened so far," I admit. "On the contrary, right now I feel more like I'm locked in a room with no windows and can't find the way out." My gaze falls on the pond. The water churned up by the raindrops looks beautiful together with the reeds along the bank and the mossy green streaks drifting lazily along. But beneath that surface it gets darker with every inch until you can't see anything at all.

As if Alex could sense my thoughts, she stops walking, pushes me a little away from her and sizes me up. "How can I help you?"

"Grandma says life is short. No more than a moment,

once you're her age and you look back and realize you always postponed the good things to some *later* that never actually comes." I exhale noisily, my shoulders giving a tired shrug. "You should see her. How sad she looks and how empty her gaze. No matter how hard I try, I can't manage to cheer her up." I hesitate because I don't know how to tell her the other thing without sounding crazy. "But that's not all…"

Alex nods knowingly. "You don't want the same thing to happen to you."

"I want to be happy, not just with Lukas but with my whole life. I want to do something that brings me joy. To spend my time on things that make sense." And I absolutely don't want to make the same mistake my grandparents did. "Quitting my job was supposed to be the first step toward that, but now…"

"You're missing the idea of what you could do." It isn't a question; Alex knows exactly where the problem lies.

I nod. "I wanted to give myself a week to figure out exactly that. But the days just passed me by, and I know absolutely nothing." I've been thinking every second. No matter whether I helped Grandma take care of her chickens or studied vocabulary for this tedious Spanish course, with only two more units left, thank God. My thoughts were always on a future that refuses to reveal itself to me. "What am I supposed to do? Do I have to work as a secretary again? Different boss, the same dissatisfaction?" I ask, frustrated.

"So what have you actually tried?" Alex wants to know, and I imagine I can hear so much courage in her voice that it's enough for both of us.

I wish I could talk about thousands of things I've thought through. About to-do lists and research. Secretary-

Marie would pull an overview of all the options out of her bag. But I'm not her anymore, and maybe I never was. Seeking help, I look up at Alex. "I've read a few articles and even done those personality tests online. Crazy, right?" I ask cautiously, because it seems ridiculous even to me.

"Not at all." Alex shakes her head firmly.

"Basically, it doesn't matter anyway, because it didn't help at all." That's it, the awful truth. The thing that drags me down, even when I try my hardest to fight it.

Incredible, but she smiles at me. "Because all you did was think. You have to try a few things out; that's the only way you can find out what suits you."

It would be so nice if her enthusiasm could sweep me along. But I can't manage more than a skeptical look. After all, I've already had a few hobbies, but neither the book club nor the baking class nor making soap truly fulfilled me.

Alex isn't put off by that. "Don't worry, I'll help you. Where do you want to start?"

"Wherever you like." I sound as if I've already given up without even trying. Why am I so lacking in drive? That's not me. I know that for sure, and yet I don't have the power to change it.

Bursting with energy, Alex sets off again and I follow her. "You love animals," she says, tapping her index finger thoughtfully against her chin. "You could work as an animal keeper."

I don't have to think for a second, because I like her idea right away. "At the zoo! That would be like visiting faraway countries every day without having to leave Vienna. And it wouldn't cost anything, it would even make money."

"You know what? Let's go straight to Schönbrunn Zoo and find out everything there is to know." With determination, Alex pulls me along, and before I understand what's happening, we're already heading for the next subway station. "This is going to be great."

Alex seems so enthusiastic that the corners of my mouth lift all by themselves. "I'm sure it will be." I try to sound confident. Because that's the only thing I want to be.

Chapter Twelve

At last we're here, right in front of our dream house. And in a few minutes we'll know for sure that it's not only on the outside but also on the inside exactly what we've been searching for in vain for almost nine months now.

Excited, I squeeze Marie's cold hand and smile at her. As so often in the past two weeks, she isn't feeling well today either. I had a hard time getting her off the sofa, but ever since we got here, her mood has changed.

She's fidgety, just like me. I hope she doesn't notice the nervous trembling of my fingers, doesn't see how hard I'm trying to smile casually, and doesn't hear how shallow my breathing is.

Quickly I turn to the real estate agent. "Ms. Molinger, would it be all right if we looked at the house on our own first?"

"But of course. Here's the key, make yourselves at home."

Her smirk tells me that everything has been prepared just as discussed. The panoramic room in the attic is decorated with wildflowers, and tall lanterns are supposed to hold burning candles.

"As I already told you on the phone, there are still a few repairs that need to be done, which the seller will cover. So don't let the various defects put you off."

I give her a grateful nod and, as inconspicuously as possible, feel for the little box in my jacket pocket.

She's still here. Everything is fine.

I quickly wipe my palm on my pants, then lace my fingers with Marie's and march off with her. When we reach the front door, we pause for a moment. "Are you ready?" I ask tensely.

Her gaze flicks to me and I can see how nervous she is. She's happy to be here with me, and after all those days when she seemed so listless, her smile is like a strip of light in the night. "Let's do it."

I have to kiss her once more before I unlock the door. "Your Highness, I most humbly present to you your new palace." With a sweeping gesture, I invite Marie over the threshold and am rewarded with an amused little giggle from her.

"Wow," I suddenly hear her breathe in awe. "Look at this staircase!"

I'm at her side in an instant. I let my gaze wander. In front of me lies a spacious anteroom with extra-wide doorways leading into the adjoining rooms. On the left I spot a living room with an open fireplace, on the right a country-style kitchen. Directly opposite the entrance, glass doors have been installed that offer a fantastic view of the garden. The dark parquet floor is partly broken, bits of plaster are crumbling from the walls here and there, and the railing of the sweeping staircase looks rickety. There's really a lot to be done here, yet I feel at home right away.

"There's another room back there." Marie sounds giddy.

Grinning, I follow her into a small, light-flooded corner room that apparently served the previous owners as a conservatory. Reverently, she turns in a circle.

Seeing her so happy makes me happy too. "What do you think we could do with this room?"

As if I'd said something wrong, the shine in Marie's eyes fades within seconds. She tilts her head to the side thoughtfully and chews wildly on her lips. "Definitely not take care of any animals," she comments bitterly, and if I didn't know better, I might think she was on the verge of bursting into tears.

I have no idea what she's talking about, but I know one thing for sure. I shouldn't let this mood arise in the first place. "Come on, let's check out the upstairs." With a broad smile on my face, I reach for her hand.

Together we walk up the stairs and first inspect the bathroom, which still needs renovating but is very spaciously laid out. Right next to it is a bedroom. While I imagine where we'll put the bed, Marie slips on to the next room.

She's leaning in the doorway when I reach her a little later. At the sight of this room, I can't suppress a sigh. Not when I imagine the two of us standing right here in a few years and the four walls in front of us no longer being empty. Quickly, I step in behind Marie and pull her very close to me. "The crib could go over there, and on the right side there'd be space for a changing table," I whisper.

She nods; I can feel it against my chest. She's probably so moved right now that she's lost for words, and in truth I feel exactly the same.

"We should buy this house. It's perfect for us, isn't it?" I don't really need to ask this question, because I already know the answer.

Marie takes a deep breath, then lays her hands on mine and gently strokes the backs of my hands. "It is."

Maybe this isn't the right moment for it, but we still have to approach this whole house-buying thing sensibly. "So, how's the job hunt going?" I ask, trying to sound as casual as possible.

Marie immediately slips out of my embrace. "Um, yeah… there's not much happening yet, if I'm honest." As if she had trouble looking at me, she averts her gaze and walks back to the bedroom, even though we've already checked it out.

A bit flabbergasted, I watch her move away from me so quickly, as if she wanted to flee from this conversation. We both knew this topic would come up today; after all, it's already been two weeks since she quit her job. She should have started looking at job ads and updating her application documents seven days ago. But when I come home from work in the evenings, I don't find a single sign that she's done anything at all. I know she's anything but okay. Her grandpa's death hit her harder than she wants to show me. She wants to be strong, even though that's not necessary at all.

I follow her, reach out my hand and gently stroke her fingers. "What's going on, Marie? Why haven't you sent out any applications yet?"

She hesitates. Bites her lip. Sighs. "I was at the zoo the other day," she suddenly says, as if that had anything to do with the topic.

I cut her off right away. "You're dodging me." Yes, I sound forceful, but if we want to buy this dream house, it has to be that way. "Tell me what you're thinking. Straight out, like you usually do."

"I don't want to just do any job, I want to find my dream job. Something that fulfills me completely." The words spill out of her like a waterfall, and I see desperation reflected in her eyes.

"You want what?" There's mockery in my voice, and at the same time my palms grow damp. And right away that wall goes up inside me, the one that always builds whenever I'm confronted with this kind of spiritual nonsense.

Thinking like that isn't good for her. And certainly not for our shared future, which is now so close. With this very house and with the ring in my jacket pocket that's waiting to finally be put to use.

"You can't be serious."

Her disappointed look hits me, and we both know which unspoken truth is suddenly standing between us. "The last two weeks went by way too fast. I was able to recover, but my batteries still need a bit more recharging."

The uncertain sound of her words hits me right in the heart. And the fact that she's changing the subject doesn't bode well either. "Hm," I mutter, racking my brain over what the right reaction would be. Her almost vanished smile, the dull hair, and all the times I've found her asleep on the couch in the evenings are clear signs that she's right. She still needs to recharge. But if she doesn't start contributing to the household budget again soon, we won't be able to afford the installments on the gray-blue wooden house with the white-painted porch we both just fell hopelessly in love with.

I have to convince her not to wait any longer. I just don't know how. "What do you actually do all day? You seem so..." I search desperately for a wording that won't hurt her.

"…dissatisfied. Maybe I'm wrong, but to me it doesn't look as if you're enjoying your break."

Marie doesn't answer, and right away I know I've just hurt her. Nervously, I shift my weight from one foot to the other. How could I make her understand what I really mean?

I miss her, that's the truth. I miss her sun-bright smile, I want to laugh with her again and feel that we're both pulling in the same direction.

"All I want is for you to be happy. I want you to shine again. And dance. Send me silly photos and burn the food." Do I sound desperate? Maybe, but I am, a little.

Now Marie presses her lips together, a watery sheen glimmers in her eyes. "Just give me a little more time, okay? Please, I just need a few weeks, then I can get going again." There's a pleading in her voice, so intense it's as if her life depended on getting those days.

I want to meet her halfway, but I still can't. "Marie, help me understand this. We have a plan, and we're already right in the middle of it." With a single sweep of my hand, I indicate this wonderful house with its dark parquet floors, the light-flooded rooms, and the lovingly decorated doorframes. "We just have to reach out and take it, but we can only do that together." Even though I try, I can't hide that I don't understand.

Shaking her head, she lowers her gaze. Her shoulders slump forward, she exhales heavily. "I don't really know what's going on myself. I only know that it is. And that I can't get going again. Not yet."

Seeing her like this lays a heavy weight on my chest. And with every passing second she stands there in front of me like this, the pressure increases. There's nothing I want more than to be there for her. I want to hold her, give her courage and confidence. So I take a step toward her. Then I wrap my arms around her and hug her as tightly as I can. "Let me help you," I whisper in her ear, "we'll get through this together."

A violent tremor runs through her body, and that's when it hits me. Marie is anything but okay. "Absolutely," she says in a choked voice.

Maybe she's only doing it for my sake, but I still breathe a sigh of relief. She's in a crisis, but soon we'll have beaten it together. We'll get back on track; after all, we're still Lukas and Marie. For now I'll put in a few more extra hours than usual. That way I can't completely make up for Marie's lost salary, but every euro helps. I also know from the realtor that the final payment isn't due until we move in. And judging by the way things look here, the renovation will definitely take several more months. Still, Marie has to get back to work as soon as possible.

I kiss her forehead and dry her cheeks with my fingertips. "Give me a smile," I ask her gently, because we both desperately need it.

The corners of her mouth twitch and I can clearly see that she's doing everything she can to grant me my wish. Still, she can't manage it. "Can we go home?"

For a moment my gaze jerks to the metal spiral staircase that must lead up to the attic room. The place we were supposed to go next. The place where I wanted to drop to my knees in front of her and ask her the all-important question. "Of course. There's nothing else to see anyway," I answer on impulse and turn to leave.

Chapter Thirteen

If the morning sun weren't tickling my nose and the wooden back of the chair weren't pressing against my shoulder, I wouldn't know I was awake at all. My body is so heavy I can barely feel it. It's as if I had no idea where my arms are. As if I couldn't feel that my legs exist. My eyesight still works. At least there's that. I watch Lukas marching back and forth through the apartment, folding shirts and pairing socks.

"Are the T-shirts still on the drying rack?" Lukas's voice only reaches me as a dull sound, just like his expectant look.

Maybe I'm frowning, maybe I'm not. "T-shirts?" I ask, trying hard to think about what he might mean.

"The white things. Last week you promised you'd wash them. We even wrote it down together in the weekly planner." He mimes a rectangle in the air with his hands, and I think I can hear a hint of frustration in his voice.

Oh right. I was supposed to do the laundry.

Damn.

Apologetically, I lift my shoulders, even though they weigh at least a ton. "I'm sorry." I've barely spoken the words when the first tears well up inside me. There hasn't been any strength in my body for days, but apparently I can still cry. Silently, the salty drops roll down my cheeks. I let them run along my neck; I barely feel the tickling, and besides, it doesn't matter anyway.

Nothing matters. Nothing works anymore. I'm broken, somewhere in there, probably in my head.

Lukas's horrified look changes instantly. Now he's watching me with such concern, it's as if my tears cause him pain. He comes closer and puts his arm around my shoulder. "It's not a big deal, I'll just pack the black polo shirts."

Harshly, I wipe the tears from my cheeks and brace my head in my hands. "No, it is a big deal."

Lukas crouches down in front of me and looks deep into my eyes. He looks as if he wants to say something, yet he stays silent and pulls me closer to him. The fact that he wants to hold me doesn't make anything better. On the contrary, I feel worse than before.

"I'm a terrible girlfriend," I force out in a choked voice, because that's the truth.

He immediately shakes his head. "No, you're not." I can hear how hard he swallows. Several times. Then he clears his throat, but he can't manage more than a whisper. "You're not doing well. I should stay here."

"Your business trip is important, and it's only three days. I can handle it." I push him a little away from me and try with all my might to smile at him. I can't do it, just like I can't manage anything else anymore. At best, it's a tired spark that lights up in my face at that moment. Like flicking a lighter that has only one last breath of gas left.

Lukas's doubtful look tells me everything I need to know. "I'm worried about you," he admits openly. For the first time since my life went off the rails almost six weeks ago, he says it out loud. "What's going on?"

I stare at the floor. "My world is gray," I breathe into the silence between us. So these are the first words with which I even try to explain to anyone at all what's going on with me.

Gently, he strokes my hair, as if he could chase away all the bad thoughts and the gloomy mood. "Tell me what I can do." The pleading in his voice is unmistakable, countless worry lines creasing his face.

"I..." I begin, but I don't get any further. What am I supposed to say anyway? What could I ask him for when I don't even understand myself what's happening to me? As if that weren't enough, I feel fresh tears forcing their way out.

No, please, not again. Why doesn't it just stop?

Impulsively, I spring up from my chair. I need a distraction. And the feeling that I'm still good for something at all. "Let me help you pack." My voice cracks a little, but we both pretend not to notice. I drag myself toward the bedroom, where his open suitcase lies on the floor in front of the bed. "What are you still missing?"

Hesitantly, he follows me and looks at the contents of the trolley. "Underwear." He seems confused, the way he runs his hand through his hair, and a little awkward. So I gather what strength I have left and walk to the wardrobe.

Everything is fine. At least that's what I keep telling myself, over and over, while we finish packing his suitcase together. Without a break I repeat the words in my head until he puts on his shoes and shrugs into his jacket. When he kisses me goodbye, I can't enjoy either his soft lips or the homely scent of his skin. Everything is fine, I tell myself again, so that there's no room in my head for anything but these three words.

"I can't wait until we see each other again." Lukas covers my forehead with kisses.

"Same here," I murmur.

Then he lets go of me and gives me one last searching look. "And it's really okay for you?"

"Oh, sure." I do it. Right this second I pull up the corners of my mouth and nod in confirmation. I give it my best shot and it seems to work. The worry lines on Lukas's forehead smooth out, he exhales in relief and says goodbye with one last kiss.

A second later the door clicks shut behind him. I'm alone, and as if my body were losing all its muscle strength, I suddenly can hardly stay upright. I drag myself into the living room, flop face-down onto the sofa and bury my face in one of the lavender-colored cushions. I feel a bit like I'm a corpse.

Dead. Cold. And without drive.

This has to stop. I know that, apparently my body doesn't. There's so much I should be doing. First and foremost helping Grandma. But I can't manage that today. The effort of visiting her in her little house on the outskirts of town and pretending everything is fine seems impossible.

For weeks now I've been putting on a cheerful Marie act for her. She shouldn't worry about me, because she's not doing well herself. So I try my best to be there for her, but like with everything else in my life, I'm failing at that too. Every one of our meetings is an exhausting effort in itself, and by now I just don't have the energy for it anymore. So I do the only thing I can still manage. I call her.

It rings, but Grandma doesn't pick up. Her phone is

probably lying on the rustic kitchen table while she's outside in the garden pulling weeds. The voicemail kicks in.

A recorded voice asks me to leave a message. I take a deep breath. I only have to sound cheerful for a few seconds. I can do that, I just have to really mean it.

"Hey, Grandma! I hope you're doing well. I'm great, it's just that the days are going by way too fast." So far this has been going well, but now my voice threatens to crack. "Call me when you have time so we can have a good chat again," I force out. Then I hang up without saying goodbye, because I can feel I can't manage that anymore.

As if it weren't dark enough inside me already, a wave of guilt crashes over me. My whole life Grandma was there for me, and now it would clearly be my turn to comfort her. And yet I'm not capable of offering her more than a ridiculous phone call.

I could burst into tears on the spot. Again. I don't want that, but I still can't stop it. Even my old life was better than what I have now. That's exactly what hits me in this moment.

I pull my legs in close to my chest and rest my head on my knees. It grows dark all around me, yet it's still brighter than it is inside me.

This was supposed to be the end of my unfulfilled days, but in truth it's just the end. My "later" turned out to be a total failure. How could that happen? What on earth has happened to me over the last few weeks, and why wasn't I able to stop it?

My head refuses to give me answers, my eyelids close. I wish my ears would follow their example, but they don't do me that favor. At full volume they register the ringing at the apartment door.

Whoever is standing on the other side of the dark-stained wooden door doesn't give up. Now there's knocking as well, first soft, then more and more insistent.

"Marie?" I hear Alex call in a muffled voice.

Oh man, Alex. I'd promised to call her. Supposedly, anyway.

With a sigh, I peel myself off the sofa and trudge to the door, which she's pounding on without pause. Only when I turn the key in the lock does it fall silent. I push the handle down, the door opens a crack. Alex takes care of the rest.

"Marie." She sounds appalled. Why?

"Sorry, I forgot to call you back." Dully, I try to lift my hand. It doesn't seem in the mood and just hangs tiredly at my right side.

For a moment Alex and I stand facing each other and look at one another. Her mouth opens, but she doesn't say anything. What more does she want from me? I've already apologized.

"Come here." She takes a step toward me and pulls me into her arms. I couldn't escape this hug even if I wanted to. Her closeness feels good and at the same time it doesn't. Too much warmth and too much affection suddenly rain down on me. My heaviness suddenly turns all soft. It's as if I were melting apart. As if I couldn't hold the pieces of my world together at all anymore.

"This won't do." With a determined look on her face, Alex grabs me by the arm. "When was the last time you were outside?"

"Why?" I sound a bit like a toddler being forced by its mother to do something it absolutely doesn't want to do.

With her lower lip pushed forward, she tilts her head to the side. "Come along, young lady." In the very next second she drags me into the bathroom. There she positions me in front of the mirror. "Tell me what you see."

My hair hangs in lank strands in my face, the skin of my cheeks has the color of the tiles on the bathroom wall. Pale eggshell. And there's something wrong with my eyes. They're so dull. And dark. A bit like the two thumb-sized chocolate stains on my nightshirt. "I haven't had time yet to freshen up."

Alex immediately shakes her head so that I feel the gust of wind her oversized feather earrings cause on my neck. "It's one o'clock in the afternoon." She says the words as if she were explaining a law of nature I've just broken.

"So what?" I wish I could let myself drop onto the edge of the bathtub, but my gut tells me Alex definitely wouldn't approve of that either.

Up to now her hands have been resting motionless on my shoulders; that's over. She shakes me, my whole body vibrates as if the earth were quaking. "Wake up, Marie!"

I ought to pull myself together, so I blink away my rising tears and bite my lip. Still, it happens all by itself, because I don't know where I'm supposed to find the strength to stop it. I start sobbing, my nose swells up. I have no choice but to let myself fall back into Alex's arms. Without saying a single word, she rocks me back and forth. As if I were having nightmares, even though it's real life that over the past few weeks has settled over me like a heavy coat that doesn't let a single spark of light through to me. Will I ever get out of this on my own?

For minutes we stand tightly entwined in the bathroom. The tears run down my face like waterfalls. Where they land on Alex's neck, she swallows suspiciously hard. I feel a bit as if time were stretching for us. But then, eventually, it's over. As if I had no tears left, as if there were nothing left of me, just my shell.

"I'm sorry." I pull away from her embrace. As soon as I

lift my head from her shoulder, I feel its weight, so heavy I almost fear I'll collapse under it. This has to stop. Please. Can't this finally stop?

"No." Alex's fingers brush my cheeks. "You don't have to apologize. Never."

I'd like to smile, but I can't. Instead, I give a helpless shrug so she gets some kind of reaction out of me. "Thanks."

Suddenly a promising grin forms around the corners of her mouth. "Now we're going to shake you out of your rut. You're going to take a shower, fix your hair, and put on the dark blue wool dress. Then you'll do your makeup and pick out one of your pretty bracelets."

No matter how convincing her words are, they already seem to be bouncing off my surface. I look at her in confusion. "Why?"

"No questions. Just do it. You've got ten minutes." Alex gives me an encouraging pat on the back. "Starting now."

From the way she looks at me, I know she means it. And maybe this is exactly the kind of help I need. So I nod mechanically and reach for the towel she hands me. She seems very pleased with herself, gives me one last grin, and leaves the bathroom, humming cheerfully.

I do what she told me to do. Every single thing.

Only vaguely do I notice how, in the meantime, she loads the dishwasher, raises the blinds, and airs out the apartment. When I step into the living room a few minutes later, she's fluffing up the couch cushions.

Why is she doing this? I don't ask, because in the end it doesn't matter anyway. Instead, I tug at my wool dress, in which I feel anything but comfortable. Maybe I shouldn't have lived on nothing but chocolate croissants and pudding today. I'm full to the brim, and the dress is way too tight.

Alex keeps going until the apartment looks as if it had a photo shoot scheduled for today. "Very good. Next, we're going to do something."

I absolutely don't feel like it.

"Oh no, don't even look at me like that. Talking back will not be accepted." Is she seriously raising her index finger and wagging it in front of my nose as if she were my nanny? "You need to get out of here. That much is crystal clear." Her voice has taken on a caring tone.

I swallow, but a watery film still rises in my eyes. No, please don't. Not again. "What are you planning?" I say quickly and blink my tears back to where they belong. This time I succeed. So I can do it, as long as I stay strong enough.

A satisfied smile spreads across Alex's face. She links her arm through mine and steers me into the hallway. "Something you've been wanting to do for a long time," is all she replies mysteriously, and points to my shoes, which I obediently put on. Because it's better to give in. Because I don't have the energy to fight anyway.

Obediently, I do everything she tells me to. I slip on my jacket, lock the apartment door behind us, and follow her to the tram stop.

"So how are things going with Lukas, anyway?" Alex wants to know as we walk.

Of course I know what she's trying to do here, and it actually works. "Great."

"Have you told him how that llama at the zoo spat on you? Or what you said when you found out what a zookeeper does all day?" I wish Alex's warm laughter would catch on with me too. The memory of our visit to the zoo is hilarious to her. But not to me. Because if you look more closely, that story is just a symbol of everything that's going wrong for me at the moment. No job seems to suit me, and by now I don't even have the energy to try something new.

Alex tilts her head to the side and studies me. "You did tell him, didn't you?" Her voice sounds a little alarmed.

Maybe she sees it in my expression, or in the way I'm chewing on my lip. Either way, she senses something, so I might as well say it out loud. "Not yet. He's really busy, we hardly have any time together. In the evenings he's tired, and honestly, so am I," I answer evasively. Of course it's a flimsy excuse, but it's all I've got.

"Excuse me? Our dream couple doesn't have time for each other? In this situation?" With a disbelieving shake of her head, Alex pulls me farther down the street.

Lost in thought, I let my gaze wander over the gray-brown façades of the houses. "How am I even supposed to explain it to him? Lukas is always so extremely sensible, he doesn't care for daydreaming, and I actually get that. If I'd had his childhood, I'd think the same way. And besides…" For a brief moment I can't go on. Because what I'm about to say is just awful. I take a deep breath, then force myself. "…besides, I don't even understand myself." There it is. I've lost my way; somewhere in the past six weeks, between quitting and today, I forgot where I am. And who I am. I only know what I don't want. To go back to my old job. To postpone my life until later. I stop abruptly. "Have I gone crazy?" I ask, my voice pleading.

"Listen…" Alex grips both my shoulders. "You're just confused, there's nothing to worry about. Give yourself a little time and everything will sort itself out."

How wonderful it would be if she were right about that. "Mhm," I murmur thoughtfully, and I'm glad that at that very second the tram comes screeching around the corner toward us.

We get on, weave our way all the way to the back, and drop into the last free seats. Even before the car starts moving, Alex nudges me encouragingly. "So, are you at least a little curious where we're going?"

I shrug.

Not really.

Alex seems unimpressed. "We're going to the gallery," she says, her face lighting up.

"The Impressionism exhibition?" I must have forgotten about that too.

"A little more enthusiasm would be appropriate." Her disappointment is obvious, so I at least try to give her a grateful smile.

We spend the rest of the drive making meaningless small talk, most of it carried by Alex. The April weather and news from her relationship with Leon provide plenty of topics, at least that's what she seems to think. Only when we enter the exhibition rooms and look at the paintings by Claude Monet together does the mood turn serious again.

"Did you look at the links I sent you?" Alex seems lost in thought as she studies the poppy field in the artwork in front of us.

The sky above the flower heads is a brilliant blue. That's exactly where I look, pretending to focus on it. "Sure." That's a lie. I haven't gone to any of the counseling centers, and I haven't done a single trial day. I couldn't; I didn't have the strength.

"And? Was there anything?" she asks, without the slightest quiver in her voice. Then she moves on to the next painting, as if my answer didn't matter at all.

She wants to give me time and space. So I can find words for what can't be said. I take a deep breath and stroll after her. My gaze wanders furtively back and forth between her and the painting with the artfully painted water lilies. "Not really."

"So what have you tried so far?" She doesn't even bat a single eyelash, even though she must have noticed how I suddenly shrink in on myself.

I clear my throat. I want to say something, but I can't.

Now she turns to me with an expression I can't read. "So little?"

"I'm sorry." Ashamed, I look down, to where my pretty shoes touch the gray carpet without leaving even the slightest trace of a footprint. As if I weren't really here at all, flashes through my mind, and a little part of me even wishes it were true.

"Doesn't matter," I hear Alex's voice, so fresh and cheerful it's as if this were a quiz show and she were the host trying to cheer up the unsuccessful contestant. "Then we'll just figure it out together." She links her arm through mine and squeezes it. "Take a look around."

Even though I have no idea what she expects to get out of this, I obey. She wants to be there for me, to reach out her hand and pull me out of my abyss. How could I take away her hope of making some kind of difference? I let my gaze wander around the room, take in the high white walls with the framed artworks and the other visitors, some murmuring softly to each other, others silently absorbing the mood of the paintings. There are seats set up everywhere, and over there in the corner stands a wingback chair upholstered in golden velvet.

"Done," I say, turning back to Alex.

"So, did you discover something beautiful? Something that brought you joy? Something you want more of?" Her confident expression pains me, because I'm sure I won't live up to her expectations.

"Don't know," I admit frankly, and glance around again so I can at least give her something. "The paintings are pretty."

"There you go, that's a start." She sounds as excited as if I had answered the million-euro question on *Who Wants to be a Millionaire* correctly. "We'll pick out the most beautiful painting together. How does that sound?"

"Sure." I suppress a shrug and try for a smile instead. I want her to see how grateful I am to her.

"Good, then come with me. And keep your eyes open. As soon as you spot something that speaks to you, you tell me. Okay?"

She links her arm through mine and we stroll on into the next room, where only paintings of the sea in different seasons are on display. But it isn't the paintings that catch my attention. My gaze lingers on something else instead.

"There."

"The tour?" The confused sound in Alex's voice would have amused me in the past.

My approving grunt has to do as an answer. Because I'm distracted. Not by the tour, but by the woman leading it. Even though neither her dark pantsuit nor her light blond hair, pinned up in a strict bun, is anything special, there's something fascinating about her. It's as if she were surrounded by an aura all her own. As if she were throwing off sparks like a sparkler.

"Look at her," I whisper, sounding as reverent as if we were standing in the middle of St. Peter's Basilica.

"Who?" Out of the corner of my eye I notice her letting her gaze sweep through the room.

"The woman over there," I say, as if that explained everything.

Alex looks more confused than before. "The gallery

employee?" She thinks I'm crazy; I can hear it in the way she draws out the "e." But I don't care, because I see something she's missing.

"Look how enthusiastically she talks about the paintings. She has so much fun at her job." I can't help but sigh. Standing right in front of me is a living example that it's possible. "That's what I want too."

Absentmindedly, Alex turns to me. "You want to work at the gallery as a tour guide?"

"Nonsense," I answer quickly, making a dismissive gesture. "No, I just want to have a job like hers that gives me that much joy. I want to smile like she does when I do my work. Go home in the evening feeling content and fulfilled. Be happy."

For a brief moment Alex wrinkles her nose. She doesn't understand me, flashes through my mind. And right after that, the doubts come back. Have I actually gone crazy? "You think that's not possible," I say, disillusioned, and immediately feel my shoulders slump forward.

Alex hesitates, if only for a moment. "I don't know," she replies, then presses her index finger thoughtfully to her chin. "What if the gallery employee only puts on that smile because of the visitors? I'm afraid you're confusing professionalism with happiness."

"But..." In truth, I have no idea what I want to say. Not even in my head do words form for this longing I carry inside me.

Protectively, Alex puts her arm around my shoulders. "Maybe work is, in the end, just something you do so you can afford a good life. Maybe it's best to look for a job you can simply get along with." She pats my upper arm as if that could somehow make anything better.

Is she right? What if I'm dreaming of something that

doesn't even exist? If I've lost myself on a path that leads nowhere?

What if *later* really never comes?

"Maybe," I murmur absentmindedly, and although Alex is still holding me in her arms, all at once I feel as if I'm completely alone in this world.

Chapter Fourteen

It's moments like this when I can hardly stand being without Marie. We haven't seen each other for three days; I haven't been able to feel her lips on mine or smell the peach-like scent of her skin. Only a few feet still separate me from her, but alongside my anticipation of holding her in my arms again, I also feel something else.

Something unpleasant.

Fear, maybe, or worry that I'll see her crying again for no reason. That I'll have to miss her sunny smile and feel all too clearly that something's wrong with her. Something she can't talk about. Not even with me.

I quickly shake the negative thoughts out of my head. Everything is fine, Marie is just going through a rough patch and maybe it's already over. Who knows, maybe she's waiting for me just as longingly as I'm waiting for her. Maybe she's cooked, set the table nicely, and put on some good music. The thought brings a smile to my face as I unlock the door to our apartment.

I step inside. The air that hits me is so stuffy it's as if

dust and carbon dioxide have pushed out all the oxygen. It's frighteningly quiet. At once, a heavy feeling settles in my stomach, along with a premonition I don't want. Still, it's there. There's only one thing I'm hoping for. Marie could be at her grandma's, enjoying the sunshine in the park, or having coffee with Alex.

I send up a quick prayer, begging that I'm right. But in the very next moment I hear a sigh, dull and heavy. It's coming from the living room.

No, please don't. I can't stand to see her suffer, not again.

There's no question I have to be strong now.

For her.

So I bite my lip and start walking. In the very second I step into the room through the grass-green painted door, I see Marie heave herself up from the sofa as if she weighed at least a ton. One more sigh and a strained exhale later, she notices I'm there.

"Hey," she mumbles, pushing her stringy hair out of her face as best she can. Her eyes are small and dull, she lets out a long yawn and seems even too tired to cover her mouth with her hand.

"Are you okay?" I ask, like a blind idiot, and sit down next to her.

I pull her against me to give her support, because everything about her is screaming for it. It doesn't take a second before the musty smell of her sweater creeps into my nose. Even the skin on her neck smells like she last showered days ago. Reluctantly, I breathe through my mouth.

"Mhm, everything's great." She nods; I can feel it against my shoulder.

Since when do we lie to each other? "Really?" I ask awkwardly, feeling unbelievably stupid as I do. My fingers wander across her back and land in a damp, soft spot. Chocolate. Whether I like it or not, this is slowly getting to be too much for me. Very gently, I push her away from me. "Out with it. What's going on with you, Marie?"

"I'm just tired, that's all." Not even her shoulders lift apologetically; they just hang there as if they couldn't hold themselves up anymore. That alone wouldn't be so bad, but together with the dull expression on her face and the missing sparkle in her eyes, she reminds me of a plant that hasn't been watered for far too long. "Let me sleep a little longer, okay?"

Honestly? We haven't seen each other for three days and all she wants to do is sleep? Did she even miss me?

"Of course, go ahead." Confused, I pull away from her. Any other day I'd stroke her cheek and whisper to her how much I love her. But today I can't. The woman sitting next to me on the sofa has hardly anything in common with my Marie. She's like a blurred black-and-white version of a woman who's usually so vivid and full of color.

I can't do this. Being here with her and not knowing how to deal with her. Experiencing how she pushes me away and having no idea what would help her. This moment feels as if a noose were tightening around my neck, pulling tighter and tighter with every second. Now Marie lets herself sink back into the couch cushions, her lids already closed again.

Helplessly, I watch her curl up as if she were a cat. There's nothing I can do but cover her up. I pull the cream-colored wool blanket up to the tip of her nose and kiss her forehead.

She doesn't react, as if I weren't even here. Even if it's not fair, I'm disappointed. I'd imagined coming home differently. Completely differently. Still, at least one thing becomes very clear to me.

It can't go on like this. Marie needs help, and so do I. And I already know who I'm going to get it from.

To be safe, I leave a message for Marie. If she wakes up again soon, I don't want her to think I ran away from her. Not when she already feels so bad. Then I sneak out of the living room as quietly as if I were a thief who didn't find what he was looking for.

Half an hour later I'm standing right in front of Anna's apartment door. Whatever problem there is to solve, she knows the answer. Hopefully this time too.

"Hi, darling. I thought you were traveling." Anna tucks a strand of her wild dark-brown mane behind her ear and looks at me in surprise. Her eyes are so wide open that her lashes blend into her eyebrows. She's wearing workout clothes; she was probably just about to head to the gym.

"Came back early." I kiss her now-free cheek and slip past her into the apartment.

"Tense atmosphere at home?" Of course Anna senses what's going on with me. After all, we've known each other since we played together in the sandbox in a tiny backwater at the end of the world. Together we ran riot in kindergarten and at school. That time welded us together; we're like siblings who are always there for each other.

"When I got home today, Marie was asleep. Probably all day. The apartment is a complete garbage dump, and I swear to you, that's exactly what it smelled like." My voice sounds so feeble, as if my energy had left me.

"I think you're in desperate need of a beer." In a friendly gesture Anna links her arm through mine. Then she pulls me out of the apartment and a few hundred yards down the street to our regular hangout, Joe's.

Once there, a terrible thought hits me right on the threshold. Walking into the bar feels more like coming home than going back to our apartment earlier. Here there's that familiar smell, guests are laughing together. The bright smack of colliding billiard balls mixes with soft background music from the jukebox. All of that feels so good that I inevitably make this awful comparison. I don't want to think like that, but it happens anyway, and immediately my worries about Marie take over. As if Anna can see that, she steers me to the long, modern bar and signals for me to take a seat on one of the stools.

"We'll skip darts and pool for now today," she says, her voice noticeably cheerful.

Sitting still is torture for her, but she does it. For my sake. Gratefully I watch as Anna orders a beer for me and her usual lemon water for herself from Joe, the owner of the little bar.

"You always know what's good for me. Why is that, anyway?" I study her thoughtfully. For as long as I can remember, all she's had to do is look at me to make any further words unnecessary.

"Is that so important? I just know. Just like that, for no particular reason. But you're changing the subject right now, darling." She smiles at me kindly.

Am I? Maybe. But I wouldn't even know what else to talk about. Lost in thought, I watch the other guests. At the last table behind the bar, a young couple is sitting across from each other. They're not doing anything except looking at one another, and I can easily imagine what they're feeling. After all, Marie and I had the same thing. At least we used to.

Joe, who suddenly appears in front of us with the drinks, jolts me out of my thoughts. "The usual," he says and sets the glasses down on the dark-stained bar. Then his gaze falls on me. "Rough day?"

"Exhausting business trip." I take a long sip of my beer. A warm feeling spreads in my stomach, the alcohol dulls my worries and immediately makes me feel a little calmer.

Joe watches me with an amused smile and looks as if he believes he knows something that not even I know myself. As a bartender, he has probably developed a good sense of his guests' emotional state over the years. Still, he doesn't ask anything and goes back to work.

While I watch Joe at the coffee machine, lost in thought, Anna starts chattering. "All right, then tell me. Were you even able to talk to Marie when you got home?"

If only I knew. "She was awake for about three seconds and then fell right back asleep. She couldn't have cared less that I was there, so I left again." I shrug helplessly; just remembering the experience is enough to make a pressure spread across my chest. It feels as if Marie's dark mood is now wrapping itself around me too.

"And…?" Anna's eyebrows climb upward, her fingertips tap impatiently against the glass of water in her hands.

I should probably just admit it; Anna already knows the truth anyway. "And now I'm ashamed of it. A little. Because I just ran off like that," I say meekly. "Why are you even asking if you already know?"

"Obviously because I'm curious whether you can see it yourself. It wouldn't be the first time you didn't quite understand one thing or another." Anna gives me an encouraging wink. Her legs jiggle nervously because she can hardly stand sitting still for even a few minutes.

"She just said she was tired. What was I supposed to do?" My voice gets quieter with every word.

"That doesn't make anything better, does it? We've

already talked about this. More than once." Anna sounds wonderfully calm and loving. Listening to her is like hearing a feel-good song on the radio. Still, her words hit me right where it really hurts.

I take a deep breath, lean against the bar and prop up my head. Because the moment has come to finally speak the truth. "I know I shouldn't run away. But I just don't understand Marie anymore. Lately she's been talking complete nonsense. I can see she's not doing well, that something's going on, and still I can't do anything about it. Because I can't reach her, no matter how hard I try." At last it's out, and just saying it makes me feel a little better.

Anna's understanding features wrap around the frosty mood in my thoughts like a warm coat. "You're helpless. And you, of all people, who can usually sort everything out wonderfully and bring order to things." She reaches out her hand to me and touches my shoulder in comfort.

With a single gulp I finish my beer and signal to Joe to bring me another. "It's like Marie suddenly lives in her own world, one that's so damn far away from the one we share. Do you get what I mean?" I take her hand from my shoulder and hold it tight. Because what I'm about to say will shake even her to the core. "And as if that weren't enough, I'm angry on top of it. I don't want to be, but I still can't help it."

"Because she's not there for you anymore?" Anna knows, I can see it in her eyes. Even so, she doesn't judge me; she would never do that.

That alone gives me the courage to open up to her even more. And to say what's really unsayable. "She doesn't take me into consideration, and sometimes I get the feeling I don't even exist for her anymore. I work myself to the bone day and night so that we're okay. She, on the other hand, wastes her time with whatever." Discouraged and tired, I slump, because right now a memory catches up with me. I sound like my mother, even using the same words she does whenever the conversation at home turns to the right way to live. And to Aunt Ulrike.

No, I don't want to think about that. Because this is something completely different. Marie has absolutely nothing in common with my mother's sister.

"Your reaction is understandable," Anna says sympathetically. She quickly moves her barstool closer to me so she can stroke my upper arm encouragingly.

"She doesn't care about any of this." I can't help but sigh. "So why should I care about her needs? Why should I still be there for her?" Surprised by myself, I clap a hand over my mouth. Did I really say that out loud? I hadn't even dared think it before, and now the words have just slipped out.

"Because that's not how love works. And you know that, too." All of a sudden she's so close that she can wrap her arms all the way around me. The safety of her nearness does me good. "Whatever's behind it, something is obviously causing a pretty serious crisis for Marie. Which means you need to put your own needs on the back burner for a while. You'd want the same from her if you fell into a deep hole, wouldn't you?"

Of course she's right, I know that myself. Still, I'm unsure whether I'm strong enough. My love for Marie is, because it simply has to be. "Definitely."

Her hand pats my chest. I feel a bit like a horse getting its reward. The image even makes me smile, and of course Anna notices that immediately. "There you go, that's already much better," she says in a tone that fits the patting perfectly. "And what are you going to do with this insight?"

"I'm going to go home and take care of her. As best I can." If only it were that easy. Even I can hear how discouraged I sound. Still, I try to think up ways I can help Marie.

"You look like you're on your way to a funeral." Anna straightens up and studies me intently with her light-blue eyes. "Think of the good times you've already had together. It'll be like that again, I'm sure of it. For now you just have to grit your teeth and sit this out together with her."

I nod almost automatically. "I'll do what I can."

A cheerful smile spreads across Anna's face, seeming to bathe the whole room in bright light. "Perfect," she says, sounding very pleased with herself. "You two can do this."

"Yeah, what we have really is something special." As soon as I've spoken the words, thousands of memories shoot through my mind. Each one more beautiful than the last, and above all I see Marie smiling. With fine little lines around her sparkling eyes and pink-tinged cheeks. I want her to be that happy again.

"Something very special. And if anyone can judge that, it's me." There's a note of her very own sadness in Anna's rapturous tone. She would never admit it, but what Marie and I have is exactly what she wants for herself. Still, most of the time her love life is a barren wasteland.

"Oh, come on, you're exaggerating." With a dismissive wave of my hand I try to play down Anna's daydreaming. For her sake.

She just rolls her eyes up at the ceiling, unimpressed, and sighs. "After you two met, you were unreachable for weeks. I still remember exactly how many get-togethers you canceled because you lost track of time. And the way you looked at each other… like… as if the world only turned for the two of you." Full of energy, she jumps up from her barstool and walks over to the jukebox standing a few yards away in the corner. "Your relationship is something really special, believe me. It's worth fighting for!" she calls over to me and fishes her wallet out of her oversized sweatpants.

As beautiful as her words sound, they remind me of what has become of our love over the past few weeks. "Over the past years we had differences of opinion now and then, sometimes even fights. But this is different. Sometimes I think the Marie from back then has nothing to do with the Marie she is today," I say thoughtfully. I take a big gulp of the freshly tapped beer Joe has just silently set down in front of me and hope the alcohol can push away the heavy feeling in my stomach.

"She's still in there, trust me! People don't suddenly change a hundred and eighty degrees." Out of her mouth, the words sound like an irrefutable truth, as if she were explaining a law of physics to me. With a satisfied nod, Anna feeds some coins into the jukebox and confidently presses a button. Cheerful reggae music starts to play at once. "From now on, no more moping. We're going to play another round of darts. Then you're going to go home and support Marie."

I watch Anna walk back to the bar and try to sort out my thoughts. Of course I want to believe her that everything can go back to the way it was. But what would actually help Marie? What would drive away her sadness? That's the one question that should matter more to me than anything else. I have to find that answer before I go back to her.

I need something that makes her happy. A perspective. A goal she'll enjoy working toward. But what could that be?

Her dream house!

Why didn't I think of it sooner? I'll finalize the purchase, transfer the down payment, and surprise her with it. That's it. That's how she'll become the way she used to be again.

"Why are you grinning like an idiot?" Anna's curious gaze lands on me.

I can't suppress a smirk, and I don't even want to. "What else am I supposed to do with such feel-good music in the background?"

"All right then. But now up you get, the darts are waiting," she says, kicking her legs restlessly. Anna needs action; as far as she's concerned, we've already been sitting around doing nothing for far too long.

"Gladly." Suddenly I feel a little freer. It's as if Anna, with her advice, has taken the noose from around my neck. As if from now on I can breathe a little easier again.

Chapter Fifteen

Listlessly, I stick my toothbrush into my mouth and peer through the narrow gap in the bathroom window that isn't covered by frosted film. Can't that stupid sun just go down? Out there it's shining, so bright and warm, as if it wants to laugh at me.

It took all the effort I had to drag myself up off the sofa and wash my face. But even the ice-cold water didn't give me any energy. On the contrary. If I had a completely normal manual toothbrush, I don't think I'd even be capable of brushing my teeth.

While the vibrations of the electric toothbrush shake me, my gaze wanders to the mirror, even though I don't want to look at myself. Because I know perfectly well what I look like. And how Lukas saw me earlier. Neglected. Unkempt. Gray.

For a long time I could only feel it; today a single glance is enough to recognize the truth. Right now my life is breaking irrevocably. Everything is going wrong.

It's as if Grandpa's death six weeks ago knocked against

a vase. Since then it has been wobbling, first a little, then more and more. One day it will have swung so far that it will tip over. The vase of my life is lurching, and in the very next moment it could crash to the floor. And still I just watch it, without reaching out my arms to catch it.

It's time to admit to myself that I need help. Someone has to stop this downward spiral before I disappear completely into the darkness.

To make matters worse, today is the first of May. As of now I'm officially unemployed, and I still don't have the energy to look for my "later." But I wouldn't find anything anyway, so what's the point of even looking?

And as if that weren't bad enough, I won't even get any support from the employment office this month, because I quit myself. I know that, and Lukas knows it too. He hasn't brought it up again, and I've spent the last few weeks pretending this day wouldn't come. Now it's here. And Lukas is gone. He wanted to let me sleep, if I'm to believe his message. Maybe he also ran away. Because he has no idea how to deal with having not only a depressed but, from now on, also an unemployed girlfriend.

If my phone didn't ring, the dejection wouldn't be able to stop itself from turning into tears. I reach for the phone. It's Grandma. I have to pick up.

"Hi, Grandma." The words leave my mouth so slowly that I almost fall asleep while I'm saying them. I should sound cheerful, but I can't even manage that with her. Is this the last sign I've been waiting for? The moment when the vase finally tips over?

"Are you okay?" The sound of Grandma's voice is unmistakable. I know exactly what she looks like right now. She's frowning and tilting her head to the side. If I were with her, she'd be giving me that motherly look of hers.

"Of course," I say, forcing myself with all my might to sound casual. The last thing Grandma needs on top of all her grief is a granddaughter she has to worry about.

For a moment the line is silent; only her breathing can be heard. It's quite possible she's fanning herself some air. Strange, she never usually does that. "We haven't seen each other in a long time." Her voice is quiet, almost on the verge of breaking.

Immediately I feel even worse than I already did. What kind of terrible person am I? How can I leave my grieving grandma alone? After everything she's done for me. "I'm sorry, I…"

I don't get any further, because I have no idea how I'm supposed to explain it to her. The woman on the other end of the line lost the love of her life before the two of them could enjoy the twilight years together they had been waiting for for decades. I don't know what's wrong with me, but compared to Grandpa's death it's certainly some insignificant little thing. I have to pull myself together; this ridiculously weak behavior has to stop.

"I'll come visit you tomorrow afternoon," I say quickly, forcing the corners of my mouth up. I push aside the fact that I have no idea how I'm supposed to muster the energy to do it. For Grandma.

She doesn't answer.

"Grandma? Are you still there?" Tired, I slide onto the edge of the bathtub and rest my forehead against the sink. The ceramic should be cold, but I don't feel anything. Maybe because my skin is exactly the same temperature.

It's still silent at the other end of the line.

I feel panic creeping up inside me. Slowly but relentlessly. "Say something!" I beg her.

All at once I hear a gasp. "Come by anytime," she forces

out. She sounds as if she can't get enough air to breathe. Either that, or she's fighting her own demons right now. "See you then."

A second later the call is over. Thoughtfully, I set the phone down on the shelf next to the sink.

Something's wrong with Grandma. She would never end a phone call so abruptly; that's just not like her.

Are her days as dark as mine? Is she, too, having to sit by and watch helplessly as her life falls apart? And if I'm not there for her, who will help her then?

I see her in front of me. She's sitting on her sofa, between the colorful cushions she embroidered herself, her hands folded in her lap. Her glassy gaze is lost where her thoughts are too. In nowhere.

She's alone, she has no one left. Not even me.

Do we both need to seek professional help? On our own, we clearly can't manage it.

Suddenly a terrible rage overwhelms me. At myself. At the fact that I didn't realize this sooner. At the fact that I can't get my act together. And at the fact that Grandma is doing even worse because of me than she already was.

Full of self-hatred, I drag myself into the bedroom, banish the sun by closing the shutters, and huddle under the blanket. But even with my eyes closed I feel that there's no ground beneath my feet anymore. That there's nothing left I can build on.

Chapter Sixteen

A twinge of guilt gnaws its way through my stomach. It's gotten late, the game of darts was the perfect distraction, and Anna's company was so wonderfully uncomplicated. Joe's supply of beer was inexhaustible, and so one thing led to another.

Now I'm standing in the cherry-red bedroom doorway, freshly showered but still drunk, and staring into the darkness. Only slowly do my eyes get used to the lack of light and make out Marie's silhouette. She's lying under the blanket in the same curled-up position as this afternoon on the sofa. I can only just hear her breathing softly.

I tiptoe over to her and lie down behind her. Propping my head on my hand, I study her delicate features. Almost automatically, I brush the strand of hair from her face that hangs across her button nose like a silky fine curtain. Then I kiss her cheek, which she answers with a grunt. It sounds as if she's sighing contentedly and growling like a German shepherd at the same time.

"I love you," I whisper in her ear because my feelings

for her overwhelm me. Amused, I watch her clumsily swat with her hand at the spot where my lips were just touching her earlobe. I should let her sleep, so I sink down behind her in the bed and wrap my arm protectively around her waist.

A heavy tiredness spreads through my body, my eyelids close. But behind them no dream is waiting for me, only a memory. Of the Marie from back then, the one I'd so love to have back.

The summer of first love lay behind us, and autumn was over as well. We were cuddled up together in front of the tiled stove in my parents' vacation house, enjoying the cozy warmth and watching the dancing flames.

In my mind she's sitting in front of me on the rug once more; I can smell the peach scent of her hair and let my fingers glide over the soft skin of her upper arms. That and the crackling of the fire are all I need to be happy.

"Do you remember your promise?" Marie wants to know and snuggles against my chest. With her head resting on my shoulder, she looks up at me.

I kiss her cheek right where her skin seems to glow. I'll never get enough of that spot, no matter how often it still touches my lips. "That I'll love you forever?"

She giggles, even though I know I'm not tickling her. "No, the other promise." What on earth does she mean? The harder I try to remember, the more expectantly she watches my reaction. "Now you look like one of those dogs with way too much fur," she comments with a smile and smooths my forehead with her index finger.

I take her hand, pull it to my lips, and cover it with kisses. "Which promise do you mean?" I ask, placing more kisses on her skin until I reach the spot between her index and middle finger. Before I can nibble on it, she pulls her hand back and fishes her camera out of her bag.

"There," she says excitedly and holds the device right under my nose.

On the display, the pictures from our autumn day behind the Gloriette play like a movie. At first it's just me in the light of the setting sun in the flower meadow. Then we're both smiling into the camera, moving closer and kissing. With every new photo, the perspective shifts. Marie and I disappear more and more from the frame until only the sky above us is visible, bordered by meadow flowers.

Now that I see the pictures, I know exactly which promise she means. We wanted to explore the world together. "Got it." I smile at her. She can't know that I only do it because she's shining like a thousand suns. Whenever I see that expression on her face, I can't help it. Not today either, even though it feels as if all my muscles are contracting at once.

I have to tell her.

At last.

When she looks at me like that, I can't do it. So I pull her back against my chest. Awkwardly, I clear my throat, my palms growing damp. "Listen …" I say gently, trying hard to breathe evenly.

"What's going on?" Marie's fine antennae are always tuned in, but at least she stays where she is. Right in my arms. "Is there a problem?"

"Not a real problem. Just…" Yeah, what do you even call it? "A little complication. So to speak."

She wrinkles her nose. "What's that supposed to be? A complication?" She stretches the word out as if that might help her understand it better.

"That's when something doesn't not work, it just doesn't work the way you thought it would. Just… differently."

What kind of crap am I talking? Even I don't get what I'm trying to say. And yet I know exactly what this is about.

Thoughtfully, she pushes out her lower lip. "You're not allowed to leave the country because you're a dangerous criminal. Right?" Giggling, she squirms in my arms, but I don't let her go. Not now.

I take one last deep breath. Then the truth I've been hiding from her for far too long finally has to come out. "If I so much as see a plane, I break out in a sweat," I admit quietly. "And just imagining handing control over my life to a stranger makes me sick."

The cramp in my upper body eases, but I still don't feel free. Traveling a lot was Marie's greatest wish, and I've just told her she can't live that out with me. For a moment no one says anything; we just stare into the fire together. While the thoughts in my head tumble over one another like circus acrobats, I can't guess what's going on behind her pretty forehead.

I clear my throat, because I can't shake the feeling that I have to explain it to her. "In a tin can like that you're at fate's mercy, there's absolutely nothing you can do about it. One tiny technical error, one brief moment of carelessness..." My voice falters, my breathing turns heavy. "I can't do it, Marie. I just can't."

What feels like an eternity later, which probably only lasted a second, she turns to me. Luckily I'm sitting down, because my knees are so weak they definitely wouldn't hold me anymore. Her expression is serious, but there's a sparkle in her eyes. What if it's only the fire I see flickering there? Just a reflection of the flames, an optical illusion? For a moment I hold my breath.

What if she doesn't want me like this?

I swallow hard, and now the strength leaves my arms as

well. If she doesn't start talking soon, I'll fall apart and disappear into the cracks of the parquet floor.

Then, finally, she opens her mouth. "That's no problem," she says cheerfully and gives me a playful punch in the side. "We'll take the train. Or we'll rent a camper."

"It's that simple?" I sit up so I can look at her more closely. I study every single feature of her face, but I don't find any sign anywhere that she just had to force herself. This woman is one of a kind. And on top of that, she's something special.

As if to prove it, she grins at me. "It's that simple."

Even today, as I lie years later next to an older and darker version of Marie, I have to smile. Once again that liberated feeling from back then tingles through my body.

As if it were nothing special, she smiled away my fear of flying. And not just that, she also kept her word. We did all our trips by car or by train. Not once did she try to force me into one of those flying monsters that stir up in me a fear of losing control against which my mind is powerless.

Who am I not to be there for her, when she's been holding back for me our entire life together?

From now on it's my turn to do something for her, and I'll start tomorrow. The dream house will pull her out of her deep hole. I'll make sure she gets it. So she can finally be happy again.

Chapter Seventeen

No matter how loudly the coffeemaker next to me hums, I can still hear Grandma's words. In my memory, her weakened voice points out to me again and again how long we haven't seen each other. Her sad tone echoes even through the dense gray veil that shrouds today as well, like November fog.

Lost in thought, I lean against the kitchen counter and stir sugar into my coffee. I have to find a way to leave the gray behind me so I can be there for her. Do I really need therapy?

No, I can do it on my own. But how?

My gaze wanders around the room. Unsurprisingly, I don't find any clues among the brightly colored plates and the pleasantly light surfaces. Behind the yellow patterned curtain a blue sky flashes. On tiptoe I peer out the window, only to realize that even right in front of our apartment everything is gray despite all the light. Here and there, patches of green grass appear between houses, asphalt, and cars. A few flowers stretch their heads toward the sky.

In a single gulp I drain my coffee, but it doesn't give me any energy either. Tired, I look at the coffee grounds stuck to the bottom. Some people believe they can see the future in the brown pattern, so I take a closer look. But of course that doesn't make any sense either.

This won't do, I'm going to go crazy. Definitely.

I quickly set the cup down next to the sink. Here in this apartment everything is at a standstill, nothing moves, least of all my thoughts. They keep circling around just the one thing. On a spiral that keeps winding downward. That has to stop, even if I have to force myself. Today I'm going to visit Grandma.

I can already feel resistance stirring inside me, and my gaze wanders to the clock. It's only ten. I still have the whole day ahead of me, so first I drag myself into the living room in search of energy. Before I get there, the phone in the pocket of my sweatpants rings. I turn the display so I can see it.

My mother is getting in touch again for once. About once a quarter she remembers she has a daughter. She probably wants to tell me today as well where she and Dad are right now and how unbelievably great it is there. As pilots, the two of them really get around the world. No wonder they never had time to raise a child and preferred to leave that to Grandma and Grandpa.

This call will only last a few minutes, and I'll hardly have to talk. I can handle that, so I answer. "Hey," I say, just because I know nothing more is expected from me.

"Marie. Thank God!" Mom sounds keyed up, almost panicked.

Instantly my stomach drops. "What's going on?"

"North Hospital. Grandma."

What is she stammering? "Grandma is in the hospital?" A wave of violent nausea hits me. "Why?"

"Collapse. Got a call. It's critical. I'm in New York." My mother still can't manage to form proper sentences.

All at once her panic crashes over me with full force. "Grandma. Collapse. Critical," I repeat haltingly. My brain is working flat out to process the information. "I'm on my way."

"Thanks. Keep me posted," I still hear my mother say while I'm already walking down the hallway toward the apartment door as if on autopilot. I don't even change my shoes, I just grab my handbag. Then I rush out of the apartment, and I don't care in the least that I haven't showered and haven't brushed my teeth. I have no idea what I'm wearing and I don't know what my hair looks like.

Grandma is in bad shape. Very bad. Because I didn't take care of her. That's all I can think about.

I don't find out how Grandma is really doing until I'm at the hospital. She's lying in bed, apparently asleep. Her forehead is bandaged, her arm in a splint. I can't tell where else she's hurt. And that's just as well, because every one of her wounds hurts me too. Just like the sight of her. Grandma's head is almost swallowed up by the white pillowcase; she looks small and fragile.

This is my fault. My damn fault.

Over and over again this sentence races through my mind and leaves indelible traces. I should have noticed during our phone call yesterday. I should have driven over to her right away; instead I went to bed like a fucking egoist.

What kind of terrible person does something like that?

Even though it won't change anything now, I take her hand, stroke it soothingly, and talk to Grandma. I don't care that the other three patients in the room hear every word. I babble about all sorts of things, but am I actually getting through to her? If I am, then I at least want her to hear only beautiful things. She should feel safe and cared for.

Because my own life has nothing to offer, I lose myself in our shared memories until I run out of words, and I hold her hand until my muscles grow stiff. She doesn't answer; there isn't a single movement from her. If I couldn't hear her breathing, I could almost believe she was…

No, I don't want to think something like that. Grandma will be better again soon. Just as the doctors assured me earlier, she will recover, and one thing is clear: I will take care of her.

"Visiting hours are over," a caring voice suddenly says. "Your grandmother needs rest."

I look up and see a nurse in the doorway. She smiles at me kindly, acting as if everything is perfectly fine. For her, this is probably everyday life. And Grandma's case can't shake her in the face of all the other fates she sees.

With a deep breath, I push myself up from the edge of the bed and lean over my grandma to kiss her cheek. "I'll see you later," I whisper in her ear and regret it immediately. There it is again, that *later* I wanted to banish. It keeps slipping into my life as if on its own. Maybe it can't be stopped, maybe *later* really never comes.

Tired, I say goodbye to my grandma's roommates, leave the room, and step outside a few minutes later. The sun dazzles me; it's hot and stuffy. I look around and feel lost at once.

What am I supposed to do? Where do I want to go?

Home? Back to those four walls where even my thoughts come to a standstill? Back to the place where I've been falling deeper and deeper for weeks?

No, this has to stop.

"Pull yourself together, Marie. You want to be a support for Grandma," I tell myself, because it's time I finally understood one thing. This world doesn't revolve around me, and certainly not around my ridiculous search for happiness, which has only led me to misery so far.

Even though I'm not sure where I want to go, I start walking. Aimlessly I wander through the streets of Floridsdorf, looking at the façades of the houses and the faces of the people, until I finally end up right in front of the Water Park. I've read about this place, but I haven't seen it yet. From the street I can make out a lot of greenery, and here and there something sparkles.

Hesitantly I step onto the narrow path that leads me deeper and deeper into the Water Park. It feels a bit as if I'm entering a new world, even though I know the sound of birdsong and I know how pretty it looks when the sun shines through the thicket of trees and bushes and paints its unique patterns on the ground.

After just a few yards I spot a glimmer between the tree trunks. There's a lake back there, and it doesn't take long before I can see it in all its splendor. The water lies before me, dark green in color, frogs croaking cheerfully to themselves. Now and then fine air bubbles rise to the surface; I don't see any fish. Instead, my gaze falls on someone meditating on the shore not far from me. In a spot that's lit by the sun in a circle, he is squatting cross-legged right on the ground. He probably hasn't cut his light-colored hair since the turn of the millennium, and the oversized glasses on his freckled nose were already out of fashion ten years ago.

Next I notice how worn his clothes look. His feet are in frayed flip-flops. On his thin upper arms I can hardly make out any sign of muscles. But that's nowhere near as interesting as what's happening further up. His eyes are closed, and there's something peaceful in his expression that draws my attention.

He has what I'm missing.

That's what rushes through my head and makes me walk over to him without thinking any further about it. He doesn't seem to notice me, so I slide down to the ground next to him and bring my body into the same position as his. Acting on instinct, I close my eyelids and turn my face up to the sun.

The gray disappears. My cheeks grow warm. For the first time in weeks it seems to be getting brighter inside me.

That's good. Wonderful. Amazing. But what comes next? I could make a new attempt at thinking about what my life is supposed to look like in the future.

What possibilities are there? I live in the largest city in Austria; nowhere else do I have so many options. So what could I try in order to find my *later*?

Over and over I ask myself this question in my thoughts. But instead of an answer there is nothing but the memory of hobbies I only ever pursued half-heartedly and the flicker of orange light behind my closed lids. I don't see anything else. Absolutely nothing at all.

A desperate sigh leaves my mouth. How could I have been so stupid as to believe this would change anything?

"Namaste," a deep, warm male voice suddenly says.

I open my lids and turn my head to the side. The voice belongs to the meditating stranger, who is looking at me kindly. "Namaste," I repeat his greeting a little awkwardly and raise my hand to my forehead to shield my face from the sun.

"I see you're trying to meditate." He's still smiling at me, a grounded undertone in his words. It makes me feel instantly at ease, even though there's really no reason for that. "It's not working the way you imagined it would."

I wrinkle my nose and let my upper body slump forward. "Is it that obvious, yeah?"

"You're breathing like a marathon runner after crossing the finish line and squeezing your eyes shut like a thousand suns are blinding you." There isn't the slightest trace of reproach in his words.

All I manage is an awkward shrug. My hands play with the blades of grass beside my legs, as if they need something to distract themselves.

"Meditation is relaxation. What you're doing is tension," he says, placing his hands on my fidgety fingers.

For a moment I don't know how to react. Of course I did it wrong. Just like I've been doing everything wrong lately. Part of me wants to give up in frustration right away, but there's another part, and that part is curious. "Are you some kind of meditation expert?"

"No, I'm definitely not an expert, I've just meditated a few times in my life." I don't buy his dismissive hand gesture.

There's something about him that I can't describe. But I can feel it clearly. "How do I learn it?"

"Meditation means letting go. Where your mind is during a deep meditation, your everyday life fades into the background. Reason and negative thoughts lose their power." A satisfied expression flickers across his face, and I'm sure that right now he's imagining that he himself is meditating.

"That's never going to work." The words leave my mouth uncontrollably. Wherever they came from, you can clearly hear the anger I'm carrying inside me in them.

For a fraction of a second he seems to gather himself,

then he gives an almost imperceptible shake of his head. "Our thoughts determine our lives." He looks deep into my eyes, wanting all my attention on him. "And how we think is entirely up to us. You should always be aware of that. Once you've really taken that in, the rest will follow on its own." Supple as a teenager, he springs to his feet. He looks at me intently. "You'll find what you're looking for. When you stop clinging so stubbornly to what you keep telling yourself."

Before I can say anything, he turns his back on me and strolls away at his leisure. I'm left behind, confused, his last words fluttering around in my head like butterflies I can't manage to catch.

What could he have meant? How does he know what I'm looking for? And why does he suspect that I'm looking for anything at all?

Reflexively, I pull my legs close to my body and wrap my arms around them. My chin sinks onto my knees. Curled up like this, I let my gaze wander over the surface of the pond, which lies shimmering in the sunlight in front of me.

And of course it happens again. The sadness overwhelms me, and with it the anger. At myself. Six damn weeks have passed since I quit my job and I haven't moved forward an inch. Because lately I haven't even managed to try anything at all. On top of that, I'm a terrible granddaughter and a really lousy friend.

As if on cue, the sun suddenly disappears behind the treetops on the other side of the lake and casts long shadows over the spot where I'm still sitting. It grows dark, not just around me, but inside me as well.

"*Your thoughts determine your life. And you determine your thoughts*," I suddenly hear the stranger whisper.

What if it really is just a matter of deciding not to give

the darkness any space in my head? What if I just have to believe that it can be that way?

There is nothing I want more than to leave behind these gray shadows that have been threading through my thoughts far too long and far too densely.

That is what I want. So I should try. Not least because I have no other choice.

Here and now I make myself a promise. From this moment on, everything will be different. From this moment on, my sadness is over.

For Lukas. For Grandma. And also for myself.

Chapter Eighteen

For the first time in weeks, Marie is awake in the early evening. Still, something is wrong. I see it immediately when I enter the living room. She is sitting cross-legged on the sofa, staring blankly; her eyes look glassy and are laced with fine red veins. The color of her cheeks reminds me of tomatoes.

Does she have a fever? Carefully I lay my hand on her forehead, the way my mother used to do with me. She is warm. "Are you sick?"

Now she touches her own cheeks. "Grandma is in the hospital," she murmurs absently, furrowing her brow deeply.

"What happened?" In one leap I'm right next to her.

"She collapsed," Marie answers with a shrug. "The doctors say she'll recover. Her arm is broken, she's got a gash on her head, bruised ribs, and massive hematomas."

Of course I pull her straight into my arms. "What can I do for you?"

She turns her face toward me, and suddenly there's a trace of what I miss so much.

Her smile.

For just the fraction of a second, the corners of her mouth lift. "I'm hungry," she murmurs.

"I'll take care of that." I can feel the joy suddenly spreading inside me because I can help her. At the same time I know how ridiculous that is.

Still, I push myself up from the sofa with energy, hurry into the kitchen, and get to work. I can cook even less than Marie, but I can definitely manage a soup. Luckily I find a packet of instant soup in the pantry, which I serve to Marie just under ten minutes later.

She's sitting propped against the head of the sofa on a cushion, leafing through a magazine. I don't think she's actually reading it, but at least she's doing something.

Whether I like it or not, a part of me is relieved. I even breathe out a little when I set the soup down on the coffee table in front of Marie. "What are you reading?" I ask casually.

She turns the magazine's cover so I can see it. "News from the world of stars and starlets."

Even though I'm not interested in gossip at all, I grin at her. "So, anything exciting in there?"

It's an attempt to have a normal conversation, and I pray it works. Because I need a sign, a reason to keep believing that everything will be all right with Marie again. But she just shrugs.

"Unfortunately not." With a sigh, she puts the magazine aside.

"What are the doctors saying? Is your grandma going to get better?" I ask, even though I'm afraid of how she'll react. But things can't go on the way they have lately. I don't want to treat her like she's a fragile little chick anymore. We're supposed to be able to talk about everything again. Because anything else would be… No, I don't even want to go there. To hide how nervous I am, I grab the cream-colored blanket, shake it out, and fold it neatly.

"She slept the whole time. Still, I have a good feeling that she'll be back on her feet soon." Marie's answer surprises me, and even more the fact that she grabs the spoon and pulls the soup toward herself. "After visiting Grandma, I went to the water park," she says then.

"That's great." I sound like I'm advertising an attraction at the fair, but I'm happy. This is real progress. Because of what's going on with her grandma, she could just as easily have had a complete breakdown. Motivated, I grab a pillow and fluff it up. "You enjoyed the sun, yeah?"

Marie puts a spoonful of soup in her mouth and nods absentmindedly. All at once she tilts her head and studies me thoughtfully. "Do you know anything about meditation?"

Excuse me? "Isn't that some kind of esoteric stuff?" I ask, and the moment the mocking note slips into my voice, I regret it. Because I immediately see dark shadows pass over Marie's expression. I bite my lip and turn to the mess on the coffee table so she won't see how tense my face is.

Marie's spoon scrapes over the porcelain plate. "Just because you can't touch it, put it on lists, and calculate it?" she wants to know, sounding as if she really does believe in that nonsense.

With all my might I suppress the resistance rising up inside me. This is dangerous territory, and Marie knows that perfectly well. "So you want to meditate. What for? What's that supposed to do?"

"Life isn't always just about reason. Sometimes you should at least be allowed to break out in your thoughts," she replies.

Frantically, I line up the remote controls next to each other. My gaze darts over to her. Silently she takes one spoonful of soup after another, and with every second the tension rises. At least for me. Because I have not the slightest idea how I'm supposed to react to this. Because breaking out is something only children are allowed to do, and we stopped being children a long time ago.

"Listen," I say finally, and hesitantly lift my head. She actually looks at me attentively. "I have a surprise for you." That wasn't the plan, but right now I don't know what else to do. This dangerous mood has to go, and the direction this conversation is taking has to go with it.

Marie immediately stops eating; all her attention is on me.

"So ..." I begin, then I have to clear my throat. I'd wanted to prepare the right words, but there's no time for that. Like an idiot I'm standing in the middle of the living room, swallowing hard. "It's about our dream house."

"Yeah?" A row of adorable little lines forms on her forehead. As if she senses that something special is coming, she straightens up a bit. "What about it?"

Thank God. Marie is curious, and there's life in her face. I smile at her—no, I practically beam. "It's ours," I announce, spreading my arms wide.

I wait in vain for a joyful, excited expression. Instead, the lines on her forehead deepen. She studies me in disbelief, as if she isn't sure she can trust me. "What do you mean?"

"Simple: we bought it." Technically speaking, I did. And so far there are only signatures on contracts; everything else still has to be processed. But that's not important right now. Effusively I take a step toward her, pull her close and hug her tight. Maybe I'm doing it to be close to her. Or only because a far too negative part of me is afraid of seeing something in her expression that I don't want to see.

"Wow," she mumbles into my T-shirt. At my shoulder I feel how vigorously she nods. So she is happy after all, and I'm happy with her. Because the positive part of me knows that she finally has something again she can hold on to. Then she pushes herself away from me and looks me over critically. "Can we even afford it?"

Inwardly I smile. The fact that this question is weighing on her mind is the best prerequisite for getting her back on board. "Because of the repair work we can't move in before November at the earliest, and we won't need the loan until then." My words are meant to sound reassuring, and yet I can't manage to hide the pressure I feel on my shoulders. "It's a goal that's worth working for. And the six months until then should definitely be enough to find a new job. Don't you think?"

She purses her lips into a pout. "Maybe," she murmurs thoughtfully, slips out of my embrace and lets herself fall back against the sofa.

Did she really just say that? Completely without passion or conviction?

"What do you mean, maybe?" I can't and don't want to hide the sober sound of my voice. The prospect of our dream house should make her happy and motivate her a little. Instead she acts as if this gray-blue wooden house with the white-painted porch no longer matters to her.

Something is going seriously wrong here. Why?

As if she didn't register my question at all, she stares into nowhere behind my right shoulder. Seconds pass in which we both sit motionless on the couch. But what could I even say? I'm speechless, can hardly believe what's happening here.

"I have to ask you something." All at once Marie breaks the silence between us and leans over to me. "Did you always want to work in purchasing? I mean, did you dream of it when you were a little kid?"

I have absolutely no idea where this topic suddenly comes from, but I still try not to let my confusion show. Instead I rummage through my memories and quickly find what I'm looking for. "As a kid I wanted to be a journalist. I imagined I'd be doing investigations underground and uncovering scandals. Like an adventurer, only with a pen and notepad instead of a horse and sword." I shake my head without even thinking about it. How stupid I was. "No kid dreams of staring at numbers on a computer screen all day," I add with a shrug. That's just how it is.

In slow motion, Marie's head moves down and back up again. She chews on her lips. Her behavior makes me nervous; I hardly dare to move, and even less to say anything. Anything could be wrong, so I limit myself to breathing, and even that is hard for me.

All of a sudden she looks at me so intently, as if she wanted to make out something very specific in my face. "But if you never wanted to work in purchasing, why are you actually doing this job? What happened to the dream of being a journalist?" While she's talking, she tugs furiously at the edge of the sofa cover.

"As a kid you dream a lot, you don't yet get that those dreams have no place in reality." The words leave my mouth a bit too harshly, and I know I sound like my mother. Still, it's the truth. Work is the only thing that counts, and nobody knows that better than my family and me. Gently, I lay my hand on her nervous fingers. Her expression shows disappointment, as if I'd answered the question wrong. "Why do you want to know, anyway?"

She exhales heavily. "On my way home from the water park today, I was thinking about it. What I wanted to be when I was a kid, what I dreamed about, what brought me joy. I thought that would give me a clue. For a job that really makes me happy." It's more than obvious that she can barely manage to look at me. I can only guess, but I'm afraid that right now she's fighting with everything she has to keep her tears from rising. "That just sounds totally stupid, doesn't it?" she asks in a choked voice.

I don't have the faintest idea what's going on here. Or what she's trying to tell me. I get the feeling I should comfort her, but all I can think of is to pull her into a really tight hug again. "Not at all," I answer, just for her sake. Because the truth is, it sounds damn stupid.

With what little strength she has left, she flails her arms in the air as if searching for help. "Yes, it does. I have an appointment at the job center tomorrow. So I just have to know what might be an option for me." Her voice breaks.

No, Marie, don't cry. Please don't.

"You're a great secretary. So why do anything else?" I ask her in a pointedly cheerful tone.

As if she were giving up the fight, she lets herself collapse against my chest. "Because I want to have a job that makes me happy. But the only thing I keep thinking of is that I always wanted to be a princess. How stupid is that, seriously?" There's an enormous amount of anger in her voice. As if there were nothing and no one in this world she hated as much as herself.

This is leading nowhere; all I can do is try to distract her.

"In that case, you've done pretty well with Sleeping Beauty, don't you think?" I ask, letting my fingertips wander down along her spine.

A deep sigh leaves her lips. "Stop joking around, please, Lukas!"

Oh man, this conversation isn't getting any easier. What on earth am I supposed to say? What does she want to hear from me? "How does it help you to know that you wanted to become a princess? You do realize there's nothing noble about the blood in my veins, right?"

At last Marie's features soften. "Don't worry, I love you anyway." She reaches her hand out to me.

I move closer to her so I can look into her eyes. "I'm doing my best," I say, and we both know what I mean.

Her gaze instantly loses its sparkle. "I know that. And I'm more than grateful to you for it." She strokes my cheek tenderly, then her expression turns serious. She keeps chewing on her lower lip and looks at me uncertainly. "Will you give me a little more time?"

That's not what I was getting at. Not at all. How could I grant her that when the expenses for the house are already so close? "How much longer?" I want to sound understanding, but do I manage it?

For a moment she studies me with a mixture of understanding and disappointment. I don't get an answer.

"You think too much. We want this house, and to get it we have to work. You'll take the job where you earn the most, and that just happens to be the one you trained for. It's as simple as that." I look at her intently. She has to understand that! Neither of us has been a child for a long time. She knows how life works and that as adults we simply have to take responsibility, no matter whether we like it or not.

Tense, I watch every tiniest movement in her face. The sharp twitch at the corners of her eyes, the tiny horizontal lines at the root of her nose. Still, I have no idea what it means.

"Our thoughts determine our lives, you know?" She sounds convinced. "And if you think like that, you might never be truly happy." There's something in her gaze that scares me.

"But I am happy already. We both are!" I have to swallow, because what's happening here right now is clearly too much for me.

"Two minutes of happiness a day aren't enough." Hardly have the words left her mouth when she curls up next to me, grabs the light blanket, and pulls it up to her ears.

Helplessly, I crouch beside her, not knowing what else I could say or do. Even kissing her would possibly be wrong, so I don't.

This wasn't how I imagined this conversation. Marie should have been happy and started looking for a new job as soon as possible. If I don't find a way to get her back on track soon, our life will fall apart. But what worries me so much doesn't seem to matter to her at all. Now she's lying next to me. Her gaze is fixed on the TV, even though it isn't even switched on. Her breathing is fast, her features still tense.

I can't go on looking at her and feeling how suddenly we've become strangers to each other. I don't want to keep living our life on my own. I want to laugh freely with her again. But that seems impossible, at least today. So I walk into the kitchen, take a bottle of beer from the fridge, and take the first swig before I've even thrown away the cap.

Leaning against the counter, I try to get my thoughts under control.

Tomorrow is a new day. That's exactly what I keep telling myself, over and over again, so that these nasty visions of the future, which keep surging up inside me, don't get a chance to break the surface.

Chapter Nineteen

I wait.

I wait until I hear the creak of the sofa and, right after that, the hurried patter of Lukas's footsteps on the parquet floor. Now he switches off the light and closes the door behind him. A moment later I open my eyes. Dusk lies over the living room, but I can still make out the outlines of the furniture. The memories of the day when we set up this room together push into my thoughts. With combined forces we spent hours screwing together the wall unit, and when it finally stood in front of us, we were so proud that we toasted to it.

I can't help but sigh when I think back to that time. When Lukas moved in here, it was as if the sun shone just for us. As if there were no clouds and even less rain.

Today everything is different.

It's as if there were a glass wall between us. We can see each other, but we can no longer understand one another. What I say seems to bounce off the smooth surface. He no longer hears me and can't empathize with my longing, even though I'm sure he carries it within himself as well. I don't want this, and yet this damn thing keeps getting thicker. What if one day we no longer recognize each other?

No, I mustn't think like that. As soon as I've found my dream job, I'll grab the sledgehammer and smash the glass structure between us into pieces so tiny that, in the end, our wall will look like a sea of diamonds.

All I'm missing is the spark of an idea. I have to stick with it, I can't let myself go any longer.

Restlessly, I roll over onto my other side, as if I could set my thoughts in motion by moving my body. Still, as soon as I lie still again and, through the grass-green curtain, watch the darkness outside slowly take over, nothing happens. Once more my thoughts wander back into the past, but this time not to my childhood, rather to myself as a teenager. In my memory I was always a happy person, even then.

What did I spend my time on? What made me light up?

At once a scene appears before my mind's eye. I see myself crouching on the deep windowsill of the skylight in the children's room. I'm holding a sketchpad in my hand. I'm so absorbed in what I'm doing that I barely register my grandma calling me.

"Marie, come on now!" She sounds impatient. Of course she is; after all, this is the third time she's called me to dinner.

With a sigh, I put the pad aside and run to the door. I open it only a crack, just enough to make sure Grandma can hear what I yell back. "Not hungry."

My stomach protests. But it doesn't get a say, because all I want is to keep working on my pencil drawing. Right now I'm practicing how to sketch fingers, and the thumb is already going quite well. The index finger is harder, but I'm close. With quick steps I return to my spot under the window, grab the pencil, and, cheeks glowing, lay down the next lines on the paper.

Even now, the memory of how it felt back then is so vivid that I get fidgety. I can clearly feel the excitement that drove me as a teenager. I could forget everything around me whenever I drew or painted.

Why did I stop?

I inevitably ask myself this question, but I don't find any answers. Was it really just that, as an adult, I no longer had the time for it?

So much has happened. My first own apartment, my job. Lukas was there and then came the promotion to secretary of the head of marketing. Then the plan to buy a house and have children. Little adorable beings who might have his features or my hair color.

It's a lovely thought; it even makes me smile a little. And yet, in the same moment, a stabbing pain shoots straight through my chest. For years we tried to garnish our responsible life with a sufficient portion of happiness. We never managed it. I can feel so clearly that something is missing. In the perfect dream life that Lukas and I painted for ourselves, I'm missing a feeling. Burning passion, all-consuming enthusiasm, and the certainty that we experience every day consciously instead of just letting it pass us by.

Through the living room window I watch the last rays of the day's sun fighting in vain for their place in the sky. They're doing their best, but they'll lose. Because they never had a chance to win.

Even if I don't know much else, one thing is clear to me. What's happening out there right now must not happen to me.

Chapter Twenty

June has come inexorably, and we're still stuck. For weeks now, our life has been as if we were riding a roller coaster that runs mostly underground. And what we're doing today could just as well be nothing more than a ridiculous attempt on my part to get Marie to ride back up to the top with me. Still, I don't want to give up, because letting go of our plans for the future would mean letting go of our love.

Against her will, I dragged her out of the apartment and steered her all the way to Gartengasse. Here, to where the house with the number 23 stands. Our house.

Curiously, I watch her features as we turn into the street. And sure enough, the corners of her mouth lift.

"Can we go in?" There's excitement in her voice, a wonderful sound. Only now do I realize how much I've missed it.

I shake my head. "Not yet." The repair work is underway, and besides, we won't get the key until the official handover in November.

She looks disappointed. "What a shame," she says, pushing her lower lip forward.

Now. This is the moment to bring up again what has gone unsaid between us for weeks. I can't put it off any longer. Marie has officially been unemployed for a month already; it's clearly time to do something.

"How's the job hunt going?" I ask, deliberately casual, and quicken my pace.

With a sigh, Marie lets her gaze wander over the neighborhood with its neatly laid-out gardens, then exhales loudly. "The employment office only sends me job ads for secretarial positions. They're putting on the pressure, but I don't want to do that kind of work anymore, I notice that with every single interview. It's like a whole resistance army is building up inside me when I find out what I'd be expected to do there." She turns her head in my direction and looks at me intently. "I need to change direction."

That's not what I wanted to hear from her. Because it sounds like a long process with no result. And like many more months of unemployment at the end of which only frustration is waiting for her. That's not going to work! Starting in November we'll already have to start paying off a loan. I'm afraid my growing lack of understanding for Marie's nonsense is clearly written on my face, but I still try for a neutral tone. "What do you mean by that?"

"I wasn't doing nothing all through May, even if it might sometimes have looked that way to you. I didn't just visit Grandma in the hospital every day and take care of the animals at her place, I also did a lot of research." She sounds as if she's proud of having managed all that. And when I think about how listless and depressed she was in the first weeks after she was let go, this active life is actually progress. "By now I know for sure that I'm not going back to my old job," she suddenly says, and it sounds a bit as if she's setting off a grenade.

I can't believe what I'm hearing. That's a damn bad idea, I'd like to explain. This has already been going on too long, I want to scream. For her sake alone, I swallow the words. Now they lie in my stomach like boulders, ramming their sharp edges into my insides.

Why is she doing something like this? And now of all times, when we're only a few steps away from our house. Over the garden fence I can already see the pillars of the porch and the tall weeping willow whose branches sway back and forth in the summer wind.

Before I can say anything, she goes on. "I'm sure this is a shock for you. I haven't been able to tell you until now, first I had to figure it out for myself. The notice of termination triggered so much in me. I started asking myself whether I'd ever really been happy with my life as a secretary. Whether at any point I'd honestly felt content."

For heaven's sake, not this topic again.

I'd most like to scream. Grab her by the shoulders and shake her until she comes to her senses. Because with every further word out of her mouth, our dream is going further down the drain. If this were a movie, at this very moment the gray-blue painted wooden house on our left would collapse in on itself. Just like that. Why doesn't she understand that?

"Let me explain this. We keep putting everything off until later. But *later* never comes." Out of the corner of my eye I can tell she's looking at me. But I'm not going to turn my head in her direction, because I have no idea what might happen then. "I want that 'later.' And I want it now."

Abruptly she forces me to stop, steps in front of me, and looks at me intently. "You're probably wondering what this 'later' is, right?"

Oh God, no. I'm not. I just want everything to be okay again. I want us to get back what we had. I want Marie to work and for us to finance our house with our two salaries. We just want to live a good life, nothing more.

Longingly she reaches for my hands. "Lukas, what do you think?"

What am I supposed to say to that? That it feels as if someone has just pushed me off a cliff? That I'm falling? That I'm terribly afraid of hitting the ground any moment and shattering like an overripe tomato?

"What do you want me to say?" I finally ask, my voice hoarse. Behind her face, through a gap in the wooden garden fence, I can see our property. What's in there is our future, so why doesn't Marie see that anymore all of a sudden? I have to swallow just to be able to go on speaking. "Why do you think you've been living your life wrong up to now? And what about our life? Is that wrong too?"

"We always tried to find a compromise between obligations and dreams. But it was never enough to be completely happy." From the way Marie says the words, I can tell she's not even sure herself whether another kind of happiness exists at all.

"Then tell me about happiness." The fear of her answer makes my words sound mocking.

Marie's expression instantly turns combative. For a moment she even clenches her fists. "The last few years have already shown that languages, hiking, and baking aren't for me. But recently I sat in on a lecture from the medical program. It was really interesting. Architecture would be great too. Or psychology."

"You want to study?" God, where did that come from all of a sudden? It will take years before Marie earns money again. She has to realize that that's impossible.

Now she wrinkles her nose. "Maybe," she murmurs so quietly that I can barely understand her. "I'm not sure yet, I'm just trying some things out."

She can't be serious. "So you've been looking for weeks for a happiness you can't find?" I summarize in disbelief. Doesn't she see that that alone is already a sign?

"Not yet. I know this is hard for you, and I don't want to hurt you. But try to understand, I can't help it." With a desperate expression, she lays her hand on my chest and massages it in slow circles.

I don't want this loving touch, and at the same time I long for it. "What about the house?" The moment I ask the question, I bite my lip. Her answer might crush me, but I still have to hear it.

Marie's eyebrows draw together. "I don't know."

And neither do I. Because the question won't even come up anymore if we can't pay for it. I won't think about that; I simply refuse to imagine that version of our life. "Let's go," I say, because I can't think of anything else we have left to talk about.

I start moving because the pressure this place puts on me is becoming too much. Still, it doesn't help me at all not to be there anymore. All the way home, numbers clatter through my head, but no matter how I line them up, in the end there's always a big minus.

I won't be able to do this without Marie. Impossible. Despair spread through me more and more violently, along with the feeling that I was completely alone with my worries and my responsibility. But that wasn't all. By now it was clearer than anything else: I had already lived through what was happening here once before, and one thing was obvious: I must not let it happen.

"So you want to reorient yourself and find your happiness that way," I suddenly heard myself say as we turned into the street where our apartment building was. The words seemed to leave my mouth aggressively all by themselves, and I searched in vain for some force strong enough to stop me.

I couldn't take it anymore. It had to be said. Now.

"But you've been looking for weeks for that one job that will make you entirely happy. Don't you think you're expecting a bit too much?"

Marie's expression darkened. "How would you know?" Staring stubbornly straight ahead, she stomped toward the cream-colored house where our two-room apartment was.

"Because I know you. Maybe even better than you know yourself. You've always worked hard for your goals, and you can't tell me that didn't make you happy. I saw you glowing with every raise. After your promotion you were full of energy. You don't need more than that. You were already happy. We were happy!" Even though I clearly saw frustration rising in her, I firmly resolved to stick with it. Because it was finally time to get her down from this crazy cloud she'd been floating on all spring. I'd been understanding the whole time, but it hadn't changed anything. I should have known from the start; after all, it had been exactly the same back then, twenty years ago. "This search for happiness is nothing but a figment of your imagination." At last I said what I'd held back far too long for her sake alone.

Marie's gaze hit me like an ice-cold spear. "What are you talking about? A figment of my imagination? You think I'm crazy, is that it?" Her voice was shrill; gesticulating wildly, she walked beside me, getting faster with every step. "You clearly don't understand anything."

I kept pace with her, rushed in right behind her through the front door of our building, and ran up the stairs after her. "What are you trying to say? That my life plans are pointless just because they're down-to-earth and realistic? And that you, since you've apparently inhaled an overdose of wisdom, can see how stupid I am for preferring a life like that?" Panting, I dashed on and caught up with her again at our apartment door. With trembling fingers and pressed-together lips, she maneuvered the key into the lock. "Just a few weeks ago you had this life too, and you never once called it pointless."

As if she were fleeing from me and my words, she shoved the door open and raced down the hallway toward the kitchen. But even that way she wouldn't escape the truth.

"Wake up already, you're getting lost in something that's not good for you at all! You had your break, and it didn't lead you anywhere. It's time you got off your ass and came back to real life," I yelled and followed her into the kitchen.

There she stands, her back to me in the corner of the kitchenette, between the colorful tiles whose sunny mood nobody cares about today. "You don't understand anything! And you know what, you don't even want to understand. You think that only your way is the right one. Have you ever once asked yourself what will be left, someday, of all the things you waste your days on?" Her voice falters, a tremor runs through her body. Even here, leaning against the door-frame, I hear the faint whimper that leaves her mouth.

"Marie, I don't recognize you anymore. Whatever kind of crisis this is, you have to get out of it again, fast. Gaps in your résumé aren't welcome, they make you look weak and unable to cope with pressure. If you don't get back on track soon, you'll never be able to go back. And once you realize how far you've already lost your way, you'll bitterly regret it." I should at least try to sound calm, empathetic, and patient. And yet I can't manage it. Not anymore. I'm right, and I know that with absolute certainty. "Your unemployment benefits will soon be downgraded to emergency assistance, and then what? What do you think is going to happen? Yes, I love you, but I'm not prepared to support you financially for all eternity."

I did it. The words that had been burning in my throat for so long are out.

Ramrod straight, Marie is still leaning against the kitchenette a few meters in front of me. "You're just like Grandpa," she says, a cold sobriety in her voice. "And if something fundamental in the way we live doesn't finally change, I'll end up like Grandma one day."

That's what she thinks? She's afraid I'll die before her because I think realistically? She's trying to deflect, but she won't get away with that. "What does one thing have to do with the other?"

Now she's even clenching her fists. Her knuckles stand out white, her hands are shaking. "You'll never understand," she hisses at me.

"Because there's nothing to understand." This is leading nowhere. I can't get through to her, and maybe I don't even want to anymore.

Marie stays silent, and that's when I know for sure.

Me, my opinion, and my wishes don't matter to her at all.

This apartment has become too small for the two of us in an instant. I need time to think, so I leave the kitchen without another word. There's no need to say anything, because I'm sure that at least this one thing is clear to Marie. Until I've found my way of dealing with our situation, I can't see her and don't want to hear from her. And she wouldn't dream of breaking this unwritten rule.

Chapter Twenty-One

The light in the hallway comes on and casts a narrow strip of light directly onto the foot of the bed, where I've been lying alone for hours.

Lukas is back.

Like always, he needed distance so he could think in peace. Is he ready to talk to me yet? Part of me hopes so, another part is afraid. Because I still don't know what I'm supposed to say to him.

All evening I've been trying hard to imagine what it would be like if I gave in to what he wants. In my mind I slipped into a neat little suit and watched myself serving coffee and lugging files around. Taking care of schedules that never work out anyway and organizing business trips that constantly need last-minute changes. Instantly I felt like I used to. As if I were trying to run in a hamster wheel that can't turn.

No, that life is over. I can't go on like that.

But even though I left it behind when I quit, the last few weeks have been hard. I've been hard. I know that.

Grandma was moved to a mental health facility, because only the wounds you can see from the outside have healed. Inside she's suffering, and I'm doing my best to be there for her. At the same time I'm feverishly trying to figure out what my *later* might be. Every personality test ends with a different result. I went to the job fair, did a trial day at an aid organization, and looked into possible training paths to become a graphic designer. Every job comes with downsides that make me doubt. I have no idea where else I should look or which direction would really suit me. Only how it would have to feel, that I know for sure. But despite all my effort, I don't feel anything. Still not.

I'm failing. Every damn time. And as if that weren't bad enough, Lukas is now blaming me too. Of course I understand his point of view. But the other way around, not a single bit of what I say gets through to him. I'm practically screaming my despair out loud, but my words die away in the endless space between us.

The barely perceptible scrape of the door on the parquet floor pulls my attention. Reflexively I close my eyes. Not just so Lukas will think I'm asleep, but also to keep the tears from finding a way out. I press my lips together and clench my fists under the blanket. My ears strain to follow what's happening in the bedroom.

Lukas lies down next to me in the bed. He's very careful about it, as if I were a wounded chick. The smell of beer tickles my nose. He was definitely at Joe's. With Anna. He poured his heart out to her, I'm sure of it.

What did she tell him, I wonder?

Now he puts his glasses down on the nightstand. Will he turn toward me in a moment? Or is he so fed up with me that he can hardly bear being close to me anymore?

A feeling even worse than before floods my body and

crashes over my head like a thirty-foot wave. I've lost a part of myself. If I lose him as well, I won't have any idea who or what I am anymore. And still I can't do it, I can't open my eyelids and turn toward him. What would I even say?

All of a sudden, like a movie scene, images start playing behind my closed eyelids. As if I were hovering above our bed, I watch the two of us in the dusk of night. With my head resting on my hands, I look at Lukas searchingly. He's lying on his back, staring up at the ceiling. We're as far apart as the bed will allow, and I can practically see the dark abyss opening up between us.

"I'm sorry," I say awkwardly in my imagination, because I can't think of anything better.

He sighs, though only softly. "Sorry for what exactly, Marie?"

There it is again, that moment when I don't know how to go on. It's his first question, and I can't even answer that one.

As if he could sense my thoughts, he doesn't let much time pass. "That you're blocking our life? That you're dumping all the burden on me?" He swallows, and so do I. "Or that I and my wishes don't matter to you at all anymore?"

That's not true, I want to protest, and yet I stay silent. Because I know he's right. About everything. But even if I wanted to, I can't ignore this longing inside me. It's as if, over the past years, it had secretly grown beneath a surface that shattered when I quit my job. Now this craving is everywhere in me, and I know it will stay with me until it's satisfied. "I'm sorry," I repeat like a cursed doll that can only say this one sentence. Of course my tears make their entrance right after that. I let them rise without resisting any longer. Because there's no point in holding them back. They run down the bridge of my nose, then along my cheek and finally soak into the pillow.

Now he turns his head toward me, and even in the dark gray night I can see the pleading in his face. “What happened to us?” he wants to know.

Those are exactly the words that wander through my head like bodiless ghosts while, in reality, I lie rigid as a board next to Lukas and hope for two things at once. That he wakes me up, kisses me, and assures me that he still loves me in spite of everything. And that very soon I’ll have answers to the questions he only dares to ask in my imagination.

I try to tell if he’s still awake, but nothing seems to move on his side of the bed. Not even the faint rustle of the sheet can be heard. It’s as if he were just as paralyzed as I am. As if our two hearts wanted to fight while our bodies refused to cooperate.

I dare to do it.

Very slowly, I roll over to the other side and look at him. Just like in my imagination, he’s lying on his back, only his eyes are closed. I wish I could reach out my hand to him, stroke his forehead and let it wander farther down. Until I arrive where I can feel his heartbeat. Then I’d know whether our two hearts are still beating in the same rhythm. But I don’t do it; I just stare at him. Because I’m afraid of how he’ll react to my touch. And I’m even more afraid of what I might feel.

Chapter Twenty-Two

With a jolt, the tram starts moving. I find a free single seat all the way in the back, weave my way through the carriage to it, and let myself drop down. Normally I never sit on my way to work, but today everything is different. I feel a bit as if a whole freight train had run me over last night. With a load of cars on top. Or trucks.

The last few hours had felt like a nightmare come to life. Of course I couldn't sleep after my fight with Marie. Instead, my thoughts were trapped all night long between a pointless sequence of scenes from the past and moments from all kinds of possible futures.

It's the latter I'm still stuck on even now, as if I were circling the word over and over again. Future. No one knows exactly what it will bring, and yet until now I've relied on one thing: that Marie will be a part of it.

In my jacket pocket I feel for the little velvet-covered box, then pull it out. I notice how the other passengers' gazes follow my movements, but I still slowly flip open the lid. The sun-yellow stone sparkles even in the artificial light of the tram. No matter from which angle I look at it, it's flawlessly beautiful.

And it suits Marie as if it had been made just for her.

Carefully, I let my fingers glide over the diamond-studded setting. I feel the smooth cut of the gemstone and the cold of the ring band. Inevitably, I bite my lip, because in that moment the memory of Anna's reaction to our argument last night pushes its way into my thoughts.

Of course she immediately knew what was going on with me this time too. Even Joe must have seen it; I could tell from his encouraging nod when he served me the beer. He didn't say anything, in stark contrast to Anna.

"Seriously?" In my memory she looks me over again, eyebrows raised, in disbelief. Then she grabs a cue and marches over to the pool table. "And you're sure she meant it that way?"

There's nothing I can do but lift my shoulders. "How am I supposed to know?" I ask with a sigh, tracing the grain of the wooden bistro table I'm leaning on. "I don't understand her anymore."

Thoughtfully, my best friend chews on her lower lip and lets her cue wander from one hand to the other and back again. "So she wants to reorient herself," she murmurs absently. "What could that mean?"

"Honestly, I was hoping you'd know." Maybe it's asking too much, but after all, Anna is a woman. And women have to know how women think, don't they?

Anna takes her shot. Two balls land in the corner pockets at once. Instead of being pleased, she squeezes her eyelids together in concentration, as if that would help her think. "She's unhappy. With her job. And with her life too? But definitely not with you." Her light-blue, round eyes lock onto me. "Right?"

Of course she says exactly what I hadn't even dared to think. I nod, although what I really want is to shake my head so hard it makes me dizzy. "Damn. What if it's actually true?"

"No," she suddenly decides, comes over to me, and takes a big sip of her lemon water. Pulp sticks to her upper lip as she beams at me. "That's nonsense. She loves you, she always has. Why would that suddenly be any different?"

"She loved her job too, or at least that's what she claimed," I point out, and immediately I feel my chest tighten.

Anna's dismissive wave of her hand and her warm laughter are exactly what I need. "Oh, come on, that's not the same. Work is just work, nothing more," she replies and turns back to the game of pool.

"That's exactly what I told her, and not just once. But she has this crazy idea that she could find her dream job." I need to move, so I push myself up from my stool and step next to Anna. "You should hear the insane things she comes out with. One minute she's talking about wanting to be a princess, then about meditation mumbo jumbo or personality tests. These pronouncements come out of nowhere and honestly, every single time I'd most like to dump a bucket of cold water over her head so she finally wakes up again."

A deep crease forms between her eyebrows. Now she's staring at me as if I were an alien. "Doesn't this shady search for happiness sound pretty familiar to you?"

"Oh, please." I don't dare say it out loud; instead I just wave it off. Because then it would finally become real. Because otherwise I'd have to openly admit that I've already thought about it myself. "Take your shot."

"It started exactly the same way with your aunt. And I

don't need to tell you how that ended." She fixes me with an intent stare.

"I don't really remember it that clearly." That's a lie and Anna knows it. Still, I don't want to talk about it right now. Because saying it out loud would make it irrevocably real. All at once my head becomes so heavy I can hardly hold it up. I lean on the cue and squint wearily at Anna. "Damn."

She's at my side immediately, puts her arm around my shoulders and rests her head against mine. "You two will get through this. I'm sure," is all she says, without giving me any more advice. She probably doesn't know what else to do either.

The memory of this conversation still makes me sigh a night later, here in the middle of the tram. I didn't get any more advice from her for the rest of the evening. Instead, she distracted me with stories from her sports club and upcoming competitions while we played pool.

There doesn't seem to be a solution to my problem. I can no longer stop the despair from taking hold of me. I'm holding Marie's ring in my hand, and yet I have no idea anymore what I'm supposed to do with it.

Do I still want to marry her?

Definitely the old Marie. The Marie whose smile can light up an entire room. The one whose sparkling eyes are the first thing I look into in the morning, certain that the day can only be wonderful. The Marie who laughs, lives, and fools around with me. That's the woman I love.

With the new Marie, I'm no longer sure. Everything about her has changed, her expressions, her movements, even what she says. As if a dark veil had settled over her sunny nature and made my dream woman disappear. Is the real Marie even still there beneath that veil? Or have I already lost her forever?

A terrible thought. With all my strength I try to push it away. I snap the lid of the ring box shut; in a split second the yellow gemstone disappears from my sight. How wonderful it would be if my doubts vanished along with it. And the fear of having to live forever without the Marie my heart beats for.

It's time to find a solution. We have to become Lukas and Marie again; anything else is unthinkable. And right now I decide that I'll do whatever it takes for us to be a couple again, working together toward our goals: our own house, financial security, a family.

Just a good life, that's all I want. Marie wants that too, she's just forgotten. I'll remind her—no, I'll show her. And I already know how.

Chapter Twenty-Three

"What are the doctors saying?" For my grandma's sake I force a smile onto my face.

She herself apparently can't manage that. As if her facial muscles no longer had any strength, she looks at me with a motionless expression. She seems absent, as if she were staring right through me out the window, where the June sun keeps hiding today behind thick clouds. At least she's wearing the bright blue sweater I brought her yesterday, even if it doesn't change the pallor of her skin.

"Grandma?" I try again and gently place my hand on her forearm. "When are you allowed to go home?"

In slow motion she tilts her head to the side. "Home?" she repeats absentmindedly. "Where is that?"

Of course she isn't crazy or even demented. She knows perfectly well where she lives. What she has forgotten is the reason why she wants to be there. It's been like this for weeks.

"Home is where your garden is waiting for you, your chickens and the cats," I remind her gently.

"How could we not see it?" Her forehead creases, her lips tremble. "Why didn't we understand what we were doing?"

There they are again, the same questions as always. And just like every other day, I don't have any answers. So I just stroke the thin skin of her wrists and let her talk.

"We should have lived our lives. Not waited for *later*, not kept putting the beautiful things off."

Her words hit me right where this longing has been sitting in me since I quit my job, like a rebel who refuses to be driven out. "*Later* never comes."

I suddenly sound absent-minded too, stuck in my very own loop of thoughts. I know it's not too late for me yet. But even though I'm ready to do anything for a happy life, it just won't come to me.

The result is the same. For my grandma and me. Neither of us knows what to do next; we can't see the path we want to take.

Just thinking about it is enough to make my frustration almost overwhelm me. I'd love nothing more than to talk to Grandma about what has happened to me over the past few weeks. Like we used to, we could sit with a glass of homemade juice on the wooden bench in front of her house. We would watch the bumblebees as they flew from lavender blossom to lavender blossom and talk for hours. Together we've always managed to find solutions to every problem so far. Now the situation seems hopeless. For each of us.

This morning Lukas left without a word. Behind my closed lids I was awake and heard him throw back the covers and pad out of the room. Very quietly he closed the bedroom door behind him and didn't come back. Not to leave me a note on the nightstand or to stroke my hair. Not to wake me for a clarifying talk, and not to kiss me goodbye.

I messed up. But I'm definitely not going to burden Grandma with this worry. Compared to hers, my problems are ridiculously small, and I should be ashamed of letting them take me over like this.

To distract us both, I reach for the special edition of Jane Austen's Pride and Prejudice and open the book.

I read to her until lunch is served. Then I kiss her cheeks goodbye and hold her tight. There's nothing more I can do for her, and I hate myself a little for that.

I leave the Center for Mental Health, where Grandma has already been for two weeks, as if fleeing. As if I could run away from myself and these awful feelings if I just move fast enough.

Without thinking about it, I march to the water park. By now I come here almost every day. Maybe only because I can't stand being in the apartment anymore. Or because part of me has fallen in love with watching the swans on the water. There's something calming about seeing how elegantly they lay their necks together and glide across the surface of the lake, seemingly without any effort.

With a sigh, I spread out the red-and-blue checkered picnic blanket in my usual spot and lean comfortably against a tree trunk. The sun squints into my face, so bright that I close my eyes. Immediately there's that orange flicker that forms behind my eyelids through the interplay of light and shadow. The branches of the nearby trees, swaying back and forth in the warm breeze, paint ever new, abstract images on my retina. Today it smells of freshly mown grass; I hear the gentle lapping of the lake and the chirping of birds. It's actually wonderful, and yet even this place can't chase away my dark thoughts. And even less the tightness in my chest that I've felt so clearly since the argument with Lukas last night.

I snap my eyes open, yank out a whole clump of grass next to the picnic blanket, and torture the individual blades until all that's left is a green juice sticking to my fingers.

I just can't have both. Lukas and my dream job, which I still don't even know what it is. Do I really have to choose?

Maybe it's stupid. Or naive. Still, I sit up and cross my legs. Sitting cross-legged, I place my hands on my thighs. I try to breathe deeply and, in the same moment, feel unbelievably ridiculous doing it.

If I really believe that alone would help me, I must have truly gone crazy.

Crazy. Ready for the loony bin. Insane.

Words like these rush through my head as if they were looking for a place to settle in. I can't let that happen, that much is clear. Even so, I can barely withstand the pressure.

Suddenly I hear the pebbles on the path crunch nearby.

The stranger. He's here! Today I can ask him my questions, and he'll have answers for me.

With far more hope than is good for me, I turn my head in the direction the sound is coming from. There's someone back there, but the bushes are still too dense to make out whether it's really him. Impatiently, I wait for the figure to come closer. The height and build fit. Chewing on my lower lip, I send up a quick prayer. I'm like a castaway clinging to the last plank of wood, drifting in the middle of the open sea and imagining he can see a lonely island appearing on the horizon.

As if my prayers didn't reach the heavens, I have to realize a few seconds later that it's only a woman walking her Labrador. Nothing more.

The stranger isn't here; I have to manage on my own and finally make a decision. What's more important to me? A happy job or a fulfilling love life?

Basically, the answer is simple. Maybe I've lost myself, but I can't lose Lukas as well. He's the only part of *Later* that I already have, and I'd be damned if I risked that. So I rummage my phone out of my pocket and type a message to Lukas.

"I'm endlessly sorry about what happened yesterday. Forgive me. I love you and I agree with you on everything."

Thoughtfully, I skim the text. I know I mustn't send it. Because if I've learned one thing in the last five years, it's that I shouldn't pressure him after a fight. As soon as he's ready to talk, he'll get in touch with me. That's how it has always been, and this time I'll stick to it too.

I quickly delete the text. I'm not even halfway through when a message from Lukas suddenly pops up.

"Can we talk?" it says, and I immediately feel lighter.

This is it, his first step. Now I'm allowed to respond in kind. I immediately finish the text I started earlier. "Let's talk about it tonight. I'll cook!" I add as well. As soon as I send the message, I feel surprisingly liberated.

It's decided.

I'm going to go back to my old life. For Lukas's sake. The constant pressure from the job center will stop, and maybe I'll actually find a position I like. With a nice boss and reasonably interesting tasks. The fact that I currently have no idea what those could be doesn't have to mean they don't exist. The last thing I was offered was a job at the information desk of a shopping mall. That's anything but a dream, but I'll earn a bit of money and at the same time keep looking for something better.

My phone buzzes. "Lasagna would be great. Love you!" I read, and I can't help but smile. Everything is fine; by tonight at the latest, not only our argument but also my aimlessness will come to an end.

The tightness in my chest disappears, but the wistful glimmer, which I don't even know exactly where I feel it, is still there. I have to ignore it, it's as simple as that.

To take my mind off things, I let my gaze wander through the water park. How wonderful would it be to work right here? While I organize business trips and prepare presentations, I could watch the lake glitter in the sunlight behind my screen. Only the quacking of the ducks and the rustling of the wind would surround me.

Clearly, I need a job where I can at least work from home part of the time. Wouldn't that be a perfect compromise? I'd at least be able to breathe a little easier, and Lukas would be happy too.

"Namaste," I suddenly hear a deep voice say. "Was your search successful?"

Although I know who's standing behind me, I flinch. My pulse speeds up on the spot. Is it just the surprise of seeing the stranger again? Or is it a flicker of my longing, which really shouldn't have anything left to say?

I quickly shake these strange thoughts out of my head and turn to face him. "I think so." With an inviting wave of my hand, I offer him a place on my blanket.

He settles down next to me, sitting cross-legged. "Tell me about it."

I furrow my brow. He's skipping over something absolutely essential here. "Don't you want to know what I was looking for before I tell you what I found?"

"I already knew when I met you for the first time." However he does it, his presence feels frighteningly wise.

There's no way he's telling the truth. "So what was I looking for?"

"For yourself." He points with his index finger to the area near my heart.

This man is a stranger; he knows absolutely nothing about me. I haven't revealed a single one of my thoughts to him, yet he seems to know them all. Better than I do. And better than Lukas, who doesn't even remotely understand what has happened to me over the past few months. Unable to say anything in reply, I stare straight into the stranger's deep blue eyes.

"What did you find?" he repeats his question, as if he doesn't notice my piercing gaze at all.

"I… um, well, I… I think I've found something I might like." Oh God, why am I suddenly stuttering like this? He must think I'm an idiot.

Despite my total failure, he smiles at me kindly. "You sound very convinced of your insight."

"I thought there was something more. Something like meaning, a calling, or whatever you want to call it." Although I try to fight it, a sad mood immediately settles over me. "But I was wrong. The basic conditions are set and can't be changed. I should make the best of it, and that's exactly what I'm going to do."

"You want to live your life at half-mast?" he asks me, and he doesn't sound at all as if he's criticizing me.

Still, his words trigger a slight pull in my stomach. "Yes, that's what I want." My voice wavers; I have to clear my throat to go on speaking. "I've been trying for weeks to find this happiness in life. And I haven't made a single step forward. Worse still, I've ended up in a dead end. It can't go on like this." With my gaze fixed on the rippling movements of the water in front of us, I take a deep breath. Because what I'm about to say hurts me more than I want to admit. "A life at half-mast is still better than no life at all."

"Do you really believe that?" His words hang in the air

between us like an annoying smell that won't be driven away.

My shoulders automatically jerk up. "It doesn't matter whether I believe it or not. Because that's just how it is. I'll have to accept that." I can hear how discouraged I sound. My head grows heavy and sinks to my chest.

Suddenly the stranger moves closer to me. As if we had known each other for years, he places his finger under my chin and guides my head upward until I look at him. "No one has to live their life at half-mast. Not you either."

My eyes fill with tears, but I don't care. Hiding anything from him seems pointless anyway. "It makes me tired. I search and search, but I don't find anything. The path is too exhausting." On top of that, I have no support. No one understands me. And I can't leave earning the money to Lukas alone any longer.

"You're tensely searching for everything that will come to you on its own once you let go. Be open. Only then will your happiness find you." With these words, he takes his hand from my chin, but his gaze remains fixed on me as if he were casting a spell on me.

"What's that supposed to mean?" I sound like a complete idiot. And I am one, after all, since I've been crouching in the dark for weeks, trying in vain to imagine it was light.

"Remember what I told you at our last meeting." It's as if he wants to believe for me, because I can't anymore. Right now, when I'd most like to give up, he's here for me with all his conviction.

The man beside me is basically a stranger. Yet he's also someone who believes in me and my happiness. "My thoughts determine my life. And I determine my thoughts."

Those were his words, and just speaking them does something to me.

He nods, satisfied. "You didn't forget. Now you just have to understand it."

He seems certain that I'll make it. I can see it in the way he looks at me, in his gestures, and not least in the clarity of his voice. So I ask the question that rules everything inside me. "But how?"

With a knowing smirk, he gets up from the blanket and raises his hand in farewell. "Never give up, then you'll be able to do anything." He smiles at me. In his face I can see all of his conviction.

There's no need to ask, because I'm sure. We'll see each other again. With a grateful nod, I say goodbye to him. I watch him until he disappears between the bushes, and even when I can't see him anymore, his words are still with me. *Your happiness will find you, never give up*, it echoes inside me.

Even if no one else does, at least the stranger believes in me. He doesn't call my search pointless, doesn't think I've gone crazy, and doesn't dismiss my wishes as unrealistic.

If he believes in me, then I want to do it too. Once more I ask the all-important question. "So, Marie, what could the life of your dreams look like?" I ask myself.

Then I pause to feel what these words do to me. No clear picture forms before my inner eye, but a delicate spark of hope stirs in me, and I can't even say exactly where. In my stomach, maybe, or in my chest. As if it were raining stars, I feel a tingling on my shoulders. It spreads in a matter of seconds across my back and all the way down to the tips of my little toes.

So this is what it feels like when the darkness recedes because suddenly there's light again. For the first time in weeks I smile without having to force it. Because I know that the answer to my question is definitely out there somewhere, waiting for me. I just have to find it.

Chapter Twenty-Four

A feeling like a warm summer rain spreads through my body. Not just because it smells like lasagna and the radio is playing, but also because I can hear Marie humming to herself in the kitchen.

There's life in our apartment. And good vibes.

Full of anticipation for an evening together, I slip off my shoes, set the bouquet of flowers I brought aside, and walk into the kitchen. Marie is standing with her back to me, her whole body swaying to the beat of the music.

"Hey, Sleeping Beauty." Leaning against the azure-blue doorframe, I watch as Marie slowly turns toward me. In slow motion I see more and more of her face, and I can hardly believe what I discover there.

She's beaming at me, just like she used to.

Now she comes closer, kisses me tenderly, and nestles against me. For minutes we stand there tightly entwined, until she lifts her head from my shoulder and looks up at me.

"Everything's ready. Come on, I'm starving!" Full of

energy, she pulls me to the dining table in the living room. I try not to show my astonishment too openly. Still, I can't help wondering when she last went to so much trouble for me.

Telling her what I thought had an effect. My Marie is back.

With a sweeping gesture she presents the beautifully laid table to me. The modern square plates are lined up neatly. Cutlery and dark blue cloth napkins are lovingly arranged beside them. She's even thought of a white tablecloth and romantically flickering candles.

"Wow, this looks amazing." I kiss her again, this time exuberantly and full of gratitude. Because this knot inside me is loosening, the one that gave me so much fear and worry over the last few weeks. From now on, it's all uphill, the signs are unmistakable.

I pull away from her and rub my chin in mock thoughtfulness. "But something's still missing here, don't you think?"

Marie's confusion is sweet as sugar. "Everything's here. Cutlery, glasses, plates, wine. Even napkins, and the good ones at that," she says proudly.

"No, no, it's not complete yet. Wait a second." I signal to her not to move and walk back into the hallway.

The bouquet of flowers is still lying there. Earlier I put it aside carelessly, so I straighten the daisies and nudge the leopard's bane back into the right place. Will Marie recognize where the flowers came from?

Eager to see her reaction, I march into the living room. "Now the table's perfect." Even before I hand her my gift, I see it in her eyes. She knows.

"A bouquet from our meadow." The dreamy undertone in her words is overwhelming, and the joyful expression on her face is exactly what I've longed for for so long. Now she buries her nose in the flowers and, with her eyelids closed, takes a deep breath. "Fantastic!"

This time everything is right. At last our life is shifting into the proper light. Gently I pull Marie into my arms again. "I love you. And I'm endlessly sorry for what I said so thoughtlessly yesterday. Please forgive me!"

I can feel her shaking her head right against my shoulder. "You don't have to apologize, I understand you and your reaction very well. It was totally fine to bring it up once."

Where had this woman who's standing in front of me now been all this time?

"Come on, let's eat." She takes my hand and twirls with me over to the dining table.

It doesn't matter where the change comes from. It's here and it's real. That's all that counts. I just have to present my plan to her, then our relationship will be as strong again as it's supposed to be.

Boldly, a few moments later, I spear a piece of lasagna. It must have been months since Marie last cooked for me. I enjoy today all the more, with the slightly over-seasoned taste of the sauce and the pasta sheets that, as always, turned out a bit too soft. That's just how Marie's lasagna is, anything but perfect, yet there's none better in this world. My thoughts drift of their own accord to the ring hidden in my jacket pocket, waiting for its moment. Is this the right time?

No. For Marie it has to be special. A nice dinner that she even cooked herself isn't enough. It's hard for me to wait any longer, but I hold back. But it's time to let the other bomb drop. And to present her with my idea, the one that's going to save us both.

"Listen, I thought about our argument yesterday," I say, not without a flicker of nervousness.

Marie immediately lets her fork sink onto the plate. Her expression tells me not only that she's curious. That glint in her eyes is also another sign that everything really is back to the way it was.

"Give me your hand." I feel my way across the table to her and lace my fingers with hers. "We're doing well. We have everything, and soon we'll be living in our dream house. We love each other and we want to grow old and wrinkly together. Right?"

Marie nods. "Exactly. No matter how many wrinkles and gray hairs, we'll stay together."

This is it. My breathing comes fast, my pulse speeds up. Because what I'm about to say next will change both our lives. For the better—no, for the best.

"We've always wanted a family of our own too. Right?" I start to gently stroke each of her fingers and look at her so intently it's as if I'm trying to conjure her.

Barely visible wrinkles formed on her forehead, she tilted her head to the side and smiled thoughtfully. "Right," she said then, and I could see her trying to figure out what would come next.

"And you don't want to go back to your job as a secretary. Right?"

All at once her face looked as if someone had dusted it with diamond powder. She sparkled. Everywhere. Full of expectation, she squirmed around on her chair and signaled to me with a wave of her hand that I should finally lay my cards on the table.

I did, and it didn't cost me the slightest bit of effort. Because I knew it was the best solution to our problems. "We should have a baby."

The confused look on her face made my knees go weak. "Wow, that's unexpected… um… yeah…"

"You don't have to answer right away. Think about it in peace; after all, it's a big thing." Lovingly, I let my fingertips glide over her cheek. I couldn't help imagining what it would be like to have a miniature version of Marie in my life. The thought was so wonderful that hardly anything else mattered.

Now Marie pushed herself up from her chair, came over to me, and sat right down on my lap. I savored the warm feeling rising inside me as she wrapped her arms around my shoulders and rested her forehead against mine. Our noses brushed tenderly, then she kissed me with an intensity that took my breath away. "Yes, let's have a baby," she breathed without lifting her lips from mine.

No one in this world could be happier than I was. Our dry spell was over, I was sure of it.

Suddenly she moved a little away from me and studied me doubtfully. "Can we even afford it?"

"I have an idea." I couldn't help but smile. Of course I had already done all the math. I didn't want to say anything yet, but if my plans worked out, we would make it.

The two of us will be happy. Forever. And that's what we wanted from the very beginning.

Chapter Twenty-Five

In this shop everything looks as if it had been made on a cloud. The colors white, light blue, and pink dominate my field of vision, my fingers brush over velvety and fluffy soft fabrics. I pull one of the miniature hangers from the silvery shining rail and take a closer look at the romper. How tiny the little feet are and how short the torso. With a few ruffles at the collar, the cream-colored romper with the embroidered teddy bear would definitely be even cuter. Inevitably I try to imagine what my own baby would look like in it. A little Lukas, a doll-like version of myself, or a perfect mix of the two of us.

What would it be like to be a mother? Would it fulfill me?

Maybe that's even what I'm looking for. For a moment I close my eyes and I already see a boy in front of me. He runs toward me, a bright child's laugh fills the room. A gap between his teeth flashes behind his slightly parted lips, he has Lukas's hair color and my jawline. His bare little feet make a smacking sound on the wooden floor as he comes closer at a run, arms spread wide. All at once I recognize the surroundings as well. Whitewashed walls, floor-length billowing curtains in an intense shade of violet, and an open fireplace. On the other side of the windowpane, the branches of a weeping willow bend down toward the ground. The green of the leaves glows in the sunlight as if it were a sign of hope. It's obvious: we're in our dream house.

"Mommy," the boy calls happily.

I crouch down and give him an encouraging smile. He already throws himself into my arms with such momentum that I almost lose my balance. I pull him close and bury my nose in his feather-light hair.

The idea of this life makes my heart beat faster even here, in the middle of the baby store. Yes, Lukas and I really should have children. But is now the right time for that?

When Lukas asked yesterday, I didn't think. I absolutely didn't want to disappoint him, and that was the only thing that mattered.

Thoughtfully, I hang the romper back in its place and let my gaze wander around the room. I see women with big bellies discussing with each other next to the shelf of baby bottles, a couple choosing a stroller together even though you can't see her pregnancy at all yet.

At that moment a young mother with a baby in a sling enters the store. Protectively, she lays her hand on her child's head and bends down to him. For a moment she closes her eyelids, as if she had to switch off her sense of sight to enjoy even more what she feels and smells. I could be like that too. In just a few months I could be wearing maternity clothes, picking out a crib, and thinking about the right name for my baby.

Beautiful and terrifying at the same time, the thought settles in my head as I stroll on into the pacifier section.

With a child there's little room for anything else, especially in the first years.

"Your happiness will find you," the stranger told me a few days ago. Did he mean a pregnancy by that?

Suddenly I hear a baby screaming at a volume that reverberates through my whole body. The toddler in the sling is crying. My gaze lands right on the mother's face. She gives me an apologetic smile and rocks her baby back and forth.

"Shhhh," she says, looking as if she's sending up a quick prayer to heaven. And in fact, the little munchkin slowly calms down again, he whimpers and finally falls silent. "Three-month colic," the mother then says to me, as if that explained everything.

Somewhat awkwardly, I nod. "I'm very sorry."

"Sometimes this little one here drives me out of my mind." She smiles, or at least she tries to.

Curiously, I look her over, and that's when I notice how exhausted she looks. The shadows under her eyes are dark, her long blond hair is thin, the skin on her arms dry. She's so pale she looks as if she might faint any moment. "It must be exhausting."

She's still gently rocking her baby back and forth. "Don't get me wrong, I love my Florian. More than anything." As if to prove it, she strokes her boy's head. "But yes, I'm bloody tired."

Of course I don't mention that that's hard to miss. Instead, I lean toward her with interest. Bracing myself against the shelf, I want to hear it from first hand. "Do you still have any time for yourself?"

She answers my question with a knowing smirk. "Me? Who's that?" she replies, winking at me.

I don't need any more information, because one important thing becomes clear to me right away:

I very clearly want children. But first I have to find what I'm looking for for myself.

It takes only fractions of a second before a bad feeling washes over me. When Lukas presented his plan to me last night, he was so full of hope. So content and optimistic. My perfect boyfriend offered me the perfect solution for a perfect life. He's willing to shoulder the financial burden all by himself, just to see me happy and to get the life he dreams of.

I definitely don't want to disappoint him. But going along with his plan would also mean disappointing myself.

This is a crossroads. No matter which direction I choose, once I start walking there's no going back, and one thing is certain: as little as I know how to go about it, I have to make this decision. Preferably right now.

So I do what the stranger advised me to do. Let go. Be open. I take a deep breath and look closely. As before, my gaze falls on the children's clothes, and suddenly they're no longer just adorable. They also give me an idea. It must be a lot of fun to design them and then sew them.

Could I do that?

Drawing had always been my passion. I'd just have to learn how to use the sewing machine, but that's surely no problem. I'd be my own boss, and the sunroom in the house is perfect for sewing. That's where I'd build a whole new life for myself. The days when Lukas had to shoulder the financial burden all by himself would finally be over for good.

Suddenly that tingling feeling from yesterday flares up inside me again. Maybe this is it. My "later," the thing I've been searching for for so long.

Should I even still go to this shopping center for the trial shift? I probably can't cancel anymore, and if I stick it out, at least I'll be contributing something to the household budget until my business really takes off. I can do that, for Lukas's sake. If I work, he'll be satisfied and who knows, maybe that'll make it a bit less hard for him that I still want to wait with the baby.

Despite my joy, a nasty feeling is slumbering inside me. Because I definitely have to tell him the truth as soon as possible. But I have no idea how I'm going to do that.

Chapter Twenty-Six

Visiting my parents feels like taking a trip into a world that has become foreign to me. Out here in the vineyards, time only ticks softly, and sometimes it seems as if the sun creates a different kind of light. I take a deep breath, then turn back to my work and routinely snap off an unnecessary side shoot from the vine so the grapes can grow better.

Only a meter away from me, my mother is doing exactly the same thing. "So, tell me, what's new?" I hear her ask.

With a broad grin, I turn to her. "You won't believe it, but I did it." The excitement in my voice is hard to miss.

She stops working and brushes her blond bangs off her forehead with the back of her hand. "You proposed to her," she says with a knowing nod. Her light blue eyes shine. "How lovely, I'm happy for you two."

I wave it off. "No, that's not it." My mother's skeptical look doesn't stop me from continuing enthusiastically. "I told you that Marie had a rough time these last few weeks. Her grandpa's death and the termination really got to her, and finding a new job is harder for her than she thought."

"If you want to work, you'll find something," my mother comments immediately. I know she doesn't mean it badly, even if her words sound strict. For her, it has always been a given to work seven days a week all year round on the family winery.

"Of course," I say soothingly. "But Marie wanted to find a really great position." I'd rather not tell her any more than that, and I definitely won't use Marie's own words. After all, I know my mother's opinion on everything that happens outside of hard work and a sense of responsibility.

Her skeptical look lets me know that just hinting at the problem was already too much. "And?"

Whenever she looks at me like that, my muscles tense up a little all by themselves. I quickly turn back to the grapevine and concentrate on looking for shoots that need to be pinched out. "Marie is going to stop looking for a job. We've decided to start a family."

"You're going to what?" Even though I don't look at my mother, I can picture her expression exactly. It's that very particular mix of astonishment, disbelief, and consternation that makes her otherwise friendly, sun-tanned face look like a grimace. "How did you even come up with something like that?"

Shouldn't congratulations be more in order? I don't even try to hide my disappointment. "We've always wanted kids, we would've started soon anyway. And Marie is looking for a new purpose. It's a perfect fit."

"Have I really not taught you anything at all in all these years?" Out of the corner of my eye I see her shake her head and throw her sinewy arms theatrically into the air.

"I honestly don't know what you're getting at." I fumble aimlessly with the grapevine, my jaw going rigid. She should be happy for me; why is she spoiling my mood with her negativity?

Now she comes closer, slips off her work gloves, and taps her index finger against my forehead. I hate it when she does that. "Just think for a second. Can't you remember?" All of a sudden her voice sounds soothing, but I still grab her finger and push it away.

I don't want to hear it; it's nonsense and we both know it. "This has absolutely nothing to do with Aunt Ulrike," I say quickly, because of course I know what she's getting at.

"Oh really? How long has Marie been looking for a new job?" As she says the word "job," she draws quotation marks in the air with her index fingers.

I shrug. "A few months. It just takes time until…"

My mother cuts me off at once. "How many applications has she sent out so far, how many job interviews has she had already?"

A handful, as far as I know, and the employment office forced her to go to every single one. But if I tell her that, she'll have exactly the proof she needs. So I stay silent; what else am I supposed to do?

"You see?" She plants her fists on her hips. "Marie doesn't want to work; she'd rather let you support her. And having a baby will make that even easier." Her probing gaze holds me captive.

"Not everyone is like Aunt Ulrike." I reach for the basket we're using to collect the broken-off leaves from the vines and march on to the next plant.

Of course she comes right after me. She won't let it go, I can feel it. "Has Marie changed? Is she talking nonsense? Does she think she's supposed to save the world?"

"Absolutely not," I answer sharply and busy myself with

the vine. Still, my thoughts immediately wander into the past, searching for exactly what my mother is hinting at. It doesn't take a second before I find it.

Damn.

"She's looking for her dream life, isn't she?" The dislike in her voice is all too obvious. All at once my mother is right next to me and puts her hand on my shoulder.

Nervously, I chew on my lower lip. Sure, I could deny it for a while longer, but what good would that do?

"She's not going to find it," my mother adds. "She has to wake up, or this is going to end badly."

I don't want to hear that, and even less do I want to think about it. Still, I can't get past my mother's words. "This is something completely different."

A contemptuous snort leaves her mouth. "This winery here should have been Ulrike's life, not mine. That's how our father intended it, but when Ulrike finished school, she started to change."

"We really don't have to go over all that again." My voice sounds raspy.

All of a sudden, my mother's usually energetic and determined expression changes. She suddenly looks thoughtful and sad, and I know she's just been overtaken by a memory that hurts her. "Ulrike was unhappy, and we all saw it. More and more, she let us down; she was often gone for days and no one knew where she was or what she was doing there. Then she started talking nonsense. All she talked about was the meaning of life and making dreams come true, about vocation and happiness." The incomprehension that resonates in her words is impossible to miss.

While my mother grows angrier and angrier, everything inside me tightens. Because what she's saying sounds familiar. Far too familiar.

"You know how much work a winery is. And that the family has to stick together. You help each other and are there for one another." She pauses for a moment. "Ulrike didn't care about that. She was selfish and vain. All she thought about was her so-called dream."

"Of course that was wrong." I try to sound just as scornful as my mother. I have no idea why I'm doing it, maybe just to support her. After all, I can clearly see how heavily the memory is weighing on her shoulders.

"She thought she was born to be a singer. We all tried to make her understand that that's not a real job. No one can make a living from singing, and besides, she was supposed to take over the winery. That was the plan, and there was nothing to be done about it."

I know how this story ends. "She didn't let anyone talk her out of her idea," I say.

My mother shakes her head, and even today I can still see the disappointment over her sister's behavior in her face. "I slaved away to keep the winery going while she chased after her pipe dreams and kept begging me for money over and over again."

"And you gave her some." I know exactly what happened. Why do we have to chew it all over again?

She nods. "I shouldn't have done that. I realize that today, but back then I couldn't help it. Despite everything, she was still my sister." Her voice wavers, and I understand all too well why.

Immediately I wonder whether her story really has anything to do with mine. I love Marie, maybe even more than my mother loved her sister. And for months now I've been the one providing for us financially while she drifts further and further away mentally.

Oh my God, is the same thing happening to me as to my mother?

No. Unlike Aunt Ulrike, Marie backed down and understood that things couldn't go on like that. She's back with me; the two of us have a shared goal.

My mother's voice pulls me back to reality. "She almost drove us to ruin. Your father and I had to work hard to keep the family business going." Impetuously she grabs the basket with the green waste and marches off with it. Either she can't stand our conversation any longer or she wants to give me time to think.

But I don't want to think. Not about what Aunt Ulrike did to our family with her ridiculous dream, and certainly not about my own situation. Because things with Marie are completely different.

Maybe from the outside there are parallels, but at the core there are very clear differences. In silence I watch my mother empty the basket and come back to me.

"Marie is just looking for a new project to keep her busy. And a small, sweet baby will do that. It'll make her happy." My hand wanders to my chest, right where my heart beats so hard for Marie. "And it'll make me happy."

With every second my mother's expression grows more incredulous; she almost stares at me in shock. Maybe she's even disappointed because I'm not following her advice.

Still, I add one more thing to make it absolutely clear once and for all that she doesn't get to have a say in this. "You're definitely not going to spoil my joy with your horror stories."

The thin skin at the corners of her eyes twitches, the corners of her mouth pull down. "I just don't want you to rush into disaster. That's all." Her voice trembles a little, but at least she turns back to her work.

"Don't worry, that's not going to happen." I shake my head firmly and smile at her.

"And how exactly did you picture this financially? Marie doesn't work. Soon you'll have to start paying off the mortgage. A baby isn't cheap," she reminds me now, even though that's absolutely not necessary.

It had been clear that this topic would come up, too. But I had already thought about that as well. "There's an open position at my company that I applied for. Very soon I'll be promoted to deputy head of purchasing."

"And that brings in so much more?" I don't miss her skeptical look, but I smile at her anyway.

"I've done all the math. We can stretch the term of the loan a bit. I'll have to put in overtime, but with the higher base salary we'll have more coming in. And Marie won't stay at home forever." I catch a doubtful look on her face, so I keep talking before she can ruin this for me as well. "I can do this." I have to, for Marie's sake. And because otherwise everything would fall apart.

"Well, if that's how it is," she mutters under her breath. I can only guess how hard she's trying to keep quite different words to herself. With jerky movements she strips the vine, as if she needed the work as a distraction. "I do, of course, congratulate you on the new job."

I raise my hands defensively. "I don't have it yet. But basically it's just a formality."

"A formality?" she asks, raising her eyebrows.

I try it with a smile, but I can't quite pull it off. Because that pressure is spreading in my stomach again, like always when I think about it. "In three weeks I'm giving another presentation to the executive board. After that, the new contract will be signed."

Her understanding nod tells me she knows what I'm

feeling. At least she's considerate enough not to harp on about that topic as well. "I've got my fingers crossed."

I'm not sure what exactly she's referring to. My new job, or my future with Marie. Whatever she means, I could more than use her good wishes for both.

Chapter Twenty-Seven

There's barely any space on our tiny balcony, but it's still in the shade. So I make myself comfortable on one of the stools at the bistro table. Almost ceremoniously I flip open the box of pencils. The set consists of ninety colors, from the palest yellow to the darkest gray-brown. They're laid out neatly in front of me; I let my fingers glide over their tips, but I find it hard to pick one.

This fiery red is great. So bright and full of energy. The shade of blue next to it reminds me of the sea after a rainy day. Or should I start with the lemon yellow? Will it even show up against the white paper?

Bravely, I grab a pencil and roll it back and forth between my fingers. It's green. Like hope. That's good. Let's see what the color looks like on paper.

Even though I try to draw a loose, sweeping line on the sketch pad, you can see the tension in my hand in the result. I've drawn a line that wouldn't even beat a three-year-old's.

Dissatisfied, I put the pencil back where it belongs. What was I thinking? That all I had to do was buy paper and colored pencils and I'd turn into the Coco Chanel of baby-clothes design?

I gnaw on my lower lip until the metallic taste of blood spreads across my tongue.

What if designing isn't what I'm looking for?

No, I'm not going to let this get me down so quickly. I dig out my phone and start researching.

A few hours later I knew that there were many paths to becoming a designer, but all of them were rocky. The training cost a lot of money, and the longer I dealt with the details, the less I liked the idea. As if the notion of designing baby clothes were losing all its colors, I ended up with a pretty bleak version of my future. I'd have to invest a lot in this business to begin with. I needed sewing machines, fabrics, patterns, marketing, and at least a website with an online shop. I didn't have the faintest idea about any of these things. Much worse, though, was that I clearly felt how much I lacked any passion for all of it.

To get rid of the bad thoughts, I snap the lid of the pen box shut, grab all my drawing utensils, and carry them back into the apartment. I don't want to see them anymore. I march into the kitchen, and shove them with trembling fingers into the trash can under the sink. The lid of the can no longer closes properly. One corner of the sketchpad refuses to bend, as if it were fighting for its right to be here. Impulsively I yank the can out of the cupboard and stomp the contents down with my foot. The pad gives way, but I keep on kicking the paper trash. I do it until my anger turns into new energy.

Why isn't anything moving forward? It's as if I'm constantly just going in circles and always ending up right where I don't want to be. I don't want to keep feeling like a failure; I finally want to find what I'm looking for.

All at once my leg feels really heavy, but I still pull it out of the trash can and then kick the can with all my strength. The container bangs noisily against the kitchen cabinets. The sound cuts through my eardrums like a knife, but I don't flinch. On the contrary, I gather all my focus. Because this is far too important for me to let a setback like this stop me.

Restlessly I pace up and down the kitchen and wait. I have no idea what for, but definitely not for what I hear in the very next moment.

Someone pushes a key into the lock of the apartment door from outside. My gaze immediately jumps to the big bright yellow clock above the kitchen door. Even if I tried to remember the last time Lukas came home for lunch on a Thursday, I definitely wouldn't be able to. I barely have time to smooth down my hair before Lukas is already standing in front of me.

"You're home early today." I give him a smile.

Lukas grins at me. "I hope I'm not disturbing you and you've got a little time for me?" He takes a step toward me and wraps his arms around my hips.

Confused, I study the mischievous sparkle in his eyes. "You're not coming home just to… work on the baby thing, are you?" My voice sounds uncertain, maybe even nervous, but Lukas doesn't seem to notice.

Instead of looking surprised, he smiles mysteriously and rocks me back and forth as if we were dancing. "Yes and no."

"Oh, come on, there's something behind this." My hand strokes lovingly over his chest. "Tell me. Why are you here?"

Instead of giving me an answer, he kisses me. So tenderly that for a moment I forget who I am and that I still don't know what I'm supposed to be doing in this world.

With a sigh, I let myself fall into his arms so I can feel light for just a brief moment.

Light and free.

Far too quickly he pulls away from me again and taps the tip of my nose with his index finger. "Don't be so nosy, you'll find out soon enough. Everything in its own time."

"You're terrible." Just like I used to, I tilt my head to the side and push out my lower lip. I'm standing in front of him like a schoolgirl who has a treasure chest held under her nose that she's not allowed to open.

Of course, that makes him sigh theatrically. "All right, but only because I can't stand to see you suffer so horribly." As if it were necessary for dramatic effect, he catches my gaze and even waits until my eyebrows are raised so high they should practically be merging with my hairline. "We're going on vacation. And we're leaving right away."

"For how long?" I ask curiously.

"I'm free until Sunday." A cheerful smile spreads across his face.

He's full of anticipation, I can see that clearly. But while he's probably already picturing in the most glowing colors how we'll be working on our baby project twenty-four hours a day, doubts I don't even want to have suddenly overwhelm me. I'm not sure I like the idea. Still, I pull myself together. It's been a long time since things between us were this harmonious, and I don't want to ruin that under any circumstances. "Grandma's chickens need to be taken care of," I say through gritted teeth.

"Exactly." Suddenly he's very close, presses his forehead to mine and looks so deeply into my eyes that I almost see the fire in his heart burning. Maybe it's only glowing faintly, I'm not sure. "What if we leave right away and come back tomorrow evening? That should work, right?"

There's no reason not to, so I nod, even though part of me would rather stay here. In our everyday life, we're functioning again. Wherever we go, it could be different there. We'll both be defenseless against whatever the hours together will do to us. Lukas doesn't even suspect that I want to wait with the baby. Because I still don't know how to break it to him.

Alongside all these thoughts, there's also a longing deep inside me. Only those who allow new impressions can gain new insights. That's what the stranger said at our last meeting. If I leave Vienna and everyday life behind, I might stumble on something that will help me. Despite the fiasco with the drawing earlier, this thought brings a smile to my face and plants a hopeful warmth in my chest.

"Where are we going?" I ask, sounding even a little overexcited.

A short while later we're sitting in the car. The afternoon traffic is terrible, but with some delay we reach the freeway entrance. We take the A2 heading south, and I watch the strips of grass dried out by the June sun in front of the sound barriers. If it were already autumn, the leaves of the many trees behind them would be glowing in every imaginable color, even on a rainy day. Then the banks of fog would also be hanging low over the fields, giving the landscape a magical aura. But in the heat of high summer, nature loses its charm, turns brown and dusty. It looks emaciated. And tired.

"I can hardly wait," Lukas suddenly says into the silence between us, jolting me out of my thoughts. "Do you feel the same?" It's only a brief twitch of his hand, but I understand immediately. He'd love to lace his fingers with mine; instead he forces himself to keep them on the steering wheel.

Is he as afraid as I am that our relationship will go downhill again?

I don't want that, not because of me. I want him to be like he used to be. Carefree, full of wit and lightness. I try to set an example by giving him the sunny smile he loves so much. "Of course I'm looking forward to it. I love the lake, you know that. And your parents' weekend house is very cozy." And free, I'd like to add, but I hold back. Money has become a touchy subject in recent weeks. The fact that we're going away at all is nothing short of a miracle.

"We'll have a few lovely hours there." He tries to hide it, but I hear it clearly. There's an undertone in his voice, as if he doubts his own words.

I absolutely don't want him to think that about us. We'll definitely find our way back to each other, I just don't know how yet. "We can take the dinghy out and drink wine together on the porch." The excitement in my voice is real, and yet it comes more from my nervousness than from any anticipation of our time together.

At last he smiles. His eyes fixed on the road, he takes his hand off the steering wheel and gently strokes my thigh. "And besides, we should work on being three of us very soon."

"Mhm," is all I manage, because I can't get a single word out. Because the very thought makes my breath catch. Whether I like it or not, everything in my head revolves around one question. How on earth do I tell him about my decision without disappointing him? For how many hours do I have to be careful not to blurt it out by accident? For how many seconds do I have to pay attention to the sound of my voice?

If it weren't for this wall between us, everything would be so simple. We could walk by the lake together and talk the way we used to. I would say out loud what's hidden deep inside me, and he would listen without rushing to judge. If we manage that, everything should dissolve into thin air in just a few hours. In my relationship with Lukas and maybe even with my *later*.

Involuntarily, I remember something the stranger only said to me yesterday.

To know where you want to go is the hardest hurdle. Once you've cleared it, all you have to do is set out, and everything will be fine.

Everything will be fine, I repeat in my head, because it just has to be. Everything will be fine.

Chapter Twenty-Eight

"I'm going to do the whole thing with you. Prenatal yoga, birth classes, just everything! I'll come to the doctor's appointments too." Whenever I think about our baby, my mood gets so fantastic that I feel like I could hug the whole world. And of course Marie, who's sitting across from me at the breakfast table on the narrow porch of my parents' cabin, slurping her coffee like she's addicted to it. It takes at least half a minute before she finally sets the cup down.

"Let's get pregnant first before we talk details." Most of her face is hidden behind sunglasses, and she's still shielding it from the morning sun with her hand. I can barely make out her expression, especially now that the summer breeze is blowing loose strands of hair across her face. "We don't even know how quickly it'll actually work."

That's true, but I still want to be a little happy about it. "Maybe it's already happened," I reply with a conspiratorial grin.

"Maybe." With a shrug, she nibbles on her lower lip.

She only does that when she's thinking hard about how

to tell me something. Even though I'd love to ignore the unease rising in me, I can't. So I lean across the table toward her. My hand makes its way between the saltshaker, the breadbasket, and the plates. Only when it rests on Marie's bare forearm and gently strokes the fine hairs there do I ask the crucial question. "What's wrong? Are you scared?"

The way she suddenly looks away is not a good sign. She takes a deep breath, then another. With every new exhale she seems to collapse a little more into the wide wooden chair with the blue-striped cushion. "I don't want to..." she says tonelessly.

What doesn't she want? Talk about it? Think about it?

I do my best not to get impatient, but I can hardly stop myself from squirming in my chair. At least I manage to keep my mouth shut.

As if she were gathering all her strength, she turns her head toward me and lays her hand on mine. "We have to take it easy, you know? Because if we put pressure on ourselves, then..." Furrows as deep as ravines form on her forehead. "Then it might not work."

So that's what this is about. Of course, why didn't I think of that right away? "All right," I say quickly. You can hear the relief in my voice and probably see it just as clearly on my face. "No problem, we just won't talk about it anymore." I press my thumb and index finger together and pretend to zip my mouth shut.

Marie exhales so forcefully it's as if she'd been holding her breath for minutes, looks away, and takes a bite of her jam roll. "What do we want to do today?"

She means it, no more baby talk. She can have that, but just because we're not talking about it anymore doesn't mean I'm not allowed to think about it. And work on it. So

I get up and take a step toward her. "There is something that comes to mind," I murmur in her ear and then kiss her neck.

Instead of giving in to my tender advances, Marie laughs as if I've just made a joke she doesn't actually find funny. Her hand reaches for my head and keeps it from wandering any farther down along her neckline. "Let's soak up some sun first. We only have this one day, and it's far too precious to spend it indoors."

With a rattling noise, she pushes her chair back and gets up. All I can do is watch in confusion as she disappears into the dark doorway of the wooden cabin. "Why don't we look for a nice little spot by the lake? You could finally leaf through your magazines again in peace," she calls back to me, when I can't even see her anymore.

I like the idea. Very much, in fact. I haven't had time to read for weeks. But that fact fades beside a problem that's much bigger.

This short vacation would be a perfect opportunity to get closer to Marie again. And yet I stand here as if rooted to the spot, next to the breakfast table outside. Above me the sun shines down from the sky, a breeze tugs at my shirt. It should be the easiest thing in the world to follow her and seize the moment. When else can we devote ourselves so intensely to the baby plan? Still, I shift hesitantly from one foot to the other. An inexplicable fear holds me back. What if I follow her and she rejects me?

Leaning against the wooden veranda, I let my gaze wander over the houses around my parents' cabin. It seems as if I see happy families everywhere, children laughing and dogs romping around in the tiny little gardens.

That's what I want too. With Marie. Only with her, and preferably right away. Every time I picture our baby's crumpled little face and see in my mind how it smiles at me when I tickle its belly, the anticipation overwhelms me.

As if it wanted to ruin my mood, my common sense chooses this exact moment to speak up. With all its strictness, it reminds me that with every additional month Marie isn't pregnant yet, things look better for us financially. With my new job I'll at least be able to cover the payments for our dream house. If we live really frugally, we might even put some of the overtime money aside. For a financial cushion that will let us give our baby the best life it can possibly have.

As much as I'd like to ignore the pressure that settles on my shoulders like an entire mountain range, I just can't. It's as if not only the future of my relationship depended on my getting this job, but also that of our baby, which might already have been conceived.

Chapter Twenty-Nine

Barefoot, I stroll along the beaten path. A mild breeze blows around my nose, the water of Lake Neusiedl laps gently against the shore. I came here alone. Lukas is asleep on the porch swing at the vacation house, and that's a good thing. He needs the rest. The wide brim of my sunhat casts a shadow over my face; the sun's rays don't reach me. Still, it seems bright inside me today as I look out over the expanse of the water's surface. I take a deep breath and savor the feeling of freedom that floods through me in the very same moment. This would be perfect, if it weren't for the baby thing that still weighs heavily on my chest. Along with the knowledge that in just a few hours we'll be driving back to Vienna. Back to where, in three days, a trial workday at the Shopping City is waiting for me. Because it simply has to.

My gaze drifts to the place where the lake and the sky meet, then back to the shore. The footpath lies straight as an arrow before me, without bends and without turnoffs. I wish there were such a straight line in my life too, so that I could always see all the way to the end. But my path is winding and overgrown. Behind the next bend there could be a precipice, a deep ravine, or a dark cave. I don't know, and that's exactly what scares me. How am I supposed to know which direction in which to march when I'm standing at a fork in the road and can only see a few yards in any direction?

At least by now I've realized that I can't let that stop me. I look around carefully and spot a mast. The white flag is hanging only halfway up. The wind tugs at it, the stainless-steel cables clink against the metal pole.

"Do you want to live your life at half-mast?" I hear the grounded voice of the stranger from the water park ask. How many times has that sentence gone through my mind in the past few weeks? Instinctively, I picture the flag moving upward. It climbs higher and higher until it reaches the top, no matter how hard the wind tugs at it or how hot the sun beats down on it.

That's how it will be for me too, I think, and push back the hair the wind is blowing into my face. Because I'm not going to give up too quickly. Even if I don't know how many more times I'll fail, I'm sure of one thing: I'll keep trying until I've found my passion.

Still searching for clues, I let my gaze wander on. There are people walking by the lake like me. They're holding hands, children are playing with balls and flying kites. Dogs' barking mingles with the cheerful laughter of the teenagers who have made themselves comfortable under a sunshade. Suddenly I'm overwhelmed by the feeling that all these impressions are rushing past me far too quickly as long as I keep moving. So I stop and sit down right on the grass. The blades tickle my skin through the thin fabric of my dress, but I ignore that. Because right where my fingers are tracing fine lines over the ground in front of me, I discover a stone. I pick it up and look at it from every angle. How pretty it is, with its brown marbling on the light background. Tiny shadows form in the grooves of the grain, and when I turn the stone in the sunlight, I find a position where it almost looks as if it were coated in diamond dust.

Beautiful.

I'll take it with me so I can look at it again and again at home. It's meant to remind me of this day and of the feeling that's spreading inside me right now, as if the countless paths at my crossroads were becoming just a little bit easier to see. Quickly I rummage my phone out of my bag and turn toward the flagpole. This memory has to come home with me too, but I can't pack it. So I take a photo. And another one, with more of the sky in it. Pleased, I realize how beautifully the white of the flag's fabric stands out against the intense azure blue. On a sudden impulse, I press the button that activates the front camera, and a second later I see myself. A gentle smile is on my lips, my eyes are sparkling even though the sunhat is casting a shadow over my face.

I look happy.

As this thought rises up in me, I start to beam. Then I know for sure.

I am happy. So much so that I take a whole series of pictures so I can look at them again and again whenever I want to get this feeling back.

Just as I'm about to put the phone back in my bag, it rings. It's Alex.

"Hello, Alex." My voice sounds upbeat; I hope Alex notices it too.

"Well, well, look at that. She's still alive after all." There's a lovingly reproachful tone in her words. I can practically see her furrowing her brow and tilting her head to the side.

The thought makes me grin. "Of course, what did you think?"

Even before she answers, I feel the mood between us shift. "Can't you figure that out?" she suddenly asks grimly.

What does she mean by that? I rack my brains trying to figure out what could be wrong, but I can't come up with anything. "No idea."

A derisive snort comes down the line. "Seriously? Are you for real?"

I bite my lip. Alex is mad, that much is clear. What did I do?

My silence is apparently taking too long for her. She takes a deep breath. "You. Were. Going. To. Call." She forces the words out in clipped bursts, as if they had been burning in her throat for ages. "You swore up and down you'd call me. And I waited, I didn't want to pressure you, and I thought you'd come to me on your own. Damn it, why did you go weeks without a word?"

Right, that phone call, I remember. "I'm really sorry," I stammer awkwardly, even though I know there's absolutely no excuse for it.

"What on earth is going on with you?" I can clearly hear the pleading in her voice. "No more excuses, understood? Tell me the truth."

I don't think I can do this. A tension builds inside me, as if high voltage is coursing through my body. I have to get this energy out somehow, but all I do is pluck individual blades of grass beside me. "Grandma is in a psychiatric clinic," I finally say so quietly that I can barely hear it myself.

"How can I help you?" All at once Alex sounds warm, and it hits me that she has basically already forgiven me.

I shake my head. "She seems to be losing herself in her grief for Grandpa. Sometimes she's barely responsive. Then again she tries to put on an act for me, but I know perfectly well she's not okay. And it's getting worse… I read to her, I tell her jokes, I play cards with her, I tell her how much her animals miss her. None of it has any effect."

"Let's have a coffee and just talk. We'll find a way to help your grandma together. Besides, you still owe me information. Don't think I've forgotten that." There it is again, that insistent note in her voice that doesn't allow any contradiction.

Alex isn't going to let this go; she's far too curious for that. "Coffee would be great, but I'm not in Vienna. Lukas surprised me with a short vacation at Lake Neusiedl."

"That's bad." She sounds contrite. "Leon and I are flying to Greece tonight. We'll be back in two weeks. Then we'll meet up and talk everything through. And I really do mean everything."

Even though she can't see it, I nod. "We'll do that."

"I just want what's best for you." Alex's voice has taken on a soft undertone. If she were with me right now, she would hug me, I'm sure of it.

All at once I understand what I've done to her over the past few weeks with my silence. I was so wrapped up in myself and in Grandma that I failed to see how much I had shut her out. At the thought of how helpless she must have felt, a queasy feeling spreads in my stomach. "I'm so terribly sorry," I force out in a choked voice. "I couldn't…"

"It's all right." She cuts me off as if she can sense what's going on inside me. "It'll be okay again, don't worry."

Her words wrap around my body like a warm blanket. I want to take as much of her confidence for Grandma as I can, and in fact, together with the flagpole in front of me, I manage it. "Definitely. Have a great vacation. Bye, Alex."

After she says goodbye too, I hang up with a sigh. Really, I should go back to the vacation house where Lukas is waiting for me, and yet I stay seated. My gaze fixed on the play of the water, I try to figure out why I don't want to leave this spot yet. There's a longing deep inside me, it pulls me away, wants to see other places and experience new adventures. It whispers in a soft voice. Almost soundlessly it reminds me of the old Marie, who wanted to conquer the whole world.

Wasn't it always just traveling that Lukas and I dreamed of? Wild beaches, foreign languages, and unfamiliar smells. Didn't we want to see steppe grass, Japanese gardens, and heart-shaped reefs? We wanted to experience the whole world. Not let ourselves be locked up. Be free.

What have we become? Has life caught up with us because that's just how it has to be? Because in truth dreams are like soap bubbles. Beautiful to look at, but untouchable. We release them into the sky and yet we know they'll never arrive there. Because even the slightest breath of air makes them burst instantly.

Our breath of air is life. The obligations that are placed on us as we get older, and the demands that society makes of us. Lukas and I no longer live in dreamland, there are no rainbow-colored bubbles shimmering in our sky, and we've simply stopped sending any more up there. Because we no longer hope that some might still reach their destination.

Suddenly a realization rises up in me. It overwhelms me with its clarity, and I know for sure that it's right. This is what has turned my days gray! What weighed heavily on my heart and brought tears to the corners of my eyes whenever I felt the pressure of our life. When I had to be what was expected of me and do what's considered proper.

More than anything, I'd like to be as free as I used to be. I want to feel like a soap bubble that not even a typhoon can harm. Like a small, shimmering work of art that fights in order to finally make it all the way to the top.

But no matter how much I wish for it, leaving everything behind together with Lukas is impossible.

Yet.

But that's going to change.

Chapter Thirty

"My recommendation would be to classify the supplier as qualified." I look over at my boss, Marianne, who, together with the other department heads and the company's managing director, is following my presentation attentively.

There's a smile on her perfectly made-up face, which is good. So I move on to my next and final slide.

"To conclude, I'd like to make one more suggestion for improvement. Here you can see the draft for a company newsletter to promote internal communication. As part of my new role, I'd be happy to take charge of implementing it."

That's it. I've finished the presentation and I can finally breathe a sigh of relief. The sweat on my palms won't dry for a long time yet, and my fingers are still trembling a little. But at least in the last half hour I managed not to trip over my words. There were no technical hiccups and no stumbling, not even a trace of uncertainty in my voice.

I did everything right. Thank God.

With a winning smile, I let my gaze wander over my

audience and land directly on Marianne, whose deputy I'll soon be. She nods at me approvingly and secretly gives me a thumbs-up from behind the meeting table.

"Thank you, Mr. …" In search of my name, the managing director flips through his notes with his witch-like fingers.

"Richter," I answer for him, and in the same moment I'm not sure I should have done that. The boss may be small and so thin you could almost overlook him, but his eyes are alert and his mind is exceptional. Cutting him off mid-sentence could earn me a black mark.

He nodded and looked up at me. "Of course. Please wait outside while we evaluate your application." His expansive hand gesture encompassed the entire room and the people sitting in rows along the long conference table.

Naturally, I immediately turned to leave. "With pleasure." A bit impetuously, I pushed the door handle down; my hand slipped over the lever, which gave off a dangerously loud click. I had to make sure I got away quickly. So far it had gone well; I couldn't afford to screw it up in the final stretch.

That was exactly why I took my time to close the door quietly and carefully behind me. Then I drew a breath, and in the very same moment joy rose up inside me. My fist clenched all by itself in a victorious gesture; I could hardly keep my legs still. I had known everything would work out. And now I could see it, the proverbial light at the end of the damn long tunnel I was stuck in at the moment.

It was only a formality now, so it was hardly surprising that just a few minutes later the door to the conference room opened.

One after another, the department heads streamed out, but I didn't see the managing director. Everyone seemed to be in a terrible hurry; even Marianne only gave me a brief nod before hurrying off toward her office.

Hardly had the commotion died down when I heard the boss's voice. "Mr. Richter, please come in."

There was no reason to be nervous. At least that was what I told myself as I entered the conference room. The stale air hit me and almost took my breath away.

"Have a seat." My boss's hand indicated the chair right next to him.

Like an obedient schoolboy, I sat down and smiled at him, even though the sight of him scared me. It had always been that way, because there was something in his expression that clearly showed you had to be careful with him. So, to be on the safe side, I didn't say anything at all at first.

He turned to me and folded his hands into a triangle. "Well, that was quite a nice presentation you gave."

"Thank you very much," slips out of me. I sound like an excited teenager, that's just not okay. And the fact that I have to force myself to keep my fingers still takes more effort than I ever could have imagined. I have to stay professional at all costs.

Basically, I already have the job anyway.

As if he wanted to stop me from talking, the managing director raises his hand. "Quite nice unfortunately isn't enough," he says in a firm voice.

Excuse me? I must have misheard. Obviously.

"You're surely aware that essential aspects were missing." Of all times, now he doesn't go on. He doesn't do anything, doesn't even leaf through his notes.

Should I ask? I don't know. He sizes me up with his gaze as if he were a snake and I his rabbit. If I make even one wrong move, he'll devour me. With a long, drawn-out clearing of my throat I buy myself some time. "Of course," is all that comes out, hoarse, over my lips.

He doesn't seem to want to add anything and gets up from his chair. All of a sudden he puts his hand on my shoulder. "Work on yourself, because there's always a next time."

Next time?

"Of course," I squeeze out once more, because I can't think of any other word. I just have to hold out until he leaves the room. I count the seconds so I don't have to think about what just happened.

One, two, three.

He disappears in the doorway, and in the same instant all the tension drains from my body. Unchecked, I let my head slam against the tabletop.

This can't be happening.

Only the pain in my forehead keeps me from giving in to my despair on the spot. I press my lips together hard and lift my head, only to let it drop again.

Damn it.

That was my chance. The only one. How could I screw it up like that? What did I do wrong?

No, I can't just let this go. I want to know what happened in there. Impulsively, I jump up from the chair, wipe my palms on my blazer, and exhale in short, sharp bursts.

Then I start walking, straight to my boss's office. The way is too short for me to calm down, so I yank the door open without knocking.

"Marianne, what was that?" I ask, even though I haven't even closed the door behind me. With long, sweeping strides I walk up to her desk and fold my arms across my chest. As if that could give me any support when my world is being shaken as if we were having an earthquake of magnitude twelve.

Her pitying look hits me, but if she thinks that makes anything better, she's sorely mistaken. Now she gets up to close the office door. "Sit down," she says heavily, smooths her midnight-blue suit, and points me to a seat at the small round meeting table.

I quickly shake my head. "No, I don't want to sit down. I damn well want to know what just happened in there." I feel the anger boiling up inside me, out of control. I can't hold it back much longer, and I don't even want to. My disappointment is too great. "Please tell me what I did wrong."

Her shoulders slump forward, she takes a step toward me, as if she's about to pull me into a hug. Then she suddenly stops and twists her mouth. "You didn't do anything wrong," she admits in a soft voice. "Come on, have a seat. Please."

I stare at her in disbelief. How can everything have been right and yet I still don't get the job? I let myself drop onto the chair because I can feel exhaustion spreading through my whole body. Propping my head on both hands, I fix my gaze on my boss's green eyes.

She exhales loudly. "The truth is, you never had a chance from the start."

She can spare me the shrug. "Excuse me?" It's no more than a hoarse whisper, yet it seems to hit her hard.

Awkwardly, she lets her subtly manicured fingernails glide over the dark gray table until she finds a spot she can cling to. "I'm so sorry."

"Sorry for what?" I can't hide the anger in my voice. "That I just made a fool of myself over there? Or that you didn't warn me?" Accusingly, I point my index finger at her.

"You threw me to the wolves." I swallow so I don't completely lose control. "Why?"

"I didn't know." Her gaze is sincere, her voice steady. "Only after your presentation did I find out that it had long been decided who would get the job. I was just a puppet, same as you."

What the hell is she talking about? I furrow my brows so tightly that the pain in my forehead returns. "Who?" is all I ask, and I'm sure she knows exactly what I'm getting at.

As if she wants to buy herself some time, she tucks her reddish corkscrew curls behind her ear. "The managing director's nephew."

My hand slams down on the table between us with full force. "Shit," I shout at the top of my lungs because I just can't hold it back any longer. "I needed that job and you know it." I don't want to sound this accusatory at all, but I can't help it. Because right now I can see my future bursting, as if it were nothing more than a huge balloon colliding with the sharp branch of a bare tree. I can even hear the bang, loud and clear.

Even Marianne's soothing hand gesture doesn't change that. "Of course I am, that's why I've come up with something."

I have no idea what that's supposed to be, so I just keep glaring at her in anger.

"We're going to try to get you a raise," she says, her voice softening. "The boss isn't an idiot, he's seen that you're good. The presentation wasn't for nothing, it'll help me wring something out for you."

Her effort moves me, but it'll be in vain. Because it won't bring in nearly as much as I need. In my desperation, I bury my head in my hands.

How am I supposed to do this?

It takes less than a second for me to realize there's only one option. We have to wait with the baby. Marie will be terribly disappointed, and that's far from all. I'll have to force her to go out and find a job again. There's no other way.

All at once Marianne is standing behind me, laying a friendly hand on my shoulder. "I'll authorize overtime for you, that'll add up to something."

I nod, but my thoughts are already elsewhere. Marie has to get back on track. She has to. Until then I'll rack up overtime, as much as I possibly can. The very idea takes my breath away, but I have no other way out. Giving up the dream house isn't an option. We searched for it far too long, and our two hearts are already far too attached to it.

What if I asked my parents for money? They wouldn't even have to give it to me. It would be enough if they lent it to me so I could keep up the loan payments after we move into the house, at least until Marie is working again. Would my mother be willing to do that? Or would she just be reminded even more of Aunt Ulrike than she already is because of Marie's resignation?

No. My parents aren't the solution. I have to manage without them. Marie is doing better; very often she's almost as cheerful as she used to be. A few more weeks and she'll be her old self again. In five months the first loan installments will be due. That's enough time to find a job. Until then I just have to hold out. For Marie.

Chapter Thirty-One

I hate the employment office.

Every time I'm in Mrs. Angelmann's office, I feel like I'm tiny. Today, too, she makes herself look imposing behind her desk in her frilly blouse and perfectly styled short hair, while I sit on the visitor's chair and search in vain for a comfortable position.

"Ms. Berger, you do realize that in a few months you'll only be receiving emergency assistance, don't you?" I already knew my caseworker's worried headshake. But today it was different. More serious. And the way she was eyeing me over the dark rim of her reading glasses told me she had no understanding for me at all.

"That job at the shopping mall really wasn't right for me." Just the memory of the trial day made me shudder. Apart from the fact that the pay was atrocious, I had to sit behind a counter all day under artificial light in the hectic world of the mall and, like a talking doll, repeat the same information over and over.

I could have put up with that. For Lukas's sake I would

have been willing to accept all of it. But what happened in the late afternoon of that day was too much.

Far too much.

I'd rather never think about it again, and yet the memory crashes over me like a storm surge.

In my mind I sort through the information brochures for the mall visitors once more. Neatly, edge to edge, they have to lie in front of the counter; at least that's what I was told. It took a whole hour to clear up the chaos that had built up in just six hours of opening time. All the more relieved, I'm glad it's finally done and that I no longer have to work unprotected in the throng of people in front of the counter. To give myself at least a brief moment of joy, I look at my work.

Suddenly everything happens very fast. Out of the corner of my eye I register a bright red cap. It belongs to a teenager. He's racing toward me on a skateboard. I take a step back; I don't want to collide with him. He shoots past me through the narrow passage between the counter and me.

With outstretched arms.

All the carefully sorted flyers whirl up into the air and drift to the ground like autumn leaves.

While I clap my hand over my mouth, the boy opens his and sticks his tongue out at me. "Ooops," he calls provocatively and speeds up his skateboard with a practiced move.

Before I can react, he has already disappeared into the crowd. Desperately, I lower my gaze. Careless visitors have already left their footprints on some of the flyers. I sink to the ground and feverishly gather up the sheets. On all fours I crawl across the dirty concrete tiles, and as if that weren't humiliating enough, someone now plants an elegant leather shoe right on the very flyer I'm reaching for.

With my head bowed, I tug at the paper, but the shoe stays where it is.

Please, not someone else who wants to have a laugh at my expense. Not now.

I clench my teeth, my gaze travels upward. A split second later I'm staring straight into the deviously smirking face of my former boss.

"Ms. Berger! How nice to run into you," he says, still not thinking of moving his foot. "So this is where you've ended up. Your friend, that… Alexandra something, wasn't exaggerating. This really is a dream." His smug grin is almost unbearable. "Congratulations on the promotion."

Damn. This can't be happening. Is this really happening right now? And if it is, why?

A thousand thoughts shoot through my head, but one forces its way to the front with all its might.

He was right.

On the very day I was fired, he predicted that I wouldn't find a better job. And here we are now. I'm kneeling in front of him, my lips trembling, my fingers shaking. And he's looking down at me like I'm a desperately struggling animal he still managed to catch in the end. If I believed in a God, I'd be asking him right now what he wants to punish me for. And then I'd beg him to turn back time for me so I'd never have to experience this humiliation.

But I don't believe in God. And I believe in time travel even less. Grinding my teeth, I let go of the folder and blink the tears from the corners of my eyes. Crying in front of him would be the absolute last thing I'd do. "Thank you very much for your congratulations," I reply, full of pride, even though an entire world is collapsing inside me right now.

I give him a triumphant smile for as long as I can stand

it. Then I spin around on the spot, walk away, and feel like the biggest failure of all time.

Since then I've been trying hard to drive the memory of that terrible moment out of my head. Today I watch Ms. Angelmann, who turns her gaze away from me and focuses on her screen. I have to distract myself. Desperately. So I look at the photos on her desk. She seems to have a large family; the little ones are probably her grandchildren. She's surely a family person, yet she's relentless with me. "In the past eight weeks we've sent you to interviews for a total of twenty open positions." There's a snooty undertone in her voice. "Apparently not one of them was good enough for you."

"That's not quite true," I object, even though I of course understand her point of view. From the outside I must look like an ungrateful idiot. But that ends now, because I didn't come here to talk about the failed placement attempts. "Listen, I have an idea I'd like to discuss with you," I say quickly.

She immediately leans forward over the desk, props her chin on her hands, and nods expectantly.

"I'd like to propose a retraining program. You offer a lot of courses—does that include a training course for set designers?" My motivated smile doesn't seem to reach her. On the contrary, her forehead creases and I can guess what's going through her head. Not another one of those. That's what she's thinking.

She takes a deep breath. "No. Unfortunately we don't offer anything like that." And there it is, that forced professional smile she uses to hide her own opinion. "But I'd be happy to give you a training catalog from the education center." No sooner has she spoken the words than she starts rummaging in one of her desk drawers.

Crushed, I clench my fists. Not just because of the way she mocks my attempt to move forward. But also because I don't have the money to pay for a course like that myself.

Should I ask Lukas?

No. He already does so much for me, I can't pile even more on him. Not when I'm not even sure this training is right for me.

Relentlessly I feel the despair crawling up inside me, and I don't know how to deal with it.

Damn it. Why can't something work out, just once, when I'm trying so hard for my future?

"Here you go." Mrs. Angelmann slides the catalog across the desk to me. Her gaze flicks to the clock; the next loser is probably already waiting for her services. "Pick a course and we'll check whether we can fund it." Or whether you'll end up a pathetic welfare recipient, her expression adds without a word. "If I may give you some personal advice: take the job at the shopping center. And you'd better forget this set-designer thing as quickly as possible. In that field you definitely won't find a job."

"Of course not," I mutter in frustration and take the catalog. I stuff it into my handbag, say goodbye, and just focus on getting out of here.

I leave this awful place and, even if I don't know much else, at least I know where I want to go next. To the water park and then to Grandma's. So I cross half of Vienna in the heat of high summer and reach my destination just under an hour later.

In the shade of the trees it's a bit cooler, but the summer air still seems to shimmer just as much. As if a single spark would be enough to make everything explode.

It suits me. Because I feel like a powder keg too. On

some days filled with fireworks powder, on others with TNT.

Step by step I wander through the park, past ponds and retirees sitting on wooden benches talking about the weather. I take in the intense scent of the rosebushes and hear the gravel crunch under my flip-flops. Even though this seems like a little paradise, I'm wistful. Ever since I remembered on the shore of Lake Neusiedl where our dreams used to take Lukas and me, I haven't been able to shake the thought. And my conversation with Mrs. Angelmann has only made it even more significant.

Just up and gone. Away from the job center, away from the obstacles that never get any smaller. Away from the worries, and above all away from the everyday life that has such a tight grip on both of us that we can hardly breathe. The mere thought of it sends a longing glow through my chest. And yet I mustn't let it turn into a flame of hope. Because running away is absolutely impossible.

Grandma needs me. With every passing day she seems to be doing worse, despite the professional treatment at the mental health facility. Leaving her on her own is unthinkable. But there's more. When Lukas and I talk to each other about happiness, we've lately been speaking different languages. He would never leave everything behind with me. Besides, you need money to travel. And God knows we don't have that.

I rack my brain for a solution as I spread out my picnic blanket and sit down. I could let my gaze wander along the pond, but I don't even care about its beauty. Because I'm stuck again, even though I'm trying so stubbornly to move forward.

Little by little I gather small branches from around me and break them one after another into pieces. As if I were addicted to that cracking sound that's a bit like something breaking. What's left of the twigs I throw into the water in front of me so it can sink down to the deepest point of the lake and be swallowed there by the muddy bottom.

Now I hear another sound pushing in between the cracking of the branches. Footsteps. I whirl around at once, and sure enough I see the stranger.

I lift my hand to greet him. That special smile is on his freckled face, the one that makes him look as if nothing in the world could shake him.

As soon as he's standing in front of me, he takes in the mess on my blanket. Countless tiny wood splinters have come loose from the broken branches and are scattered all around me. I immediately feel caught out and hastily run my hand over the woolen surface to get rid of the fragments. But it seems like the things are practically glued to the fibers.

"Rough day today?" I hear him ask. I don't have to look at him to know he's still smiling.

Even though it's obviously pointless, I start plucking the splinters off the blanket. "A little."

"Do you want to talk about it?"

My hand invites him to sit down next to me. Silently he joins me. He waits for my answer. "I'm frustrated," I say, pull my legs up to my chest, and wrap my arms around them.

"Your half-mast life turned out to be an illusion." He doesn't smirk, and the fact that he was right weeks ago doesn't seem to please him. On the contrary, I feel his compassion, but there's something else. I can't quite make it out; maybe it's confidence.

"Yes… and no… kind of." Of course that's not an answer, but it sums up what I'm thinking. Everything and nothing is drifting around in my head, and it just won't sort itself out. Only one thing is certain: my longing for happiness is still overpowering.

He nods, a warm breeze blows a few strands of hair into his face, and for a moment he looks at me intently. "You can't find your way." It's not a question. He knows it, from wherever. "Not yet."

"Not yet, yes," I repeat, because that's exactly how I want to think about it. No matter how hard it is for me. Automatically, I start picking at the tiny wood splinters again. It's as if my fingers have to do something so that I at least feel, just a little, as if I'm making progress.

"Look at me," he suddenly urges me in his velvety-soft voice. All at once I feel his hand on my shoulder. It lies there motionless, yet it feels as if something is happening to me at that very spot. There's no tingling and no heat. I would never tell anyone this, but I could swear it feels as if, where he's touching me, I'm shimmering in rainbow colors. Am I finally going crazy after all?

Uncertain, I look up at him. His gaze tells me that nothing I say could be wrong for him. That I'm allowed to say exactly what I'm thinking. Without any fear. I draw a deep breath one last time.

"Sometimes it's there. That sure feeling that there has to be real happiness for me. I feel it everywhere inside me, I'm convinced that there's still something waiting for me. And then, all of a sudden, from one second to the next…" My voice falters. Still he remains silent, as if he's waiting for me to go on. "Then it's gone again. Vanished without a trace! I can't hold on to it. No matter how hard I try, it doesn't work."

I don't even try to play down my frustration. For far too long I've been tormenting myself, constantly standing on the border between hope and disappointment. With legs that don't seem to obey me and arms that just hang uselessly at my sides.

The stranger nods knowingly while my expression is probably turning more and more into a giant question mark. Now he places his other hand on my other shoulder as well and moves a little closer. "Close your eyes," he tells me.

"Why?" The word leaves my mouth faster than I can control it.

His smile looks as if he could end wars with it alone. "Close your eyes."

Nervously, I chew on my lower lip, then I force myself. He's probably the only one who's able to help me. Despite my closed lids, my eyes twitch back and forth as if they wanted to see more than just the bright flicker of orange-red light.

"Try to picture a butterfly. Think of the fragility and the beauty of its wings. Of the unique patterns in thousands of shades of color and the perfect elegance of its shape," he says suddenly, as if that had anything to do with the matter. "Do you see it in front of you?"

An actual peacock butterfly flutters up before my mind's eye. Together with a brimstone butterfly and an azure-blue butterfly whose name I don't know. For whatever reason, this sight moves me. I nod, ready to go on.

"They're free and they won't let themselves be caught. If you take them by force, it means their death."

Soft and insistent, his words hit my eardrums and from there travel straight into my chest.

I stay silent. Because I sense there's more to come. The pretty creatures go on fluttering through my thoughts unchanged. Maybe precisely because I'm silent. Because I do nothing but watch them, don't reach for them and don't call to them.

"Well, happiness is quite similar to butterflies. You can't chain it to you. As soon as you try, it'll leave you. Enjoy it as long as it's with you, and let it go with gratitude when it leaves you. Then it will come back."

I don't know what to think. What he says sounds so simple. And absolutely logical. I'd love to believe him, but my mind disagrees. It wants to convince me that everything you can't see doesn't exist.

Still, the butterflies are here with me. They dance among the blossoms of a meadow in bloom, in front of a deep blue sky without a single cloud. Then it suddenly occurs to me that there is absolutely no wind at all in this picture. If the air really doesn't move there, couldn't soap bubbles drift unhindered up toward the sky?

Maybe I'm smiling. Or grinning. I don't know, and I don't care. Because right now I understand something. Only when you leave the disruptive wind of everyday life and the crosscurrents of our conformist world outside does it become so quiet that dreams, like soap bubbles, can rise all the way to the top. To the place where they ultimately come true.

That's it! Until now I've only thought about which dream job could be reconciled with the rest of my life. What if I allowed myself to dream without any limitations at all?

A hopeful feeling overwhelms me, but then I feel the stranger take his hands from my shoulders, and in the very same moment I can't see anything at all anymore. It's as if he has just switched off the film in my head without warning.

I tear my eyes open and I'm back again. Right where so much doesn't seem to make any sense. My brows knit together all on their own. “What’s happening to me?” I hear myself ask, and with that at the latest, the magic is over. Because here, in the real world, different laws apply. Here the storm of life blows with full force. It can’t be blocked out and even less stopped. “To dream without limits is impossible,” I whisper, sobered.

“Where do your limits come from?” He looks at me intently.

“In my thoughts.” Even though I have no idea where these words come from, I do know that they’re right.

“Exactly. And you remember who’s in charge of your thoughts, don’t you?” A confirming smile appears on his face.

Whether I like it or not, I have to admit I have nothing to counter that. This knowledge alone dissolves the vague tension that just a moment ago had started to build inside me. And that even though I have no idea how I’m supposed to put his advice into practice.

“Trust yourself, nothing more is necessary,” he suddenly says, as if he could read my mind. Then he unfolds his legs from the cross-legged position and pushes himself up.

“No, wait, don’t go yet!” Instinctively, I grab his hand. “I don’t know how this works.” My words sound like one long cry for help, and that’s exactly what they are. Maybe even more than that.

Instead of giving me a clue, the stranger just shakes his head. “You want a plan from me. Fixed instructions and clearly defined guidelines.” He keeps getting to his feet. “But no one can tell you where your butterflies will fly, not even me.”

Thoughtfully, I nibble on my lower lip and try to read from his expression what he’s trying to tell me. But it’s so neutral, as if he doesn’t want to give me any hint at all. So I say the only thing that comes to mind, no matter how ridiculous it sounds. "Because I'm the only one who can see my butterflies?"

His satisfied smile radiates more warmth than the sun above us. "Aha, someone's understood something. Wonderful. My work for today is done."

I can feel that I have to let him go, no matter how much I'd like to learn more. But he could still give me something to think about. "Will I at least get a hint?" I beg him.

"Everything in life has its time." He sounds terribly wise.

"Is that the answer or the hint?" I just manage to ask before he starts walking. Still, he only raises his hand in greeting and sets off.

Only when he's already a few yards away from me does he turn back to me once more. "You have to find that out for yourself."

I probably do. I wave goodbye to him, shape a silent thank-you with my lips, and watch as he disappears, in his loose, worn clothes, between the trees of the forest. Everything in life has its time, he said. And mine has come now.

I have to know if my butterflies are still there. So I take a deep breath and close my eyes.

They really are there. I see all three of them, and in the background even more appear. With a broad smile on my face, I watch the delicate beauties. Maybe our planet keeps turning in the meantime, but in this moment that loses all significance. Because inside me, every trace of gray disappears. And what appears behind it looks like watercolors running into one another, showing me the most colorful version of this world.

All at once I'm sure I'm going to make it. I'm going to find my *later*. And turn it into my now.

Chapter Thirty-Two

I park the car in front of the Center for Mental Health. With an extended yawn, I flip the sun visor down and glance into the mirror.

It has been a long day. Too much has happened, and I can clearly see it in my face. The lines are etched deep into my skin and the tiredness weighs heavily on my eyelids. Everything that happened today around my presentation has drained every bit of strength from me. The nicest thing would be to stay home instead of going to this party. But I promised, so how could I just cancel at the last minute? Maybe it's even an advantage, because I could get drunk without having to explain anything to anyone. Then I'd forget what happened today, and the memories of the last few weeks would blur beyond recognition. For one evening I could just drift, hand over responsibility, and finally feel good again for once.

No matter what's going on with me, at least Marie seems to be doing better. Ever since we got back from Lake

Neusiedl almost two weeks ago, she's been out and about more and more often. She seems more content, and sometimes I even see that glow from before on her face. Today she also asked me to pick her up directly at her grandma's so we can drive to the party together. All of that is a good sign for our future.

At least it would be. If the situation with my job were different.

I bury my face in my hands and let myself fall back into the car seat. With slumped shoulders and heavy limbs, I try to breathe calmly, but I can't quite manage it.

In the very next moment I hear the passenger door open. Marie gets into the car with me.

"Hey," she says, reaching for the seat belt to buckle up. As always, I try to read from the sound of her voice how she's feeling. Good, I'd say, maybe even very good.

I quickly straighten my back. "How's your grandma?" I try to sound casual. As if a large part of my world hadn't collapsed today. I have no idea if I'm pulling it off, and I don't have the energy to think about it.

"She needs to finally accept Grandpa's death, but she refuses to." Marie nibbles on her lower lip.

She must feel helpless. For weeks she's been trying to help her grandma, but she doesn't seem to be succeeding. "How can I help you?" I ask anyway, even though right now I don't know where I'm supposed to find the strength for it.

"I can do this, I just have to figure out how." There's a determined look on her face. But before I can be happy about this progress, she studies me intently. "You look pale," she says, tilting her head to the side.

Can that really be? Is it possible she's worried about me? "I'm fine. Everything's okay." I stifle a yawn and smile at her. How could I not, when this warmth is spreading in my chest? A feeling of hope grips me, no longer as delicate as the first shoots of a shrub, but as strong as a fully grown tree.

Marie is back.

On top of that, she wraps her arms around my shoulders and leans toward me. Our noses touch, her skin gliding over mine, soft and warm. A second later we're kissing, and it's as if, after a long journey, we've finally arrived back with each other.

And yet at that exact moment my heart clenches painfully. Because I suspect why. Ever since she found out that the dream house belongs to us, her dark mood has gradually lifted. But it's the idea of having a baby with me that ultimately helped her overcome her crisis. If I can't manage to give her both, she'll crash again, and I absolutely can't let that happen.

"We could just drive straight home, too." With her fingertips, Marie gently strokes the lines on my forehead. "Have a cozy TV evening or cook together?"

"Bernd's turning thirty and he's my closest coworker," I say with a wrinkle of my nose, "we just have to show up there. Or at least I do."

Marie immediately shakes her head, so vigorously that it must almost make her dizzy. Her chin-length hair falls into her face, but it doesn't hide the shine in her eyes. "There's no way I'm leaving you alone. Besides, I'll drive so you can get a bit more rest."

"Who are you? And what have you done with Marie?" The questions leave my mouth unfiltered. She doesn't even seem to hold that against me; a mysterious grin appears on her lips. Instead of answering me, she opens the car door and signals for me to do the same.

We both walk around the car and, where our paths cross, we kiss each other tenderly. Just like any other happy couple would. As if we had no worries and would never doubt.

Chapter Thirty-Three

As we weave our way through Vienna's evening traffic, Lukas's attention stays on me without a break. Sometimes his mouth opens, but then he closes it again without saying a single word. He looks a bit like he has something on his mind and doesn't know how to bring it up. The light in front of us turns red, I step on the brake and give him an encouraging look.

He forces the corners of his mouth up, his hand searches for mine. "How was your day?"

"Before I visited Grandma, I went to the water park. You know, the place with the pretty ponds I told you about once." The memory floods through me and with it the feeling that, ever since the conversation with the stranger, has been rocking my body again and again, like the tides rock the waves off the coast of Hawaii. Yes, I feel good. Better than I have in a long time. My butterflies are with me. They won't leave me; soon they'll show me the path I have to take. Everything would be perfect if Grandma and Lukas could see their butterflies too.

Lukas nods, pulls my hand to his lips and covers it with little kisses. "That sounds lovely," he says at last, and I think I see a gleam in his eyes. Then he clears his throat. "I'm a bit jealous, I have to admit, when I'm sitting in my plain office all day and you're out there letting the sun shine on your nose."

If that's supposed to be an attempt to talk me into working as a secretary again, it's more than clumsy. So I just grunt in agreement and focus my attention on the road ahead of me. The light turns green, I drive off. The traffic is just as heavy, my gaze flicks back and forth between windshield and side mirror. I change lanes even though I don't have to. As if that could help me avoid this conversation that's creating a mood between us like a thundercloud is rolling in.

To my dismay, a level crossing stops us a few minutes later. I turn off the engine, and a frightening silence spreads through our car.

Maybe this is the moment. Maybe I should just do it. Smash this glass wall between us and finally share everything that's on my mind with Lukas again.

Seconds pass while I pull my courage together, then I voice the one question that has been weighing on me ever since the short trip to Lake Neusiedl.

"Are you happy with our life?" My words cut through the silence as if someone had dropped a coin. They echo, at least in my chest. Because so much depends on his answer. Maybe even everything.

Out of the corner of my eye I see him swallow hard. "Of course I'm happy. Why wouldn't I be?" He doesn't sound convinced, and he looks even less so. On the contrary, I can clearly see how much effort it takes him to smile.

He's lying to me. Why is he doing that?

I don't want to waste any more time on empty phrases and untruths. I lean over to him and force him to look at me. "What exactly makes you happy, I mean right now, today, or this week?"

His helpless shrug hurts me. Because I can see that he doesn't know what I'm talking about. "I have everything I need. A good job and soon a nice home." Affectionately, he places his hand on my upper arm and lets his thumb wander over my skin. "And besides, I've got the most amazing woman in the whole world. What more could I ask for?"

Can that really be his only truth? Doesn't he remember how we used to define happiness? "Do you know that feeling?" I ask in a steady voice, "those moments when you're so happy you feel it all through your body? It floods you completely, right down to the tips of your hair."

He immediately waves it off. "Marie, I already told you, I'm always happy." Not just the words themselves, but also the annoyed undertone in his voice is like a death sentence for my attempt to tear down the wall between us.

I still don't want to accept that. I can't, because letting go of this conversation would be like giving up on my dreams without a fight. "You're not, I can see it in your face. The tiredness and the stress. Your damn job is killing you." I lean back in the car seat and chew on my lips to get rid of at least a little of my tension.

"You're wrong." Out of the corner of my eye I see his fingers digging into his thigh. "It's not the work that's killing me, it's you. Just stop it. We can't be whoever we want to be. We have to do whatever's necessary. That's the truth, the only one." His pronunciation becomes clearer and clearer, the sound in his voice more and more urgent.

I press my lips together. "Don't you see what's happened

to us?" I ask in a steady voice. "How everyday life has driven us out of our paradise over the years, tied and gagged us? And that the two of us even let it happen?"

He doesn't answer, just silently watches the train rushing past in front of our windshield. In that moment I only wish it would take me with it. And Lukas too. It could take us both to a place where we can feel each other again.

And yet we're trapped here. The barrier opens, I start the engine and drive off.

I stay silent for the rest of the drive because I wouldn't know what else there is to say. Lukas seems to feel the same. Over and over he rubs his forehead, his expression almost desperate. He's probably wondering how he can save his girlfriend who's gone crazy. But I'm not the one who needs saving. It's really him who needs someone to show him the truth.

These thoughts stay with me all the way to the house of Lukas's colleague from work, Bernd. From a distance I can already see that there's a huge party going on. Torches are set up in the garden, colorful lanterns hang everywhere, and music reaches my ears through the open window. It smells of grilled food, people are laughing. I take all of this in, and I know immediately that I can't handle it tonight.

I can't go in there and pretend that everything's perfectly fine. As if Lukas and I were a happy couple.

Slowly I let the car roll up to the front door. "Listen, I…" How am I supposed to tell him?

"Migraine?" is all he asks.

I nod and lower my gaze. "I'm sorry."

Lukas turns to me, and I'm sure he's studying me intently. "What are you sorry for, Marie?"

"Everything." Now it happens, I start to sob. Because I can't keep the despair locked inside me any longer.

"Me too. More than you can imagine." He takes my face in his hands and looks at me searchingly, as if, despite the darkness of the falling night, he wanted to find something in my expression that he could read as a sign. Now his thumbs stroke over my damp cheeks, and we're probably both wishing for nothing more desperately than that he could chase away my sadness with that touch.

"How could this happen?" The words leave my lips tonelessly, even though I should be screaming them. Because I can't stand it anymore. That we still hear each other but no longer understand. That we want to hold on to each other and still can't reach one another. We're drifting apart like ice floes off the coast of Iceland in spring, and there's nothing we can do about it.

What if the current isn't kind to us? What if we don't find each other again, no matter how much we want to?

Desperately, I try to ignore the tightness in my throat. "But I love you," I whisper hoarsely. There's a heartbreaking longing in my voice, and it comes straight from my heart.

A wistful smile flits across his face, but the look in his eyes stays sad. "And I love you."

I'd like to believe him, but for the very first time in our five years together, his words feel empty.

Chapter Thirty-Four

Only the dull rushing of the cars reaches my ears; otherwise everything is quiet. Too quiet. I listen closely again, but there's nothing. No one is breathing beside me. Sleepily, I let my hand glide over to the other side of the bed. It's empty.

A tired sigh left my mouth. I glanced at the clock on the white-lacquered nightstand, saw that it was only half past six, and I wanted just one thing: to sleep. The week had been long and hard, today was Saturday and I finally had time to recover.

Still, I couldn't manage it. Because I couldn't stop asking myself when the last time was that Marie and I slept in together on a weekend. A warning tug spread in my chest. It was unnecessary, because I had long since known that something was going wrong. I would have liked best to let my eyelids fall shut again right away. Not just because of the sleepless nights, but also so I wouldn't have to think about how strange we had become to each other over the past few months. Eight weeks ago I had made my suggestion about the baby to Marie. For six weeks we hadn't even been working on it anymore. A silence had pushed its way into our lives. And for the past two weeks it had felt as if this apartment was just a shared flat of two people trying to cross paths as rarely as possible.

Lying on my back, I stared hard at the ceiling, but I still saw the empty bed next to me out of the corner of my eye. The cold that emanated from the poppy-covered duvet made me shudder. It couldn't go on like this. Not with me and not with us.

My thoughts stuck on exactly this problem like a needle on a record that kept playing the same notes over and over. Hearing this sound had by now become torture. Since my meeting with Anna last week, I hadn't been able to switch it off, even at night.

Once more I went over our conversation in my mind. In an instant, in my memory I was back sitting on Anna's sofa, letting my exhausted gaze wander around the living area. Although it measured not even twenty square meters, it was crammed with sports equipment. Basically, the living-dining room with integrated kitchen looked more like a gym. Only the light wooden shelves and the cream-colored upholstered furniture didn't fit in. And the countless photos showing Anna on the go, which usually made me smile with her energy.

Today they didn't manage that.

Because I still felt as if I were wearing a lead belt that dragged me heavily downward and squeezed my stomach tight.

"I have no idea what's going on with us," I whispered hoarsely, because just saying it out loud made it even more real.

Anna eyed me skeptically and pursed her lips. Whatever

words were lurking behind her closed mouth, she didn't let them out.

Since everything was already pointless anyway, I simply let my head drop onto the coffee table. Cool, damp, and a little sticky was how it felt against my forehead, but I didn't care. Even if someone emptied an entire keg of beer over me, it would have been all the same to me.

"After she quit her job, she was so depressed it was as if all available worlds had ended, then all at once she was the old Marie again and I started to feel hopeful. But for a few weeks now she's been constantly coming to me with insanely esoteric suggestions. And when I remind her what really matters in life, she looks at me as if I were betraying her. We've had to have the same conversation countless times until she finally got it."

"I understand that you're angry, darling." Anna untangles herself from her strange posture and moves in really close to me. She holds on to me, maybe because she knows it's the only thing she can do for me.

I breathe in and out deeply, as if that would help me say it. "That's not all. Her new way of destroying our relationship is ignorance. She only says what's absolutely necessary. By now I'm sure: the old Marie is gone and she's not coming back." My voice grows quieter and quieter, but I still have to say it. The thing that rushes through my head like a whole herd of horses. The thought that leaves nothing in me but churned-up earth where nothing will ever grow again. "It's time I finally admitted that to myself and faced the consequences."

For a moment Anna's body goes rigid. Her arms around my waist feel stiff; I even think she's stopped breathing. "Are you really sure about that?" she asks carefully.

Now I straighten up and look directly at her. "Who

could ever be sure? All I know is that it can't go on like this. Not for her and not for me." That's what I say, but I'm sure my eyes are desperately begging Anna for something I can still hold on to. I've got nothing left myself. There's no life raft, not even a straw to cling to.

Anna swallows and her expression darkens too. As if she were my mirror, as if her world were going down together with mine. "I'm the last person who'd try to talk you into anything," she says hesitantly, nervously picking at the hem of her sweater. There are words she doesn't want to say, I can see that clearly. We've always told each other openly what we think. Faced with this situation, even Anna seems to be struggling to find the right words.

With her lips pressed together, she finally lets out a noisy breath. "You have to find out what's behind her behavior. Ask her, and don't let go until you have the answer. Only when you know what the problem is can you find a solution."

There's nothing I want more than for her to be right. But if it were that simple, I'd have tried it long ago. I turn my head toward her; I want to see how firm her conviction really is. Behind her featherlike lashes I see a warmth that gives me support. She's my anchor, no matter how rough the seas are.

On top of that, Anna gives me an encouraging jab in the side. It's only a small gesture, but I know exactly what she's trying to tell me with it. "You've got this."

A wave of gratitude rushes through me; I press closer to her and carefully bump my head against hers. "Have I ever actually thanked you?"

"Oh, come on, what for?" she says, waving it off awkwardly.

"For being who you are," I answer just as sincerely as I

mean it. Suddenly she seems to find it hard to meet my eyes, so I slip my index finger under her chin and make her lift her head. "Look at me, Anna."

She only slowly opens her lids. Then at last she looks at me, as skittish as a wild hare. I understand why right away. Of course she's sad too, she's hurting with me. It's a bit odd, but all at once I feel like I have to comfort her.

I pull her into a friendly hug. "I don't know what I'd do without you. Where I'd be, or who I even am. You're my rock in the surf, the place I can always come back to and where I can always find something to hold on to."

"I... um... I..." My usually so cool and laid-back friend is out of her depth. Either that, or she's playing the speechless one on purpose to cheer me up.

To spare her, I force a smile onto my lips. "Thank you."

Even though Anna makes a dismissive gesture, I hug her as tightly as I can. Still, she slips out of my arms and claps her hands together in a commanding way, as if this were a party and not a wake. "Okay, that's enough with the mushy stuff. Go home, wait for a good moment and just ask her what's going on with her. Don't back down until you know the whole truth." Her tone is so firm it's like she has to convince not only me that this is the right way to go. I can clearly see how forced the smile on her lips is and how fake the upbeat mood she's trying to project. Even if she won't admit it, she's at least as doubtful as I am.

Still, she's right. What do I even have left to lose that isn't already lost anyway?

I have to confront Marie and go all in. It's time to clearly define the color of our relationship. Black or white, that's all I want to know. These grinding shades of gray in between have to stop once and for all.

Seven days have passed since my talk with Anna, and so

far I haven't had a chance to put my plan into action. As I lie here and now all alone in the bed where Marie and I used to be so close, I wonder if today is the right day to finally lay it all on the line.

Through the open bedroom door I suddenly hear someone entering the apartment. Without any conscious thought, worries immediately start crawling up inside me. What kind of mood is Marie in today? Cheerful or crazy? Ignorant or a know-it-all? Tense or so high it's like she's on drugs?

She already appears in the doorway. "Hey," she says.

Flushed cheeks, straight back, gentle smile. Today is a good day. At least that's what I want to believe, and I send a silent prayer up to heaven that it's true.

"Good morning." I signal for her to come over and sit down on the edge of the bed next to me.

She actually comes closer and doesn't seem to have to drag herself over to me by force. All at once I notice that she's wearing workout clothes. Did she go jogging? That doesn't fit with Marie. Still, I can see the sheen of sweat on her cleavage when she joins me. No matter how sweaty she is, I wrap my arms around her and pull her as close as she'll let me.

I hold her tight, with all my desperation. As if I could save our relationship that way. As if it were enough for our bodies alone to be close.

It doesn't take long before Marie gently pushes me away. "I really need to shower." At least she smiles. Without waiting for my reaction, she pushes herself up from the edge of the bed.

In a reflexive movement I grab her hand and hold her back. "Stay with me," I say, and even I can hear the pleading in my voice. Because I want to express so much more with it than just that Marie shouldn't leave this room right now. It's possible my hand is holding her a little too tightly. But it's worth it to experience a few minutes of normality. Just for a single moment we could feel like we used to.

"I'll be back soon." Her smile is gentle, her voice friendly.

What else can I do but let her go and watch as she leaves the bedroom without turning back to look at me even once? As so often, I feel like I'm a ghost to her, one that only appears now and then.

That might even be true, because in fact I only ever come home to sleep anymore. It's August, my coworkers are on vacation, and I'm the one covering for all of them. I volunteered for it because of the extra pay. At least that calculation seemed to work out, thanks to the raise Marianne managed to get for me. If I keep this up, our dream house will stay within reach. But a baby, that we can't afford. No matter how I crunch the numbers, I end up with a deficit that just can't be overcome.

Maybe none of that is even necessary anymore.

Just the thought of it makes me tired. My eyes close; I allow myself that much while Marie is freshening up.

Somewhere between dream and reality I hear, a little later, the water in the shower being turned off, and right after that the patter of bare feet on the parquet floor.

"Do you want to do something today?"

Even though my eyelids are closed, she talks to me as if I were standing in front of her, wide awake and full of energy.

I blink and see her leaning against the doorframe. As if she wanted to keep a safety distance between us, flashes through my mind all on its own. She's wearing a floor-length summer dress. The turquoise fabric glows almost as brightly as her eyes.

"What are you in the mood for?" I try for a cheerful tone and suppress a yawn.

Thoughtfully, Marie puts her index finger to her chin and looks up at the ceiling as if she might find the answer to my question up there. "We could go visit our flower meadow," she finally suggests.

Fine little lines form at the corners of her mouth. In the past I would have said something funny without thinking. "Your wish is my command," for example. I would have added a servile gesture. She would have come over to me and gallantly offered me her hand so I could kiss it. We would have grinned at each other and kissed so passionately, for so long, that the earth would have quaked beneath us. And we with it.

"Yeah, that would be nice. Let's grab a coffee on the way," I say instead and feel like some uptight banker while I'm at it. All I'm trying to do here is not offer any target and not put a foot wrong. Because I don't want to be the bull in her china shop anymore.

For a moment she pulls her eyebrows together in a questioning look, then she nods. "All right, out of bed."

I peel myself out of bed. All by itself, my mind is already searching for the perfect moment to confront Marie. Once we've cleared up what's going on with her, I'll confess the truth about our financial situation. And talk her into working again.

It has to happen today, I can't wait any longer.

My desire for this conversation shrinks down to the size of a pinhead. Even so, I pull myself together, jump in the shower, brush my teeth, and twenty minutes later I'm standing in front of Marie, fully dressed.

"You ready to go?" Marie opens the shoe cupboard and does something I haven't seen her do in months. Thoughtfully, she lets her gaze wander from top to bottom, as if she's considering which of the sandals go with her dress. Is it suddenly important to her again how she looks?

All at once she turns to me. "What is it?" I can't make sense of the skeptical expression on her face.

I probably shouldn't have been watching her, and only now do I realize how obviously I did it. I snap out of my paralysis at once and give her the most casual smile I can manage. "Nothing at all," I say and slip into my shoes. At that same moment, the phone in my pants pocket starts vibrating.

A message from the junior boss pops up. In his very first week on the job, the boss's nephew already turned out to be a complete write-off. Even though he's surprisingly likeable, he's more than unsuitable for his job. Not only does he fail to handle any of his tasks on his own, he also brings chaos into what had been running perfectly up to now. I immediately feel my shoulders slump. I probably even pull the corners of my mouth down.

"Work?" Marie's voice sounds neutral.

I skim the text of the message. There are problems with an Egyptian supplier that absolutely have to be resolved today.

Part of me rebels, another part breathes a sigh of relief. With my lips pressed together, I look up at Marie. Our eyes meet, a deep crease forms between her eyebrows. I'd love to know whether it's sympathy or disappointment I'm reading in her face right now. And yet it doesn't matter. Because the mere fact that I'm no longer able to tell is devastating enough.

"We'll have to postpone our trip." I can only hope she knows how sorry I am. And that there's just no other way.

Her forehead smooths out, the expression on her face suddenly turns very soft. She even comes over to me and lays her hand on my cheek. "I guess there's nothing we can do about that," she says understandingly. "How long will you be gone?"

I wish that just her reaction alone would lift this terribly heavy boulder from my chest. But it feels more as if only small fragments are breaking off. "Definitely a few hours. When I'm back, we'll have a nice evening together, okay?"

"Of course. I'll go visit Grandma. By the time you come home, I'll be back too." As if she wanted to cheer me up, she gives me a wide smile now. To me it feels as if the almost transparent ghost I usually am to her suddenly turns into a living being.

A wave full of hope crashes over me, breaks above my head and pours down on me like a warm summer rain. "Thanks," I say in a toneless voice and reach for my keys.

I don't dare kiss her, and only touch her forearm for a moment. Then I march off to do my duty.

Chapter Thirty-Five

Before I can form a clear thought, Lukas is gone. I only hear his footsteps in the hallway, growing quieter and quieter until they disappear completely.

Indecisively, I look at the sandals in my hand. Should I go over to Grandma's now? At once, the memory of my last visit with her catches up with me. No matter how hard I try with her, nothing seems to get through. I read to her, tell her about my failed attempts to bake apple strudel on my own, play cards with her and show her videos of her animals. But no matter how often I tell her how much the chickens miss her or how lovely it would be to harvest the strawberries in her garden together with her, it doesn't work. She looks at me with the same neutral expression every time. I can't see any emotion in her eyes.

She's sad; she just can't get over Grandpa's death. And every time I'm with her, I become sad all over again too. It frustrates me, some days far too much.

With a sigh, I put the sandals back in their place and

wander through the apartment. I could tidy up, clean the bathroom, or finally clear out the drawers of the living room cabinet where, for years now, everything has ended up that doesn't fit anywhere else. The fridge probably needs cleaning too, and the freezer compartment defrosting.

The longer I think about it, the less I like the idea of tackling even one of the open items on this list. Because none of it will help me get on the track of my *later*. And that's what I really have to do. I want to take a step forward; I finally need to know which job is right for me. The job interviews the employment office keeps sending me to are all awful. At least I know that for sure.

I stop at the window and take a deep breath to see whether the butterflies will come to me here in our apartment too. I wait what feels like an eternity without anything happening. But then, quite suddenly, one of those delicate creatures flutters up right in front of my mind's eye. And with it comes the thought that has been on my mind since my last meeting with the stranger.

If there were no limits, if absolutely everything were possible, where would I go?

At once I see myself walking along the Great Wall of China, diving at the coral reefs off the coast of Australia, and crossing the Sahara on a camel. I'm not doing any of this alone. Lukas is with me, and he looks as happy as he used to look once upon a time.

That's where I want to be, that's my future. All I need for that is a job I can do from anywhere.

Of course!

Why didn't I think of this much earlier? I can have all of that without having to start over. There's a connection between my old life and the *later* I've been desperately searching for for so long.

I'm going to work as a virtual assistant.

To earn money, all I need is a laptop and the internet. I'm my own boss, I create presentations for clients, book business trips, and organize events.

That does sound promising!

I immediately start looking for my phone to find out how I can get this business started.

My plan is abruptly interrupted by the ringing of the phone. It's Alex, and she's definitely back from vacation. Of course I remember my promise, and I know I have to keep it if I don't want to risk this relationship as well. So I answer the call.

Alex gets straight to the point. "We're meeting today," she says, and that's definitely not a question but an unshakable fact.

I hesitate, because the fire of enthusiasm inside me is blazing so strongly that I don't want to ignore it. I'd much rather take the first steps into my future than see Alex.

But before I can say anything, she goes on. "No objections. In half an hour we're meeting at the lido on the Old Danube."

I almost have to smile. From the outside, Alex looks like a delicate elf, but inside her slumbers the heart of a lion. I can't cancel on her, so I postpone my research until later. "All right, I'll be there."

"Very nice, I'm looking forward to seeing you. Finally." I hear how insistent her voice has suddenly become, and I immediately feel bad. Because it's entirely my fault that she has to fight at all.

"I'm happy to see you too," I say anyway, deliberately cheerful, and say goodbye to her.

A short time later, Alex and I fall into each other's arms. A cloud of sunscreen scent surrounds us both, but despite how unfamiliar the smell is to her, I immediately feel at ease with her.

"Oh man, it's only now that I realize how much I missed you." I pull her a little tighter against me.

An amused snort leaves her mouth. "Don't lie to me. You haven't thought about me for a second, to you I'm just a fleeting acquaintance from another life. I, on the other hand, actually miss you every day."

I loosen our embrace. "That ends now."

It's only a small crease that forms between her eyebrows, but I still see it. Right after that, though, she gives me an encouraging smile. "Let's go inside first." Alex nods toward the entrance, then she grabs my hand and pulls me along behind her. "I want to know absolutely everything, okay?"

"Yes, ma'am," I confirm in a military tone. Together we burst out laughing, just like we used to.

As soon as we enter the pool, the typical smell of sunscreen and frying fat hits me. It reminds me of vacation, cloudless skies, and relaxation. Unerringly, we head for the wooden lounging islands and spread out our towels. I've barely made myself comfortable when the first words are already bubbling out of Alex, as if there were enormous pressure building up inside her.

"So… fire away!" she says, folding her hands behind her head as she lies there.

I push my sunglasses up onto my nose, grab a hair tie, and pull my chin-length bob up into as high a ponytail as possible. "What exactly do you want to know? You'll have to be a bit more specific, I'm afraid." How wonderfully light my voice sounds. And that's not just because of the atmosphere surrounding us here. From laughing children to old people playing cards to teenage sun worshippers, everyone's here. None of them seems unhappy.

"As you wish." All at once Alex turns her gaze to the sky. Is she afraid to address me directly? Nonsense, we're both lying on our backs and she'd only get a stiff neck if she kept looking over at me. "Let's start with an easy question. What on earth do you do with all the time you have? That must be an absolute luxury problem you struggle with every single day."

I just have to keep her in suspense a little. "I'm at my grandma's, then I take care of her animals and the garden. And the job center keeps sending me to even more horrible job interviews." Alex looks like she doesn't believe me. "Don't look so disappointed, what answer were you expecting?"

Alex shrugs her shoulders for a suspiciously long time. "Maybe that you do crazy things, scare people in the park, jump off bridges on ropes, or learn to ride a unicycle. Maybe also that you're bored by now and in truth you can hardly stand it anymore. That you're out and about a lot, conquering the world. Something like that. Come on, don't tell me you like this monotonous life. I really can't believe that."

She can't seriously think I wouldn't see through what she's trying to do here. The woman with the glittering navel piercing next to me knows exactly where this conversation is supposed to lead. She probably deserves extra credit for not barging straight in the way Lukas does far too often. "Just because I don't have a job right now doesn't mean I'm not using my brain." I shake my head firmly.

"So go on then, tell me. What plans have you made for the future?" Even though she tries to hide it, I can clearly see her curious grin.

"Congratulations, you set that up perfectly," I comment with a chuckle.

Nothing is holding her back now; she props herself up on her forearms and smiles at me openly. "Thank you very much." Giggling, she gives a little bow, and I can't help laughing with her.

"You surely remember that I wanted to change direction. My old job wasn't bad, but it definitely didn't make me happy. And supposedly there are people who earn their living with their passion. At least that's what I've heard."

"We already covered that topic at the exhibition. And if you ask me, a job like that is still pure fantasy," she says seriously and nudges me with her elbow.

With my gaze turned to the bright blue sky above us, I do everything I can to ignore her joking remark. I know these arguments from Lukas all too well. "Just wait and see. Since I had a bit of time, at least I was able to think about it."

"Well? What did you decide? Come on, don't keep me in suspense like this!" From her tone I can tell she'd love nothing more than to grab me and shake the words out of me.

By now I hardly even expect it myself, presenting my idea to Alex. I slide my sunglasses down so she can see in my eyes that what's coming next is the truth.

"I actually found the perfect job that combines everything. I'm going to travel the world and earn my money as a virtual assistant." A satisfied grin spreads across my face, and suddenly I'm overflowing with ideas. "Maybe I'll start a blog on top of that. Or I'll become a travel influencer."

The words bubble out of me in a rush of excitement.

"Wow…" I've never seen Alex speechless before; this incredulous "wow" seems to be the only thing she can manage right now.

"It's perfect, isn't it? I'll put up with the secretary job for a few hours a day. In return, the rest of the time will be one big dream." I'm not looking forward to the work, but everything else makes me shine brighter than the sun above us.

Alex, on the other hand, doesn't seem happy for me. Instead, she studies me closely.

"What's wrong? Cat got your tongue?" I try to sound funny, as if that could somehow chase away her weird mood. It doesn't work.

"In a way... sort of... um..." Alex stammers. She sits up, crosses her legs, and tilts her head to the side. "Please don't be mad at me, but I just have to ask you this: What the hell is wrong with you?" The seriousness in her voice is unmistakable, and the way she draws out each word gives them even more impact.

"I'm working on my happiness. Is that a problem for you?" Defensively, I fold my arms across my chest and press my lips together.

She throws her hands theatrically into the air. "Marie, I don't recognize you anymore! You have practically nothing in common with the woman who used to be my absolute favorite colleague. First I have to drag you out of your apartment to make you do anything at all. Then you don't get in touch for weeks, even though you know I'm here for you. And now you come to me with some crazy idea like this?" Her reproachful gaze hits me, but she doesn't give me any time to explain. Accusingly, she points her index finger at me. "What about your grandma, huh? Do you just want to fly away and leave her to her fate here in Vienna?"

"Of course not!" I shoot back. How can she even think I'd leave Grandma on her own? "The treatment will work one day, and until then I'm staying."

Unimpressed, Alex shakes her head. "And what about Lukas? Are you just going to force him to quit his job and get on a plane with you?"

I stare at her in disbelief. Why is she trampling all over my dreams like this? "It's not fully thought through yet, I only had the idea today. I'm sure we'll find solutions once I get started."

A scornful snort escapes her mouth. "And do you seriously think you just put your profile on some virtual assistant platform and then it all runs by itself?" she goes on, as if she hadn't registered my objection at all.

"Stop it!" Yes, I'm yelling at her. The group of old people playing cards next to us notices that too. They all look over at me at the same time, but I don't care. Alex can spare me this kind of doomsaying. "This is the best idea for my *later* I've ever had. At least let me try."

Her hands whirl theatrically through the air. "My God, how naive are you?"

"And how stuck in your head are you?" This can't be happening. Not even Alex is on my side? I scan her face, notice the tight muscles around her mouth and her quivering nostrils. Higher up, though, something else catches my eye. Her expression gives her away. She's eaten up with envy. "You just want to bad-mouth my *later* because you're stuck in a damn hopeless hamster wheel yourself."

All at once, every trace of life drains from her eyes. "Drop this nonsense about *later* already," she snaps at me. As she says the word "later," she draws quotation marks in the air. "Don't you get that you're ruining everything with it?" Our friendship too, her eyes add without a single word.

What am I supposed to say to that? I don't know, and apparently neither does Alex. An unbearable silence suddenly stands between us like a thick, impenetrable wall.

We stare at each other, and with every passing second, everything just gets worse.

I have to get out of here. Now.

"Just forget it." In a rush, I pull my summer dress out of the bag and slip it on. I just bunch the towel up in front of my stomach, then I turn around. I can't look at Alex and I have nothing else to say to her. All I want is to escape this situation. So I start running as if my life depended on it.

But no matter how fast I run, Alex's words follow me on the way home. They sit on the back of my neck the whole time, weigh heavily on my chest, and make my stomach drop.

Drenched in sweat, I finally get home, shove the apartment door open, and fling the bag with my swim things into the corner next to the shoe cabinet. With my hands braced on my thighs, I stand in the hallway for minutes, gasping for breath, then I drag myself over to the couch and let myself fall as if I were a stone plopping into shallow water.

Of course now, on top of everything, fat, hot tears carve their way unchecked down my cheeks.

Is the whole world really against me?

Lukas, who just doesn't understand me. Alex, who accuses me of having lost my mind. The job center, which keeps putting pressure on me. And then there's Grandma, who would definitely have good advice for me if she herself weren't doing so badly that I can hardly contain my fear for her. I'm surrounded by resistance that only ever seems to grow.

No one believes in me. Only the stranger is on my side, and maybe he's actually even crazier than I am. What if I only wanted to believe him by force and in the process really fell for a fraud?

Am I chasing an idea of life that doesn't exist?

All at once I'm full of hate. For myself and my own naivety. I feel more lost than ever before. Because I no longer know which direction there even is for me anymore.

As if through cotton wool, I suddenly hear, to top it all off, the jangle of a bunch of keys in the hall. Lukas is back. At a moment that couldn't possibly be worse.

Chapter Thirty-Six

Curled up like a wounded deer, Marie is lying on the sofa. A terrible suspicion rises in me, but I still slip down beside her and try to give her a sincere smile. My hands stroke along her shins, and at last she looks at me too.

It takes an effort not to flinch. Her eyes are bright red and badly swollen. Her lips are trembling, her breathing is uneven. Only now do I notice the crumpled tissues scattered all around her on the sofa and on the light parquet floor.

Oh no, please not. Not today.

"What happened?" I actually don't want to know, because even her posture is a warning to me.

"Nothing," she answers through clenched teeth.

"Please, not so much information at once. I can't possibly process all that." I try to sound funny, because a gloomy, depressed afternoon is the last thing I want.

Not even a twitch stirs at the corners of her mouth. Instead, she pulls her legs away from under my hand and chews on her lower lip.

She's angry, and slowly it dawns on me why. I suppress a

groan, reach for her hand, and brush gentle kisses over her fingertips. "You're disappointed because I had to work. I'm sorry."

She doesn't even bother to look at me. "No problem," she says, shaking her head, and sounds as sober as a Monday morning.

Why is she making this so hard for me? And why am I even apologizing to her? For working so we can build a good life for ourselves because she can't hold down a job for longer than a day? She should appreciate that and not punish me on top of it for having so little time for her.

"What's actually going on? It usually doesn't bother you when I'm not here. This morning I even had the impression you were fine with it. And now you're making a scene?" I can hear myself how tired and exasperated I sound. But I just can't hold these feelings back any longer.

"I'm not doing that at all, everything's fine." The words coming out of her mouth don't match her expression in the slightest. If this is her way of making an effort for our relationship, it's damn well not enough.

"No, I want to know! What's changed?" I'm not going to let it go. Not this time. The secrets have to end.

For a moment Marie just stares at me, horrified. Her mouth opens and closes, yet no words come out. Then her expression darkens. "Can't you see what's going on? You go on and on about how excited you are that we'll soon be a family, and you tell me all the things you will and won't do when the time comes. But you're constantly just working. Do you really think that's ever going to change?" She sounds like she's looking for excuses, like a thief caught red-handed.

Something is seriously wrong here. And not just since today. "Oh, come on, someone has to earn the money so

Sleeping Beauty has everything she needs here. Or not?" The sharp undertone in my voice leaves no room for doubt. I've held these words back for far too long, swallowed them down with effort and let them fester inside me. "I'm the one who keeps everything running here!"

Furious, she straightens up in front of me. "You once again don't get a single thing."

Unbelievable. She even dares to scream right in my face. I no longer know what I'm doing, have no idea what I'm saying, and forget who I am.

"No. You're the one who doesn't get it. For fuck's sake, finally open your fucking eyes, Marie!" My anger knows no bounds anymore. It has sat in my gut for far too long; now it has to come out. "I wouldn't have to work nearly this much if you'd deign to contribute something to the household budget."

"I'm sorry. I'm doing my best, but…" The despair on her face knows no bounds. As if this place were a pit of venomous snakes, she suddenly springs up and runs out of the living room without finishing her sentence.

Not a minute later she slams the apartment door shut behind her with full force. The silence she leaves behind with me is ruled by a single question.

What the hell happened to us?

Chapter Thirty-Seven

Blindly, I race up the stairs in the Center for Mental Health, chased by a feeling as foul as the stench of rotten eggs.

Oh God, why did I do that?

Without thinking, I picked at his only wound and watched as the blood forced its way out. And I did it just to distract myself.

This is the final proof. I'm a terrible girlfriend. And a horrible person.

Somewhere between self-hatred and fear, between doubt and despair, cruel thoughts sweep through my head. They're like clouds that herald a storm. Much too fast to grasp, and far too dark to ignore.

There's only one place left for me to run to. To Grandma. She's my last lifeline. She's all I have left. I stop in front of her door and try to breathe calmly. Only then do I go in.

My gaze finds Grandma and instantly a shock wave spreads through me.

She is injured, far worse than during her last collapse twelve weeks ago.

What happened to her? And why?

I rush over to her without paying attention to the other patients. Maybe the beds are empty. Maybe several pairs of eyes are watching me as I reach Grandma.

I hardly dare touch her. Not just because her lids are closed, but also because I can't find a single patch of skin that isn't hurt. Her arms are covered in bruises and bandages, and an IV has been placed on the back of her hand.

"Grandma," I whisper in dismay, because I don't know what to say, and all I can wish for is that she wakes up.

But she lies motionless in her bed, the blanket over her chest rising and falling almost imperceptibly. I carefully brush her hair away from her scratched forehead. She must have collapsed again. Why?

"How could this happen?" I ask, even though I know she won't answer. "What happened to you?" And what happened to me? I add silently. Because one thing becomes painfully clear to me.

We're no longer who we were before Grandpa died. And the way she lies there in front of me, wounded and curled up, she's like a symbol of our shared downfall.

When Grandpa died, her joy in life went with him, along with her courage to go on and all her hope. That spiral of despair and grief dragged her further and further down, and no one can say whether, with this collapse, she has finally hit rock bottom.

She has lost everything.

And me?

I am lost.

With Grandma I did everything wrong. In my relationship with Lukas a storm front has built up that could finally break over me at any second. Neither he nor Alex understands me, and the truth is that I don't even understand myself anymore. My search for happiness is nothing but a story of constant failure.

That has to stop. The two of us, Grandma and I, have to get our lives back in order.

I bend over her and kiss her forehead. "We took a wrong turn," I whisper in her ear. "But together we'll find our way back."

Even though I have no idea where these words come from, the tears in my eyes are the final proof.

I tried and I simply gave it everything I had. But in this moment that comes to an end. Here and now I bury this damned idea of a *later* that can't exist anyway.

I close my eyelids for a moment and my butterflies are with me. Deep blue, white, and brightly patterned, they flutter through my thoughts. No matter how beautiful they are, I have to drive them away. They don't lead me anywhere.

So I do it. I set the creatures free and watch them disappear on the horizon. Maybe we'll see each other again. In another year. Or in another life. Or never. I don't know; only one thing is perfectly clear. As soon as I open my eyes again, I have to be the old Marie, no matter how much effort it takes.

Now.

My eyelids flutter. Then I open them and look straight into Grandma's light-blue eyes. She's awake. As if fate wanted to show me that, in the end, I really did choose the right path.

"Good morning," I whisper in a trembling voice and

smile at her. Because it finally has to stop mattering how hard that is for me.

She doesn't smile back, just stares sadly into nowhere.

Gently, I smooth down the green-patterned blanket, even though it's already straight. "What happened?"

A shrug. A brief groan. That's all I get from her.

It can't stay like this. It's time for her to let go too, and that's exactly what I want to make her understand.

I try absolutely everything. I tell her about the past, remind her of the beautiful things in life, and try to imagine a future for her that can still be fulfilling despite Grandpa's death. Even so, I leave the hospital two hours later without having achieved anything. I'm more tired than I've ever been, and I already miss my butterflies.

"You'd better get used to it, Marie," I scold myself sternly. Even so, I hesitate for a moment at the entrance.

Should I go to the water park again? One last time? I could say goodbye to the stranger. And to my dream of a better life, adds a wistful voice inside me that, from now on, isn't allowed to have a say anymore.

No. This has to stop!

I quickly turn to leave. *Later* never comes, and I'll be damned if I let myself be dazzled by that stranger again. It doesn't matter how many tears I cry on the inside at the thought. How heavy my head gets and how tight my chest feels.

I'm sticking to it. Today my search comes to an end.

Chapter Thirty-Eight

For hours I waited in vain for Marie to come back until I finally fled the apartment myself. Exhausted, I lay my hand on the door handle of Joe's. I push it down and hear the scraping sound of the door. As if in a trance, I walk to the bar and slide onto one of the stools. Apart from me there are hardly any guests here, and I'm glad about that.

"Hi, Lukas." One look at my face seems to be enough for Joe. His easygoing expression freezes; even the little lines at the corners of his eyes don't move. "One large beer, coming right up," he says, with a knowing tone in his voice.

Not a minute later he sets the ice-cold drink down in front of me. "Do you want to talk?"

Do I? Maybe. I don't know. Still, I have no choice, because it just has to come out. "You know Marie." I look to Joe for help, who is leaning on the other side of the bar, and lift my shoulders.

Joe nods, giving me his full attention.

"At first I thought she was just having a little life crisis. She quit her job in a rush and wanted to take some time off. But this break has already been going on for more than four months, and the end is nowhere in sight," I say, and at the same moment I feel how good it is to talk about it with a neutral person. The urge to tell him more overwhelms me. "We keep fighting. And every new argument is worse than the one before. I have no idea where this is going to end." The fact that all of this now reminds me all too clearly of my aunt's story I keep to myself. Because it's already enough that I constantly hear my mother's voice in my head, warning me not to support crazy pipe dreams that only lead straight into the abyss.

Joe stays silent; he only signals me with a hand movement to keep talking.

"We hardly see each other anymore. I work a lot; after all, someone has to earn the money. And when we are together, there's only pointless small talk, long silences, or arguments."

"You've lost your connection to each other." Bull's-eye. It's the first thing Joe says, and still he's absolutely right.

That gives me the courage to go on. I want to entrust everything to him so I can finally get it off my chest. "I don't see how we're supposed to get out of this. I never let her feel that I wasn't exactly happy about her decisions. On the contrary, I even tried to support her. But the more I tried, the further she pulled away from me." I want to shrug, but I don't even have the strength for that. So how am I supposed to have any energy left for Marie and her crisis? "This fight is making me tired. I don't want it anymore." Exhausted, I rest my head on my arms and take a big gulp of my beer.

For a moment, nobody speaks. I stay quiet because there's nothing left to tell, and Joe probably because he can't find the words. "You're thinking about giving up your love?" he suddenly asks.

I run my fingers through my hair, grab it, and pull until it hurts. "Is there any other way? Marie doesn't understand that she finally has to start being reasonable again. On top of that, my job takes so much out of me that I hardly ever get any rest." And the worst of all is that Marie is probably even right when she accuses me that, as a father, I'll never be there for her and the child anyway. "All I ever wanted was to be happy together with Marie. In our own house, with children and good jobs that keep us secure." I have no idea why I'm letting Joe look straight into my soul like this. Maybe because I don't know what else to do. Maybe because I'm hoping he'll have a solution for me.

"Being happy doesn't come from the outside. It's a decision we make for ourselves." Joe's voice sounds unusually calm, the corners of his mouth tug upward.

I immediately shake my head, because one thing is certain. He's wrong. "We had a good life. And we had plans. If only Marie would finally start pulling in the right direction again, everything would be fine. I've been fighting for that for weeks now, but she just keeps daydreaming."

Joe hesitates; I notice that clearly. Several times he starts to say something, but then seems to think better of it. Finally, he opens one of the drawers under the counter and pulls out a cutting board. "What makes you so sure that your direction is the right one?"

"That's obvious," I answer quickly, because this question is more than easy. "No money, no life. No work, no money. That's just how it is; there's no getting around it." Yes, I sound harsh, but I'm right. Dreams are like abysses. They make us fall and break every bone in our bodies.

Unimpressed, Joe grabs a lemon and slices it. Only

when he's finished does he look at me expectantly. "What's stopping you from at least looking at Marie's strand? Don't you think she'd want that?"

I can't help but snort derisively. "She even wants me to go along with her madness. More than once she's pestered me with that esoteric nonsense."

A knowing smirk plays on Joe's lips, even though there's so much he doesn't know. "What are you afraid of, Lukas?" he suddenly asks, hitting unerringly on that one wound in me that I'd hidden for years from the world and from myself.

I'm not going to answer his question. Because what I'm afraid of is so overpowering that I don't even want to think about it. "If Marie doesn't come to her senses, we're going to lose each other," I say evasively instead.

"Because you would never follow her into her madness." His tone is completely neutral, as if he doesn't want to give me any hint of what he thinks is right.

"Never," I confirm with absolute conviction. Because whatever is slumbering deep inside me, I'm not going to let it out under any circumstances. This panic about losing control of my life is already overwhelming as it is. "Marie has to be reasonable again; there's no other option for the two of us."

Just a small sign would be enough. A moment in which I recognize the old Marie again. A few hours in which we are who we used to be. She has to show me that I mean something to her. So that I can believe in our love again, too.

All at once Joe looks gloomy. He tilts his head to the side and gives me a wistful smile. "We are who we are. Until we decide to change it."

I have absolutely no idea what he's talking about. But my mind tells me not to question it any further. So I just raise my now empty beer glass. “Will you get me another one?”

For a moment Joe seems uncertain. Then he takes the glass from me. “Sure.”

Hardly has Joe turned away from me when I quietly pull my phone out of my pocket. The screen is black, no light is glowing anywhere. Several hours have passed by now, but Marie still hasn’t been in touch.

Of course not. She’s waiting for me to make the first move, because she knows she mustn’t pressure me. I need space to think. I should give myself this time, but today I can’t. I can hardly bear the uncertainty and the doubts.

“I have to be straight with Marie,” I say to Joe, who has just set the freshly tapped beer down in front of me. Wherever these words come from, with them a fear grips me. A fear of what will happen when I go home.

Maybe Joe is still muttering something under his breath. I don’t understand him, because the fear is pushing its way to the forefront with full force. It fights its way to the surface and spreads so powerfully that I can’t see anything else. To calm my worries, I drain my beer in one go and order another right away. Because either way, it’s as if I don’t know anything anymore. As if I’ve forgotten how to hear, to smell, to see, and to taste. My head is full of questions, all of which have to be asked today.

How will Marie react when I confront her with the facts? What will she say and what, for God’s sake, am I supposed to answer?

Chapter Thirty-Nine

On the way home from the Center for Mental Health, my legs feel heavy. Not just because from now on my old life is waiting for me. On top of that, I'm gnawed by a guilty conscience. I owe not only Lukas an apology, but also Alex.

I want to get it over with. Right now.

Reluctantly, I turn into a quiet side street, pull my phone out of my pocket, and dial her number. It takes a long time, but eventually she answers my call.

"Don't talk, just listen. Please," I say instead of a greeting, and Alex actually falls silent at once. If she were with me, she'd definitely cross her arms over her chest. Her facial expression would tell me how hurt she is. "I'm so incredibly sorry. You only want what's best for me, and I was unfair to you."

I listen to what's happening at the other end of the line. But only her breathing reaches me. She's waiting, and I know what for.

"All your arguments are right. Grandma is still sick, and Lukas won't just quit. Besides, he can't be the only one responsible for our financial security anymore. Trying to build a livelihood as a virtual assistant and be on the road a lot was a crazy idea." Saying the words hurts, but I pay no attention to that pain. It will pass. At some point.

"Mhm," she says, then a pause falls, and I have no idea how to fill it. "So what happens now?" Alex asks the overriding question to which, in truth, there's only one answer.

"Until Lukas and I start a family, I'm going to work as a secretary again." And with that, after a long, unsuccessful journey, I'll end up right back where I no longer wanted to be. "I'll apply for every open position I can find today."

Now I hear her sigh of relief, and I realize at once that her question earlier was a test. "That's the right decision. Just because you're making sure you're secure for now doesn't mean you can't keep looking for your dream job."

I don't even want to let thoughts like that in. After all, I know from the past that it doesn't work. For years I tried to reconcile obligations and dreams. I kept failing, and there's no reason why that should suddenly change now.

"No. My *later* doesn't exist. But that's okay." It's not! screams the voice in my head that has clung to me like a dark shadow ever since I made my decision.

Alex doesn't seem to notice the battle raging inside me. "Let me know if I can help you." She sounds so loving, as if she wanted to pull me into a hug.

"The fact that you're my best friend and always will be is more than enough," I say, my voice choked.

No matter how terrible the thought of going back to my old life is for me, at least I'll get the good things back too. Above all Lukas. I'll fight for Grandma, and Alex will be by my side, no matter how hard it gets for me.

We say goodbye to each other and I end the call. Then I look up. The sky is a brilliant blue. Not a single cloud is in sight, but inside me shadows keep gathering. I'll have to get used to that from now on. I don't have any other choice. I take a deep breath and start walking.

Half an hour later, I carefully open the apartment door.

"I'm back," I call out, putting on a cheerful tone.

Nothing but silence comes back to me. And nothing but emptiness is what I find, no matter which room I enter. Lukas isn't here, and there isn't a note on the kitchen table either. Of course not.

I let myself sink down onto the sofa. My gaze drifts to the window and then farther outside. Somewhere out there he is right now, disappointed in me and sobered by what has happened to us.

We have lost each other. It was my fault alone, I know that. He was never able to understand my search, but he doesn't have to anymore. It's over. From today on, the time has come to stand up for our love. As soon as he comes home, we'll talk as honestly with each other as we haven't in far too long. About the dream house, the finances, and the right time for a baby. He'll understand that his Marie is back. And that she won't leave him again.

Will I manage to hide how disappointed I am in myself? Or will he see that I broke inside when I gave in?

Hours of waiting pass. I know this time is important for him, so he should have it. At least it's clear how I have to fill it. I comb through job platforms, update my résumé, and write a cover letter. I send off one online application after another, and every time I press the button to send it, I have to swallow. It gets harder and harder to keep going. But it's what I promised myself, and I'll keep that promise. So it's only logical that I throw the employment office's training catalog in the trash and deactivate my profile on the virtual services platform.

Once that's done, I pace up and down the living room in my floor-length turquoise summer dress. Over and over I think about what I want to say to Lukas when he's ready to listen to me. With words, gestures, and my gaze. Alongside a spark of hope that we can restore our love, worries spread inside me. I don't let them get the upper hand, keep them small, and don't listen to what they whisper to me.

We can do this.

"Hey." Lukas's feeble voice suddenly pushes into my thoughts. I whirl around and see him standing in the grass-green doorway. His eyes are shining, his chestnut hair sticking out in every direction.

"Hi, my prince," I say lovingly and take a step toward him. "It's good to have you home again."

"Yeah." The muscles around his lower jaw twitch. At least he doesn't back away when I come closer and rise up on my tiptoes to kiss him. But his lips stay motionless, and when I pull away from him, I see the deep lines on his forehead all too clearly.

As if I hadn't noticed his rejection, I reach for his hand. "Sit down. Let's talk."

"If we have to." Only reluctantly does he let me steer him to the dining table.

I take a chair and place it right next to Lukas. So he can feel physically, too, that I'm here. For him. And for us. "I'm so incredibly sorry. I was frustrated and I overreacted." I search for his gaze before I go on. "Of course I know you're going to be the best father any child could ever wish for."

"Do you really think that?" There is doubt in Lukas's eyes.

"Don't you?" The question slips out of me unfiltered.

He gives a tired shrug. "I'm afraid you were at least a little bit right in what you said. I work a lot. Too much."

Now the moment has come to address the things that have gone unsaid between us for so long. I draw a deep breath. "Because we need the money and I don't earn any."

With a surprised look on his face, he studies me. Then he straightens up in his chair. "I can't do this on my own anymore." Maybe it's that he doesn't want to. But the sober undertone that was so clear just a moment ago is gone. He looks as if, in this very moment, an unimaginably heavy burden is falling from his shoulders, just because he's saying the words out loud. "The house and the baby together…," he says, then falters, and suddenly I understand what has really been going on with him these past few months.

He wanted to be perfect. Handle everything on his own and share the responsibility for me. I don't know whether it's gratitude or an oversized sense of guilt that is flooding my body. Whatever it is, it sweeps me away with it.

How could I do this to him? And how did he even manage to stay strong for me for so long?

In utter despair, I wrap my arms around his waist and snuggle up to him. "I'm sorry. I was horribly unfair to you." My voice breaks, and there's nothing I can do about it.

Lukas clears his throat and pushes me a little way from him. "What would you say if we waited a bit longer with the baby?" he asks.

I look at him intently and suddenly see in his face so much of what he has been hiding for months for my sake. "We have all the time in the world."

"You have to go back to work," he says bluntly, and I can hear the hope in his voice so clearly that it would break my heart—if I hadn't already torn it to pieces myself earlier at Grandma's.

I nod. "The applications are already sent off. And now kiss me already, or I'll be forced to jump you." Carefully, I press myself closer to him and stretch my upper body so I can reach his face with mine.

He can't quite believe me; I can see it in the flicker of his eyes. So I nod even more emphatically. I nod and smile tensely, until he copies me. Then I kiss him, as passionately as if I were sealing my promise with it.

In that moment, it happens. It feels as if the glass wall between us shatters into a million tiny pieces and comes raining down to the floor like diamonds. Silent tears of happiness well up at the corners of my eyes.

I can breathe together with Lukas again without choking, and cry with him again without drowning in it.

That's what matters most to me. Experiencing this love has to make my failed dream of *later* fade with time. And once I've finally forgotten it, the painful wound inside me will heal too.

Gently, Lukas dries my cheeks with his thumbs, then his expression suddenly changes. "I've been carrying this around with me for way too long," he says and pulls something black out of his jacket pocket.

I blink away the tears so I can see clearly.

A ring box. It's a ring box!

My breath catches instantly.

Very slowly, he opens the lid. My gaze darts frantically back and forth between his face and the black case in his hands. I couldn't have decided which sparkled more—his eyes or the sun-yellow stone that gradually appears.

"Marie …" His voice breaks, he blinks hard. And in that moment I know it for sure.

Our two hearts may have fallen out of rhythm for a moment, but now they're beating together again.

"Yes," I breathe, and nothing more is necessary. Because

we both know it's the only possible answer to that one question he doesn't even have to ask.

With trembling fingers, Lukas takes the ring out of the box and slips it onto my finger. It fits perfectly.

Even if the rest of my life isn't perfect and never will be. This is the best I can achieve for myself.

It's time for a new promise to myself. No matter what I have to endure at work, I alone decide about my free time. At the very least, I want to enjoy the beautiful sides of life, and I want Lukas to be able to do that again too.

I block out the rest. With all my strength.

Chapter Forty

I'm not fully awake yet, but I can already tell that Marie is watching me sleep. Even though the sun behind the bedroom window only bathes the world in diffuse light, it feels in here as if it were already shining. Thanks to her smile.

We've woken up next to each other ten times since our engagement. And every morning had its own special magic.

"You must've had an amazing night, or why are you grinning like that?" I mumble sleepily.

With a smile on her lips, she scoots closer to me and rests her head on my shoulder. I immediately wrap my arm around her hips. The scent of her skin reaches my nose, and everywhere we touch, everything turns wonderfully warm.

"Why are you even awake already? It's only five in the morning," I ask her and cover the crown of her head with gentle kisses.

"Because I want to enjoy every minute we're together." She sounds so full of longing, as if she were telling me the most beautiful story of all.

Her hands wander over my bare chest, so tenderly that I just can't help it. I exhale loudly and don't even want to say what needs to be said. "I've got a few more minutes. But then I have to go. Duty calls."

"Does it?" Marie's hand stills, she turns her head and peeks up at me. The radiance in her face has faded.

With my fingers I trace the contour of her cheek. I'd love nothing more than to stay with her, forget the whole world and, with her, everything that drives us. "I'm sorry. I'd so much rather spend my time with you, you have to believe me." As if to prove it, I hold her gaze.

Her gentle smile doesn't even come close to reaching her dark brown eyes. "Of course I believe you." For a moment she hesitates, bites her lip and drums her fingers uncertainly on my shoulder. "Do you ever wonder what all those ridiculously long hours at work are actually worth? I'll probably get a job offer soon, and now that the baby plan's been postponed, you could treat yourself to a bit more free time again," she says suddenly, very quietly, without looking at me, and she seems as if she were afraid of her own words.

What could I say to that? That it doesn't make sense to think about things like that? "The faster we can pay off the house, the better. It's only a few more years until I've fought my way up at work. With the corresponding raises, life will get easier again." I hold her tightly in my arms. Almost as if my words would otherwise push her away from me.

"But… you're alive today. Here. Now. You want to miss all of this just to get something out of it sometime *later*?" In truth it isn't a question she's asking me, because it doesn't sound as if she's expecting an answer. "Isn't life too short not to savor every breath to the fullest?" she asks me so intensely that a shiver runs down my spine.

What is she trying to tell me? Confused, I look at her, but in her face I see nothing but love. "Maybe," I answer curtly. For the sake of peace. "Either way, I really have to get up now. Will you have breakfast with me?"

"Of course." She stretches her body like a cat after an afternoon nap. I have to kiss her one more time, then I climb out of the soft warmth of the bed and head for the bathroom.

While I run through my morning routine, I hear life returning to the kitchen. Porcelain clinks, the coffee machine whirs. It's the tenth day in a row now that Marie has managed to get up in the morning. Like any other normal person. I shouldn't feel this relieved, but I do.

The new Marie isn't an illusion. Even if she still asks strange questions now and then, I can rely on her again.

A little later we're sitting together on the balcony. The July sun warms my bare toes, and the dull sound of the city's busy rush reaches us between the apartment blocks. I grin at Marie over the top of the newspaper, trying not to get caught. "So, Sleeping Beauty. Have you already decided which castle I'm allowed to wed you in?"

Her giggle tells me I struck the right note. She loves this game and so do I. Only today do I notice how long it's been since we last played it. Her regal expression is so perfect I could believe I'm sitting opposite a real queen. "My lord, I still need to compose myself to imagine the place. For now, have them bring me the butter without delay."

"Of course, Your Highness. Would you also care for some of the finest honey in the land with that?" I present the jar of honey to her and bow.

Marie plays her role perfectly. "Go ahead, go ahead." With a royal wave of her hand she signals me to pass her the honey.

Let's see how far she'll go. "But, Sleeping Beauty, leave that to me. Of course I'll butter the bread for you. You don't have to do such menial work yourself."

Her amused grin is answer enough. "Damn, I can't keep up my role like this," she says, giggling, "and now give me my plate back, I'm a big girl and as a matter of principle I spread my bread myself."

I laugh with her, and it just feels fantastic to be able to do that again. In a flash our love is as free as it used to be, without fear and without caution. There's only the two of us, Marie and me. A warm tingling spreads through my chest. "I'm really relieved about that. Just imagine where that could've ended."

"Stop grinning or I'll come up with something." Pointing the butter knife at me accusingly, she looks at me mischievously.

Instinctively my hand goes to my forehead. "Yes, ma'am. Understood." I pretend to salute her.

All at once Marie's features soften and I even think I see a damp shine in her eyes. "And now, report for cuddling duty," she murmurs hoarsely.

She doesn't have to tell me twice. With a single step I'm at her side and cover her forehead with kisses. I work my way down to her lips and when I reach them, it feels as if I've traveled all around the world and am finally coming home again.

"I love you."

"And I love you." She wouldn't have to say it, because I can tell anyway. It's the way she looks at me, and the tenderness with which her fingers wander over the back of my braced hand. In this moment I want to lose myself, and yet I don't have the time.

What time is it, anyway?

I sneak a look at my watch. "Already six thirty?" How is that possible? With my nose wrinkled, I look at her guiltily. "I have to go."

"How about you take the day off on a whim? We could hide from the world for a few hours." Her expression reminds me of a child who's excited to play with their favorite toy.

At the thought of my jam-packed schedule, I quickly shake my head. "I'm sorry. We'll make up for it on the weekend, okay?"

"We will." She swallows; I can see it clearly. "Have a nice day," she still trills, exaggeratedly cheerful.

"You too. Do you have anything nice planned?" I ask casually.

Suddenly Marie looks tired. "Grandma and I are going to take a walk today. She's finally making progress, and I hope the change of scenery will do her even more good." There's worry in her expression.

"I'm sure it will," I say with complete sincerity. "When will she be able to leave the Center for Mental Health?"

"I'm going to talk to the caregivers today, but I think her medication is finally properly adjusted now. Soon she'll have to manage on her own at home." Marie is sad. Seeing her like this makes me shiver, even though the warm sunlight is tickling my back.

I quickly take the last sip of my coffee. "Are you going to spend the whole day with her?" We both probably know that I already know the answer. After all, I wrote her appointments in the weekly planner a few days ago. Still, this topic has to become part of our normal life again, and today I feel that this is actually possible.

Marie's mood is still clouded. "I've got two job interviews in the late afternoon. Keep your fingers crossed that it works out this time."

Until a second ago there was still a part of me that didn't want to believe in our new peace. But it dissolves into thin air in an instant, just evaporates like a puff of smoke in a bright blue sky. Encouragingly, I stroke her upper arm; after all, I know how frustrating all the rejections have been for her. "You've got this, I can feel it."

The fact that Marie is chewing on her lips in a depressed way isn't good. "I don't understand why no company wants me. Maybe it's because of my age. Most of them probably think I'll get pregnant right away and that my training would just be a waste of valuable time."

That could actually be the case. Even where I work, women Marie's age hardly stand a chance of being taken on. "Not everyone thinks like that," I say anyway, because I can see how dejected Marie is.

"I'm not going to give up." With clenched fists and a determined expression, she looks at me. She even seems as if she might burst into tears at any moment. I haven't seen her this combative in a long time. It's another sign that everything will soon be back to normal. "You have to go," she reminds me.

I actually don't want to leave her alone. But you just can't stop time. "That's unfortunately true. Have a nice day, Sleeping Beauty." I kiss her forehead, look deep into her clear eyes one more time, and then, heavy-hearted, I head out.

It's only when I close the apartment door behind me that I really become aware of what just happened.

With how determined she's tackling things, Marie is guaranteed to have a new job soon. She'll be earning money and we'll be able to pay off the mortgage on the house together.

A burden as massive as the Himalayas falls from my shoulders, and just a moment later I no longer know how I managed to carry it for so long.

Chapter Forty-One

My joy is forced, the smile nothing but a façade. But I don't have a choice. Not with Lukas, and certainly not with Grandma. Ever since I picked her up at the Center for Mental Health a little while ago, I've been playing the cheerful Marie. Before Grandpa died, I could always cheer her up with my good mood. So I'll manage it today too; I just have to fight for it. Just like I do for so many other things.

Putting on a show of energy, I take Grandma's travel bag from the back seat of the car. "Ready?"

My gaze shifts to her. She's still sitting apathetically in the passenger seat. The same gloomy expression as always lies on her face.

That doesn't make it any easier, because I don't feel like laughing either. On the contrary, I'd most like to burst into tears as I walk around the car with the bag over my shoulder. But my feelings don't matter. Not even the ones that have been making my life even harder for the past few days than it already was.

They're the result of an unshakable truth. I'm out of options.

No company wanted to hire me, even though I gave it my all in the interviews. From Alex I know that my old position is becoming available again. My successor lasted only a few weeks with the boss, the two of them are just as incompatible as we were.

Whether I like it or not, I have to do it. As soon as tomorrow I'll be on my knees begging my former boss to take me back.

A wave of nausea runs through my body whenever I think about how much my failure will boost his ego. In one stroke he'll have more power over me than ever before.

How am I supposed to pull this off? How can I sacrifice forty hours of my life every week and still fight to be happy in the time that's left?

Suddenly everything inside me goes dark, but I don't want to let that happen. Job hell won't break over me until tomorrow. Today I'm here in Grandma's garden, between raspberry canes and rosebushes. A little way off the chickens are clucking, the sun warms my skin. This moment is one of the good ones. I mustn't ruin it for myself by mentally drifting off into my crushing future.

Besides, only Grandma matters. She's the one I want to take care of. So I push the darkness back and force a smile onto my face. I open the passenger door and help my grandma out of the car; at least that way I'm doing something meaningful. As we walk together toward her wooden house, I beam at her, even though it's anything but easy for me. At some point a little of it will rub off on her, because it just has to. She's made progress over the past few weeks, but she still lacks the energy for life. Bringing it back is my big goal. I have to manage it so she can cope here on her own.

My grandma's sorrowful sigh pulls me out of my thoughts. She must have spotted the welcome sign and the decorations. I've decorated the entire entrance area of her little house with balloons.

"Thank you, sweetheart, that wouldn't have been necessary," she says, sounding so wistful that I'm no longer sure it was really such a good idea.

I quickly shake my head. "I was happy to do it. Come on, let's go inside."

Of course I know how hard this must be for her. But for all of us the day comes when we have to confront reality so that things can move on. For me that day will be tomorrow. For my grandma it's today.

Her lips tremble, but I still take her hand and we enter the house together. I steer her into the living room, where she lets herself fall onto the sofa between the hand-embroidered cushions and looks around so incredulously it's as if she can't grasp where she is.

That doesn't stop me either. Because the welcome sign was only one part of my plan. I also want to remind her of the good times with Grandpa so she doesn't think of him only with grief. What could be better for that than my grandparents' photo album? Looking at the pictures of their life together will help Grandma cope with Grandpa's death. So I pull it out of the bookcase and sit down beside her on the sofa. I move closer to her and open the album.

The very first picture shows Grandpa's laughing face. The straw hat on his head sits crooked. The straps of the overalls he wore for work can be seen in the portrait, just like his sun-tanned skin.

"Do you remember this day?" I ask carefully. "That was when Grandpa built the chicken coop." He did it for her so she would always have fresh eggs from happy chickens. But I'd rather not mention that. Not yet.

My gaze wanders to Grandma. She stares unblinkingly into nowhere, paying no attention to the photo. Clearly her thoughts are in a place where Grandpa's death has no access.

"He hit his thumb with the hammer. His finger was swollen and blue for weeks, remember?" I take her hand and squeeze it. I smile as best I can while I do.

There's no reaction from her. Just like with my countless attempts before, she blocks this one too.

As if I didn't notice her refusal, I turn the page. "Here you two are together on the Grossglockner mountain." I study the picture more closely. A happy glow lies on their faces. Next to the photo I spot a year. "It says June 1990. That was your first ascent, right?" Yes, there's a pleading note in my voice. Because I have no idea what else to try if this doesn't work either.

Hopefully, I look up at her. Deep furrows have formed on her forehead.

"Look, Grandma," I try again. "Grandpa made this album to capture your most beautiful moments. He wanted you to look at it every day and relive those moments. 'For later,' he always said, grinning mischievously. You remember that, don't you?"

"There is no *later* anymore," she suddenly murmurs, and at once the first tears roll down her cheeks.

It isn't the reaction I'd hoped for, but at least some life returns to her face. This is my chance to help her. "But these pictures here, they still exist," I reply passionately, and immediately wonder where it comes from despite the frustration inside me. "They show our memories so they never fade in our hearts." I hesitate, but then I say it. "Through them, Grandpa won't fade either, even if you go on living your life without him."

All at once she looks straight at me. "I can't let him go." There is more despair in her eyes than a person can bear.

The sight of her gives me a stab of pain. Right there, where my own dream refuses to come to rest. "We can't have everything, no matter how much we wish for it." I have to sound convinced, yet I can hear the longing myself, forcing its way out from the furthest corner of my soul. So I clear my throat quickly, because there is only one truth. "All we can do is accept what life does to us and make the best of what we have."

"It can't be over yet." Grandma's voice is thin, but at least she's talking about what happened. That's a good sign. A very good one, in fact. "I still wanted to experience so much with him."

"But you did!" New courage stirs in me. I turn to the next page of the album and tap my index finger on the picture of Grandma and Grandpa working in the garden. "Look, here. This was when you planted the flower bed in front of the porch together."

Just looking at the photo makes me smile sincerely for the first time in weeks. I took it myself. It doesn't just show two people with dirty hands and sun-tanned skin kneeling among freshly planted forget-me-nots, daisies, and periwinkles. There is so much more that you can't see, but can feel all the more clearly. Even now, although the picture is already quite a few years old.

"Look at your faces. Do you see the love in Grandpa's expression? Do you see the mischievous grin on his lips because he's just about to tear off a blossom from the pansy?" Anyone who looks at this photo knows what happened next.

Grandma's mouth twitches. "He stuck the blossom in my hair and looked at me as if I were an angel."

I take the album off my thighs and hold it up. "You'll find countless experiences like that in here. The two of you had a wonderful life, the pictures prove it."

I'd never realized how powerful photos can be, but in this moment it becomes clear to me what they mean for all our lives.

A wave of exhilaration sweeps over me. With ease it carries away everything I've been forcing myself to do these past few weeks, and I don't even try to resist it. Because behind the dissatisfaction and the pressure, where disappointment in myself and the desperate suppression of my dreams have no power, a brilliantly bright light suddenly burns.

Before I realize what's happening to me in these few seconds, I jump up from the sofa. I run up the stairs, storm into my old childhood bedroom, and open the drawer of the waist-high cabinet next to the bed. There I search for one very particular protective case. It doesn't take long before I find it.

Small, square, and purple, it now lies in my hand. I hold my breath, then reverently open the Velcro fastener and let the contents slide out.

There it is. My old camera.

With this camera I captured so many of the moments that will help Grandma overcome her grief. It was with me when I fell head over heels in love with Lukas. Like a relic from a time when we still allowed ourselves to dream, it now lies in my hand. My fingers wander over the matte golden surface to the power button. I press it down, and even though it's really nothing special, my heartbeat skips a beat.

The screen actually flickers on. It still works!

Even though I don't understand why I'm so incredibly happy about it, I savor this feeling of joy. It doesn't last long, because a second later the screen is black again. A blinking battery symbol is all I can still see, but that too disappears the next moment.

I immediately rummage the spare battery out of the drawer, because I can hardly wait to take a few snapshots. In my mind I'm already doing it while I swap the batteries. With the camera in my hand I walk through the city and snap all the wonderful things I discover. I can already feel what that's going to be like.

When I'm done, I press the power button again. The spare battery is almost empty too, but this time the camera works. A feeling of happiness, as golden as the light of a thousand autumn suns, seizes me and carries me away with it. Because all of a sudden I know one thing for sure.

This inconspicuously small thing in my hand is my future.

With photos I want to show happiness to those who otherwise wouldn't recognize it. I'll capture what we all miss when we chase, day after day, the illusion of a life society forces on us. And if Lukas sees my pictures, maybe he'll be able to understand exactly that too. Not a single word will be needed anymore for him to realize how much our life in recent years has played out in a hamster wheel we never wanted to end up in.

Beaming with joy, I run back into the living room, where Grandma is now leafing through the album herself. With tears in her eyes that speak of more than just grief. I quickly take a picture of her and then another one right away.

"Just look what I found." My voice cracks.

Grandma looks up at me, the corners of her mouth even lifting a little. "Does it still work?"

I nod, then give her a conspiratorial look. "And not just that." My legs are jittery, I can't breathe calmly any longer. "It's time, Grandma," I blurt out excitedly. "I'm absolutely sure which job is right for me."

"You're going to be a photographer." Now a smile spreads across Grandma's face as well. She picks up the photo album again. "You definitely have talent. These pictures prove it."

Maybe I really do, but that isn't important right now. Taking photos will make me happy. It probably won't be easy to make a living from it, but I'll hold on to it, no matter what comes.

My old job, my former boss, and the employment office no longer have any place in my life. Because I know exactly which path I'm going to take from now on.

That alone is enough to lift the heaviness from my shoulders that has been with me for months. I feel light and free. No wonder the next thought immediately bubbles up inside me.

"I have a fantastic idea," I say to Grandma as I start looking for paper and pens.

Grandma's skeptical gaze meets mine. "What are you up to?"

Instead of answering, I just give her a mischievous grin. With notepaper and ballpoint pens in hand, I steer her outside onto the porch and point to the balloons that are waiting for their turn, tied to the wooden posts like a colorful rainbow. "We'll let them rise up into the sky. Together with our wishes."

"That sounds very lovely, sweetheart." It's only a small smile, but to me it feels as if the sun is now climbing over her horizon too. On top of that, Grandma pulls a sheet of notepaper toward her.

I follow her example. Be as happy as possible every day, I write on the first sheet. Tell stories with photos that move other people, on the second. Then I pause. Because a wish rises up inside me, one whose fulfillment still seems far away despite everything.

The past few months have proved it. Lukas would much rather live in an artificial world full of pressure and stress than give up control for even a single moment. He doesn't even want to ask himself why, in recent years, we stopped jumping in puddles and marveling at everyday miracles.

That's going to change from now on. With photography I can finally help him see the truly important things in life.

Full of confidence, I put my pen to the paper one last time. Dream together with Lukas again, I write, imagining the moment when he realizes how different life can feel. Light as a Sunday morning, bright as a cloudless spring day, and colorful as the autumn that gradually settles over nature. He'll come to this realization soon too, I'm absolutely sure of it.

Beaming with joy, I turn to Grandma. "Shall we get started?"

She nods, a spark of hope in her face. "I'm ready."

I know her grief isn't over. Even so, today she's taking the first step into a life in which she'll find a new kind of happiness. With our wishes safely held in our hands, we leave the wooden bench and head over to the balloons.

Not five minutes later we're both standing in the middle of Grandma's garden. Surrounded by raspberry canes and lavender bushes, each of us is holding three balloons, each one tied to a wish. We don't have to say anything, we just look at each other and nod. Then I focus entirely on myself and think about my three wishes.

To be as happy as possible every day. To tell stories with photos that move other people. To dream together with Lukas again.

That's it. That's my *later*. I've found it. A deep feeling of gratitude spread through me. Smiling, I let the balloons go and watch them rise up into the sky. White, blue, and yellow like the butterflies that, from now on, are allowed to flutter through my thoughts again.

I want to capture this moment. I lift the camera and fix the memory of the feeling that's flooding through me now on pictures forever.

Even after the balloons have long since disappeared from view, Grandma and I are still standing side by side in the meadow. Our eyes turned to the sky and our thoughts where our happiness finds us.

Chapter Forty-Two

Shopping for groceries together is not one of my favorite things to do. Still, we headed out together today. There was something in Marie's expression. A radiance so overpowering that I couldn't say no. Even though the supermarket is packed and we can hardly get through with our cart, she's still laughing. She's so happy that I'm almost starting to worry again.

"Look at this." With an expression of reverence on her face, Marie holds up a bunch of grapes. Then her gaze wanders to the fruit, which she slowly sets spinning. "Great, isn't it?"

I have no idea what she means. Should I ask her?

She doesn't give me time to react but chatters on right away. "The way the light breaks on the deep red of the grapes is absolutely fantastic." Thoughtfully, she tilts her head to the side. "You'd have to position them directly in the slanting morning sun… yeah, that would be good. Maybe with a few leaves, or better yet, completely minimalist in a shallow bowl."

To do what? I keep the question to myself and just watch her continue to stare at the fruit, alternately squinting, nodding, and smiling. She looks a bit like she's on one of those drugs that make the whole world appear in rainbow colors. Extremely strange.

I clear my throat. "Should we buy them?" I ask as casually as possible and put a bunch of bananas into the shopping cart.

"Definitely." With a proud grin, she grabs the grapes and lays them in our cart as carefully as if they were the finest porcelain. Then she dances on down the aisle, but she stops again as soon as we reach the tomatoes. She snatches up a particularly big one and studies it from every angle.

I feel a bit like I'm out with a child who sees miracles everywhere and seems to have all the time in the world.

But that's exactly what we don't have.

My gaze wanders to the clock; it's already half past one. I have to get to the office. High time to move along. "We still need pasta, honey, and cheese," I read from the shopping list and hope it'll distract her from her tomato. It's not on the list, so there's no reason to spend much time on it.

"Mhm." That's her answer, then she suddenly spins around in a circle. As if she's looking for the right position, for whatever.

This won't do. With one step I'm beside her and lay my hand on her forearm. "Marie, I'm running out of time."

She jerks her gaze away from the tomato and looks at me. The shine in her eyes softens everything inside me, because it's exactly the way she used to look at me. "Of course," she says suddenly and strokes my cheek. "Time." There's a weighty undertone in her voice, but I still have no idea what she's trying to say with it.

I can't deal with that right now anyway, so I grab the cart and head for the next aisle. "We have to keep going."

Did she hear me? I don't know, because I'm waiting for a reaction in vain. Exasperated, I start walking. Wherever she is with her thoughts, in my world the clock keeps ticking relentlessly.

It takes a moment, then she suddenly stands next to me. I'm already in the middle of deciding on a type of pasta. "Time is the only thing we can't buy." All at once she sounds terribly know-it-all.

I shrug. "But with money you can buy lots of other things. Pasta, for example." Without further ado I grab a pack of penne, because basically it doesn't matter what shape the stuff has. It all tastes the same. "Or a house," I add with a wink.

No sooner is the pack in the shopping cart than Marie blocks my way. With a serious expression she studies me. "And what if in the end there's no time left?"

"What if in the end there's no money left?" I raise my eyebrows pointedly. She can go ahead and explain that to me, my frighteningly blissful Miss I-live-in-my-very-own-world.

Her vehement headshake surprises me. "That's not going to happen," she says with utter conviction and beams at me, wonderfully content.

Does that mean…? Oh yes, finally!

"Because you've got a job?" Even I can hear the joyful surprise in my voice, and to be honest, I don't want to hide it at all.

The corners of her mouth lift, deep laugh lines form at her temples, and her eyes sparkle as if millions of gemstones lived there. "I've got big plans," she answers mysteriously, and I don't need to know anything more.

"That's great." I can't help it; I just have to pull her close and kiss her with all my passion.

Our dry spell is finally over.

When I pull away from her, she gasps for air. Her cheeks are flushed and she gives me a furtive smile. "I want more of that."

I'd love to kiss her again, but even without looking at the time I know it's already way too late. Maybe it's the hope that I'm wrong that makes me glance at my watch anyway.

"Hey," I hear Marie say, and suddenly her hand slides over the watch face. "Come on, leave that. We only live now, and no moment will ever come back. We should enjoy that, don't you think?"

"Of course we should," I answer evasively. I don't want any stress with her. Especially not now that everything is going so well again. "Still, there are obligations, and we can't just ignore them." Carefully, I push her away from me. Everything in me hopes she'll understand, and I'm pretty sure she can see that in my face.

"Then rush off, I'll finish up here on my own," she says thankfully, with a sweeping gesture that takes in the whole shop.

My gaze lingers on her. She seems as if she knows something. As if she were able to see things I'm blind to. She doesn't judge me; it's a different feeling she's sending my way.

But which one?

I don't have time to think about it, so I kiss her goodbye and head out. But even though I try to focus on what's waiting for me at work, I can't forget the look on Marie's face. Together with her strange behavior in the produce section, it worries me. What if she's drifting off again? What if she doesn't stop doing crazy things?

No. Thoughts like that are unnecessary and completely over the top. The last few months were difficult; it's hardly surprising that I suddenly suspect problems everywhere that don't actually exist.

Marie is happy and she has a job. Everything is perfectly fine.

"Don't be so paranoid," I scold myself and quicken my pace so I won't fall even further behind.

Chapter Forty-Three

Yes, our weekly planner has a TV night together scheduled for today, and we were actually going to watch Star Wars, Lukas and I. We've made ourselves comfortable on the sofa, popcorn and drinks are ready. But even before the movie starts, my thoughts begin to drift. To the place where, after five long months of searching, they've finally found their new home.

Accompanied by the epic film music, I go through everything once more. It's a bit as if I had a checklist in my head that exerts a magical pull on me.

My camera is clearly outdated. I've already taken many good pictures with it over the past few days, and for the time being I'll keep using it. Still, I should look for a DSLR camera. Maybe I can find a used one at a good price and also the lenses to go with it. But which ones are the right ones? I need a specialist shop, someone has to advise me. Also about software for editing the pictures. So I grab my phone and type the words "camera shop" and "Vienna" into the browser's search function. It shows me five stores in the old town at once.

"Hey, what are you actually doing?" Lukas's voice reaches my ear so faintly it's as if he were sitting in another room.

I tap on the first homepage that comes up. The shop is on Getreidemarkt, right next to the Kunsthistorisches Museum. Strange that I've never noticed it before.

Lukas shakes my leg. "Mhm," I mumble absentmindedly and look at the next store. It's only a few streets further on. How convenient.

"Hello? Earth to Marie, please wake up."

Something moves in the corner of my eye. My gaze jerks in that direction and I realize Lukas is giving me very clear hand signals. He's also eyeing me with raised eyebrows.

He looks unbelievably cute when he's this confused.

"Nothing." I give him a beaming smile. At the same time, it's almost unbearable not to continue my research. Now that I finally know where my path is leading me, there's only one thing I want.

To get started.

With every passing day I feel more of a new kind of energy. And sometimes everything about me feels light. As if I could fly. The world turns colorful and I know perfectly well that these colors shine just for me.

Happiness finds me. More and more often, and more and more intensely.

"But that's not what it looks like, Miss Red-in-the-Face." There's a mixture of curiosity and love in his expression.

Should I tell him? No, I'll stick to the original plan. It's better to present him with my new future when I've got everything together. So he can see that it's been thought through responsibly. Exactly the way he likes it. It's a compulsion I can't resist, so I turn back to my phone and tap on the next link. "I'm just surfing the internet a bit," I mumble with a grin, then I start reading the text.

This might be the right business for me. I save the address and look at the opening hours. Tomorrow I'll go check it out, and already the anticipation overwhelms me. It feels like it's raining again for the first time after a long dry spell. It's liberating.

All at once I feel his hand on my forearm. I look up and meet his questioning gaze.

"We promised we'd tell each other everything," he reminds me, his voice warm.

Wc did. And we do. Always. Just not in this one thing.

Hesitantly, I pull up the corners of my mouth. "It's supposed to be a surprise. But I need a few more days for that."

He snuggles up to me and strokes my hot cheek. "And what if I can't wait?"

Whenever he looks at me like that, everything inside me turns soft. I love this man more than I could ever put into words.

Maybe my hesitation is unfounded. Because if he loves me the way I love him—and he does—there's nothing I should have to worry about.

Expectantly, he raises his eyebrows. "Come on."

I should do it. Here and now I should tell him about my dream. About what photography means to me. And about this passion that I know for sure will never let me go again.

About my *later*.

I'm going to work toward earning my money as a travel photographer. I want to capture the whole world in pictures and bring my impressions home to share them with others.

In my mind, I'm already running my hand over the glossy cover of my very first photo book, and I know exactly what will be on the cover image.

Colorful scarves, red deserts, golden bangles.

India.

For a moment I pause and mustered all my courage. I lock my gaze on him. He nods at me trustingly. "Come on," he repeats impatiently.

Now or never.

I don't know how he'll react, but I know one thing for sure: that our entire future depends on this.

Afterword

Many of us strive for happiness. Sometimes we forget that we first have to find what makes us happy before we can start working on fulfilling our dreams. And often we're not aware of how rocky the road there can be. *Promise Me* is meant to encourage all readers never to give up the search and to allow themselves, every now and then, to let their thoughts fly to places where reason has no say.

The end of *Promise Me* is not yet the end of Marie and Lukas's story. In *Show Me the Stars* you'll find out how things go on for the two of them. Is the once so great love lost forever? Will Marie really be able to live her dream?

You'll find all the information about *Show Me the Stars* on the following pages.

All that's left for me now is to say thank you. Once again, many wonderful people accompanied me during the creation of this novel. A huge thank-you for all the help and support goes to my family. And also to the tireless book professionals, beta readers, bloggers, and release helpers, who by now are so numerous that I can't even name them all.

A very special thank-you also goes to you, dear readers, for choosing this book. I hope you enjoyed reading *Promise Me* just as much as I enjoyed writing it.

All the best,

Belinda

Next in the Marie & Lukas Series

vinci-books.com/ShowMeTheStars

She chose her dream—but it may cost her love.

Marie left safety behind to chase the life she wanted, but ambition hasn't paid the bills. As she struggles to stay afloat, Lukas—the man she still loves—slips further away. Can she build her future without losing her heart?

Turn the page for a free preview…

Show Me the Stars: Chapter One

Yes, our weekly planner has a TV night together scheduled for this evening, and we were actually going to watch Star Wars. We've made ourselves comfortable on the sofa, popcorn and drinks are ready. But even before the movie starts, my thoughts drift away. To the place where, after five long months of searching, they've finally found their new home.

Accompanied by the epic film music, I go through everything once more. It's a bit as if I had a checklist in my head that's magically pulling me in.

My camera is clearly outdated. I've already taken many good pictures with it over the last few days, and for the time being I'll keep using it. Still, I should look for a DSLR. Maybe I can find a used one at a good price, and also the lenses to go with it. Only, which are the right ones? I need a specialist shop, someone has to advise me. Also about software for editing the pictures. So I grab my phone and type the words "camera shop" and "Vienna" into the browser's search function. It shows me five stores in the old town at once.

"Tell me, what are you actually doing?" Lukas's voice reaches my ear so faintly it's as if he were sitting in another room.

I tap on the first homepage that comes up. The shop is on Getreidemarkt, right next to the Kunsthistorisches Museum. Strange that I've never noticed it before.

Lukas jiggles my leg. "Mhm," I mumble absentmindedly and look at the next store. It's only a few streets further on. How convenient.

"Hello? Earth to Marie, please wake up."

Something moves at the edge of my vision. My gaze jerks in that direction and I see that Lukas is giving me very clear hand signals. He's also eyeing me with raised eyebrows.

He looks unbelievably cute when he's this confused.

"Nothing." I give him a beaming smile. At the same time, it's almost unbearable not to continue my research. Now that I finally know where my path is leading me, there's only one thing I want.

To get started.

With every passing day I feel more of a new kind of energy. And sometimes everything about me feels light. As if I could fly. The world turns colorful and I know very well that these colors shine just for me.

Happiness finds me. More and more often, and more and more intensely.

"That doesn't really look like it, Miss Red-in-the-Face." There's a mixture of curiosity and love in his expression.

Should I tell him? No, I'll stick to the original plan. It's better to present him with my new future once I've got everything together. So he can see that it's been thought through responsibly. Exactly the way he likes it. It's a compulsion I can't resist, so I turn back to my phone and tap on the next link. "I'm just surfing around on the internet a bit," I murmur with a grin, then I start reading the text.

This might be the right business for me. I save the address and look at the opening hours. Tomorrow I'll go and check it out, and already the anticipation overwhelms me. It feels as if, after a long dry spell, it's finally raining again. It's liberating.

All at once I feel Lukas's hand on my forearm. I look up and see his questioning face.

"We said we'd tell each other everything," he reminds me, his voice warm.

We did. And we do. Always. Just not in this one thing.

Hesitantly, I pull up the corners of my mouth. "It's supposed to be a surprise. But I need a few more days for that."

He snuggles up to me and strokes my hot cheek. "And what if I can't wait?"

Whenever he looks at me like that, everything inside me turns soft. I love this man more than I could ever put into words.

Maybe my hesitation is unfounded. Because if he loves me just as much as I love him—and he does—there's nothing I should have to worry about.

Expectantly, he raises his eyebrows. "Come on."

I should do it. Here and now I should tell him about my dream. About what photography means to me. And about this passion that I know for sure will never let me go again.

About my *later*.

I'm going to work toward earning my money as a travel photographer. I want to capture the whole world in pictures and bring my impressions home to share them with others.

In my imagination, I'm already running my hand over the glossy cover of my very first photo book, and I know exactly what will be on the cover image.

Colorful cloths, red deserts, golden bangles.

India.

For a moment I pause and gather all my courage. I lock my gaze on him.

He gives me a trusting nod. "Come on," he repeats impatiently.

I don't know how he'll react, but there's one thing I know for sure: our entire future depends on this. Even so, I don't want to put it off any longer.

Now or never, I think to myself in silence as I clear my throat at length. Then, my heart galloping, I start to speak.

"I take photographs," I announce bluntly, full of pride and with all my conviction.

There's no change to be seen in his face. "Application photos?" he asks, without moving even an inch.

"No, not for applications. I photograph nature. Interesting faces, everyday scenes, basically everything that catches my eye."

In the next few seconds I can practically see the information seeping into his consciousness. Instead of being happy for me, his expression darkens. "What for?" he wants to know, with a mocking undertone.

There it is again, that expression that tells me without a single word that I'm crazy. Marie Berger, a case for the head doctor who's supposed to drive out unwelcome daydreams.

This can't be happening. Please, no.

Why the hell can't he drop the role of the dutiful adult for just one single moment? If he did, he wouldn't have to ask anything else. And I wouldn't have to tell him anything more. He'd understand right away, and it could be the beginning of something completely new.

I know my goal, I can feel exactly where it's driving me. If he would give me the chance to show him how amazing it is, then he would come with me. But he doesn't. Not yet.

"What for?" I repeat his question and try to put a loving tone in my voice. "Because photography is my passion and I want it to become my profession." His skeptical look scares me, so I hurry on. "Lukas, I finally found what I was looking for. When I take pictures, I'm just happy, you know?"

"You already have a profession." His words are full of panic, his hands keep moving restlessly over his thighs.

I quickly shake my head. "But it's wrong for me. Try to understand, I'm not a secretary, I'm a photographer."

My joy seems to bounce off his stony façade. Is not a single one of my words getting through to him? He suddenly jumps up, as if he can't bear the situation any longer.

I hold my breath.

What happens next can destroy everything. Or make it whole again.

"Are you completely out of your mind?" he asks, sounding as if I had just announced that from now on I intend to live a polygamous life.

His words drill painfully through my eardrums, my shoulders grow heavy.

No, no, no. This wasn't how it was supposed to go.

"I'm not crazy at all. There's nothing wrong with me. I think you're the one who's crazy here!" An accusatory tone had slipped into my voice all on its own. What else could I even do? Beating tolerance into him is the last option. This situation is almost unbearable. Nervously, I grab one of the lilac cushions and knead it in my hands.

"Oh no, don't you dare try that on me. This is about you. And about the fact that you want to throw your whole life away. For some nonsense that only exists in your imagination." He practically spits out the words, as if they were disgusting slime that had built up in his throat and now finally wants out. "And about the fact that you're throwing our life away."

I stare at him in disbelief. That's what he thinks? That I'm throwing our life away? Which life does he even mean? The one in which we'd recently done nothing but function? "I'm doing what?"

A strained groan leaves his mouth. "Don't you notice it? For months you've been sending me on a roller coaster ride that just makes me want to puke all the time. Marie is depressed, Marie is overjoyed, Marie is cuddly, Marie is distant. And where, my dear Marie, where is Lukas, huh?" Now he's pacing up and down the living room like a lunatic.

No, this won't do. "Where is Lukas? He's where only reason lives, right?" Gesturing wildly, I throw my arms up. How can he accuse me of something like that? He, who in the past few months hasn't made a single effort to really understand me. He, who has constantly nipped my attempts to tell him about happiness in the bud.

"I'm the one who has to keep everything running while you pretend you're looking for a job, but in truth you just lean back and keep chasing pointless fantasies!" With his index finger pressed against his chest, he blinks at me in anger.

"They're not pointless fantasies, why don't you get that? I was unhappy in my old life, and I'm finally able to breathe again." I'm yelling at least as loudly as he is. Everything has to come out until there's nothing left.

He stops abruptly and folds his arms across his chest.

There he stands, right in the middle of our colorful living room, as motionless as a statue. "I really can't listen to this esoteric crap anymore." His voice is clear and firm, just like his expression.

"But I'm not going to stop just because you don't like it. I have a right to live my *later*," I whisper in a choked voice. Instantly, hot tears carve their way down my cheeks. They're back again, bringing with them that sadness I thought I'd already left behind.

Everything is going wrong. Again.

Unimpressed, Lukas looks me over and starts moving again. Even more agitated than before, he paces up and down in front of the coffee table.

"And what about my wants? Have you ever thought about that? For so long I've been understanding about you and this insane crisis. I've held back, given you all the freedom you wanted. Again and again I tried to motivate you, and again and again you slapped me in the face." His arms drop to his sides, dragging his shoulders down with them. All at once he looks tired, and drained. Despair and hopelessness suddenly appear in his eyes. "My mother was right. She really was right," he murmurs softly.

I wished I could go over to him and wrap my arms around him, rest my head on his chest and feel his heartbeat. Then he could pull me close and we would both know again that one of us can't exist without the other. Still, I don't do it. Because I'm at least as frustrated as he is and probably twice as helpless.

Is no one capable of stopping what's happening here right now?

"I wanted to save you. I wanted to save us," Lukas whispers in a trembling voice, "but in between all your daydreaming, did you think of me even once?"

It would be easier if he looked at me accusingly. And yet there's only disappointment in his eyes. No hatred and no reproach.

"So no. Fine, then just answer one more question for me: What is this relationship even worth anymore?"

Paralyzed, I crouch on the sofa, unable to think clearly and not knowing what to say. "Is there really nothing left of us? Of the two people who, in the middle of a meadow of flowers behind the Gloriette, dreamed of conquering the world together?" I finally manage to say. Where has our love gone, the blind understanding and the feeling of togetherness? Helplessly, I look at him through the vale of tears in my eyes, but he turns away with a stony expression on his face, as if he didn't care about any of it.

"Go find yourself another idiot you can take advantage of. We're done."

His words pierce my whole body like a thousand stab wounds. I should fight back, but I can't. Because what this overthinking man wants to hear from me will never cross my lips. Helplessly, I watch him leave the living room. I listen as he rushes down the hallway at top speed, and a few seconds later he slams the door with such force that the walls shake.

Now everything is quiet. I don't move and I don't breathe. Because I need all my strength to understand what has just happened here.

What if our relationship really isn't worth anything anymore? What if this realization is the only thing we still share?

Is it really over between us?

"Over, over, over," it echoes in my head like an echo breaking against the abysses deep inside me. And very slowly I begin to understand that my "later" might just have dissolved into thin air once again.

Show Me the Stars: Chapter Two

I nod to her. So she knows that the two of us can still be who we were. When this game is over. Here and now. "Come on."

As if she had to summon all her strength, she holds her breath for a moment. "I take photographs." Defiance is written all over her face, as if she wanted to prove something to herself.

Still, I feel relief rising inside me. "Application photos?" I ask hopefully.

Her conspicuously strained groan is a warning to me. "No, no applications. I photograph nature. Interesting faces, everyday scenes. Basically anything that catches my eye."

Excuse me? What is she talking about? "What for?" Maybe my question sounds mocking. But I don't have the energy to hide my frayed nerves from her.

She doesn't answer. Instead she looks at me so accusingly, as if I'd said something wrong. She has no right to do that. I'm still allowed to ask where this is suddenly coming from. And what she wants to do with it. In truth I'm the one who could be looking at her reproachfully.

"What for?" she repeats my question, and I can clearly hear that she'd like nothing better than to fling the word back at me. At least she holds herself back; maybe all of this still means something to her after all. "Because I like taking photos and I want to make it my job."

As much as I'd like to, I'm not going to react to that. Because I don't understand what that's supposed to mean. Photography as a job? You can't earn any money with that. Do you really want to go on being the one who keeps everything running while she loses herself even more? I immediately hear my mother's voice asking. But that isn't even necessary, because by now I know myself what's wrong and what's right.

For the sake of peace I ignore this idiotic behavior and instead reach for her hands. In contrast to her expression, they're soft and warm. Marie doesn't meet me halfway but pushes her lower lip forward. Just a little, but it's enough for me to know that right now she's simply annoyed with me. As stiff as a shop-window mannequin, she sits on the dark gray mottled woven-fabric sofa, directly in front of the oversized picture of the two of us. In this photo we're smiling at each other. It looks as if we don't even notice that there's someone else there pressing the shutter.

That's who we used to be. Marie and Lukas. Forever. How on earth did we both forget who we are? I'm sure she knows just as well as I do that we can't go on like this.

"Lukas, I've finally found what I was looking for. When I take pictures, I'm just happy, you know?" Marie doesn't just sound like a crazy person, she looks at me that way too.

No. That can't be true. I let go of her hands and draw

back. Panic flares up inside me, unstoppable, but I still have to clear this up. "You already have a job."

Her vehement shake of the head can't mean anything good. "But it's wrong for me. Don't you see, I'm not a secretary, I'm a photographer." Suddenly there's this sparkle in her eyes. I know it, even if I can barely remember it anymore.

That's exactly how she used to look at me. Back then.

In that moment one thing suddenly becomes clear to me: the woman sitting in front of me on the sofa is no longer the Marie I fell so madly in love with back then. She has turned away from me. I can't make her happy anymore, and she probably can't make me happy either.

Everything around me froze, the cold tearing my hopes away with it. And with them the vision of our shared future. All that was left was my incomprehension, mixed with the anger that had been seething inside me for so long and now finally had to come out. I jumped up, because the days when I met her on my knees were over as of now. "Tell me, have you completely lost it?" I sounded agitated and stern, but that was exactly how it needed to be.

"I haven't lost it at all. There's nothing wrong with me. I'd say you're the one who's lost it here!" The shrill tone in her voice shot through my whole body. Agitated, she grabbed a cushion and squeezed it with all her strength.

There was no reason to talk to me like that. Absolutely none.

I was supposed to be the crazy one, when just a year ago I had been the best man in the world for her? I hadn't changed one bit since then. On the contrary, more than ever I had tried to be there for her. To support her when she needed someone to lean on, and to show understanding when she drifted off to places I couldn't follow.

My God, what an idiot I had been to stick by her for so long!

"Oh no, don't you dare try that with me. This is about you. And about how you want to throw your whole life away. For some nonsense that exists only in your imagination." I couldn't help it, the words had to come out. They had been lying in my stomach for so long, sitting on my throat and blocking my mind. Why I had held them back all this time was a mystery even to me. It hadn't done any good. "And about how you're throwing our life away," I added, with all the fury I carried inside me.

She stared at me as if she didn't recognize me anymore. At least for once she was feeling in her own body what it was like when you no longer knew who the other person really was.

"I'm doing what?" Her hands kept digging into the cushion. I heard her fingernails scraping over the fabric.

How could she pretend she didn't know what I was talking about? "Don't you notice it? For months you've been sending me on a roller coaster that just makes me want to puke the whole time. Marie is depressed, Marie is over the moon, Marie is cuddly, Marie is distant. And where, my dear Marie, where is Lukas, huh?" The words left my mouth louder and more forcefully with every sentence. I couldn't stand still any longer, so I paced tensely up and down in front of the coffee table. My head felt as if it were about to explode.

With her eyebrows drawn together, she watched my every step. "Where is Lukas? He's where only reason lives, right?" Now she was also flailing wildly with her arms in the air.

I stop moving abruptly and point my index finger at myself. "I'm the one who has to keep everything running while you pretend you're looking for a job, when in truth you just lean back and keep chasing stupid pipe dreams!"

Of course, there it is again, that defiant expression on her face. As if she were a little girl who isn't getting what she wants. "Those aren't stupid pipe dreams, why don't you get that? I was unhappy in my old life and I can finally breathe again." She yells so loudly I'd still hear her standing next to a plane taking off.

All at once it feels as if the living room walls are closing in on me. They're coming closer and closer. They're taking the air from my lungs and the clarity from my thoughts. I have to get away from her, away from this apartment. Away from this life. Marie will never get that the world doesn't revolve around her alone.

"I really can't listen to this esoteric crap anymore." Strangely enough, my voice is completely clear and so steady it's as if none of this could touch me.

As if she had to hold on to herself, she pulls her legs up to her chest and wraps her arms around them. "But I'm not going to stop just because you don't like it. I have a right to live my *later*," she whispers in a choked voice. To make matters worse, tears are running down her now horribly pale cheeks.

How can she? Why is she acting as if she were the victim here, when in truth I'm the one who's in the process of losing everything?

"And what about my wants? Have you ever thought about those? For so long I've been understanding about you and this absurd crisis. I've held back, given you every freedom. Again and again I tried to motivate you, and again and again you slapped me in the face." If she doesn't get it this way either, I don't know how else I'm supposed to explain it to her. "My mother was right. She really was right," I mutter, even though I hadn't wanted to say the words out loud. But it's the truth, surging so violently through my whole body right now that I can't fight it.

If she would just once stop thinking only about herself, we'd still have a chance. The two of us, Marie and Lukas, forever. That was all we ever wanted, nothing else.

All I need is one small step from her. Just once she should come over to me. Stop my pacing through the living room, put her arms around my shoulders and smile at me. Apologize and admit that she's lost her way.

Still, she does nothing.

She stays where she is. On that damn sofa between the damn purple cushions and the damn soft blanket. That's where she sits with her damn honey-blond hair, looking at me out of her damn dark brown eyes as if she'd run out of damn feelings for me.

"I wanted to save you. I wanted to save us," I say in a choked voice, because a part of me can't believe that this can't be stopped anymore. "But between all your daydreams, did you think of me even once?"

She doesn't answer. Her eyes are empty, her shoulders slump forward. She looks like a lost chick that has just been cast out of its warm nest. But that's exactly why I can't let myself go soft.

I stop at the living-room window, my gaze drifting outside. Behind the pane of glass, the day is just coming to an end, while in here something entirely different is ending. Without turning back to her, I go on speaking. "So no. Fine, then just answer me one last question: What is this relationship even worth anymore?"

That was it, the all-decisive question. And now that it's out, I can barely stay upright. We've arrived at the place we never wanted to be.

Forever. That was our goal. And what did it turn into? A never again.

I whirl around to face her. Over on the sofa, Marie is rocking herself back and forth. No matter how hard I try to read anything in her face, I can't. When did I stop knowing what she's thinking and feeling what she feels?

All I can make out is her empty gaze and the trembling of her lips. She doesn't reach out her hand to me and she doesn't come toward me. "Is there really nothing left of us? Of the two people who, in the middle of a meadow of flowers behind the Gloriette, dreamed of conquering the world together?" she asks in a choked voice.

She'll never stop resisting growing up. But that's reality, whether she likes it or not. I can't stand it any longer. And there's no strength left in me to keep believing in us. "Go find some other idiot you can use. We're done." The words leave my mouth wearily.

I give up.

She can go wherever she wants. I'm not going to go with her anymore.

I'd love to say, "If I leave this apartment now, I'll never come back," but I don't have the energy for that anymore.

I look at her one last time, but still there's no reaction from her. So I start walking. Away from Marie's madness. Away from the pain and the disappointment. Out of the apartment. Out of this relationship that hasn't been one for far longer than either of us would ever admit.

Show Me the Stars: Chapter Three

He's gone. The apartment is quiet. My head, on the other hand, is full of questions.

What if our relationship really isn't worth anything anymore? What if this realization is the only thing we still share?

Is it really over between us?

Rigid with horror, I sink back into the sofa cushion that suddenly smells only of Lukas.

Did he just tell me that everything I dream of is nonsense? Did he turn around and just run off as if he had nothing more to say to me?

Of course he did.

When he can't be the perfectionist who knows exactly what to do, he runs away. Right now he's probably wandering through the streets of Vienna, breathing in the exhaust-laden night air and looking for a solution to something that in truth isn't a problem at all. I can see him in front of me, with that petrified expression he gets whenever he has to think. The more time passes, the calmer his breathing becomes, the tension eases, and he starts to understand how idiotically he behaved. He just has to, there's no other way.

I have to move too, because I can't stand just sitting here doing nothing until he comes back. So I push myself up from the sofa and march into the kitchen. There's a stack of dishes waiting to be loaded into the dishwasher, and the trash really needs to be taken out as well.

That will distract me. That way I can keep the awful feeling in my stomach somewhat in check and stop these terrible doubts from spreading any further inside me. I can't let them get the upper hand. Because I'm afraid of what that would do to me.

At top speed, plates and cutlery go into the dishwasher, I scrub pots and wipe the light wooden countertop with a damp cloth. Anyone who could see me would think I was a lunatic who believes her life depends on getting this kitchen clean.

But I don't care. I'll do anything not to think about Lukas and our fight. Still, I can't forget him. And even less his disregard for my dream. My gaze darts quickly around the room. Next to the fridge there's a half-empty glass. I grab it, yank open the dishwasher, and cram it in with trembling fingers.

Too hard.

With a clinking sound it shatters into thousands of tiny fragments. Everything is covered in shards, the whole dishwasher and the floor all around it too.

How fitting.

I need all my strength, but I still refuse to let it get me down. The broken glass doesn't mean anything at all. I was just clumsy, that's all.

I throw myself into the work, frantic. I have to clear up the mess. Make everything clean again.

Not twenty minutes later, it happens. The kitchen is perfectly tidied up. I'm hot, my breathing is heavy.

Slowly, a sense of calm returns, I look at my work and all of a sudden I'm just sad. Because what my eyes see is such a stark contrast to the state I'm in inside that I feel like a foreign body. Out here everything is in its place, but inside me there's so much chaos, as if a burglar had turned every last corner upside down beyond repair.

I mustn't think like that. I breathe in deeply and out again in a shaky sigh. Then I reach for my phone. If I don't talk to someone about what happened right now, I'll go crazy.

I dial Alex's number. Luckily my best friend picks up right away, and even faster she notices what's going on with me.

"You two had a fight," she says, sounding not at all surprised.

"He totally freaked out!" The moment the words leave my mouth, my nose starts to clog up. The pressure in my head keeps building. There's a war going on up there. How could Lukas be so ignorant? He trampled all over my dream. Why?

"Is it possible that, once again, you ambushed him just a tiny little bit?" she asks carefully.

Leaning against the kitchen counter, I let our argument run through my mind again like a movie. "No," I decide then. I couldn't have told him any more gently.

On the other end of the line I hear Alex breathing. She's thinking, and it's already taking too long. "Oh, you know what he's like." There's a soothing note in her voice. In the background I hear bangles clinking; she's definitely making that typically dismissive little hand gesture of hers. “Give him a bit of time to calm down.”

“He just needs to straighten out his worldview,” I add thoughtfully. That’s just how he is. Lukas, the rational guy, who has to calculate every tiny detail and write it down on lists before he knows what he’s supposed to think.

“This isn’t the first time he’s behaved like this.” She sounds convinced. Thank God.

Of course Alex is right about that. And the fact that she’s saying exactly what I already thought myself gives me a sense of security. Even though I’m barely capable of forming a clear thought, there’s at least one thing I can see clearly in front of me.

Lukas will come back and we’ll sort this out calmly. That’s how it was before, and that’s how it’ll be this time too. Because who are we if we don’t have each other anymore? We’re Lukas and Marie. Forever. And nothing else.

Just like always, he’ll be back with me in a few hours. We’ll hold each other in our arms, kiss tenderly and then, then we’ll talk.

Openly and honestly.

The two of us will say what we’re thinking, and he’ll understand how much photography means to me. It’ll become clear to him that it isn’t a pointless dream but a real goal. Our difficulties will come to an end. And what happened in the last few months will be behind us once and for all.

About the Author

Belinda Benna is an award-winning author whose moving romance novels are filled with emotion, allowing you to lose yourself between the lines and find yourself at the same time.

Experience stories that will make you cry, laugh, and fall in love—each with a message that will stay with you for a long time.

www.ingramcontent.com/pod-product-compliance
Lightning Source LLC
La Vergne TN
LVHW040213110826
845155LV00031B/718

* 9 7 8 1 0 3 6 7 3 3 8 1 0 *